THE HAWTHORNE WITCH

A. L. HAWKE

PHANTOM HEART, LLC

ISBN: 9781953919007 (ebook)

ISBN: 9781953919014 (paperback)

ISBN: 978-1-953919-27-4 (hardcover)

Library of Congress Control Number: 2020950029

This is a work of fiction. It comes directly from the author's imagination. Witchcraft is included to infuse a sense of realism to the novel, but in no way is it supposed to represent actual practicing witchcraft, witches or the religion of Wicca. The book also includes fictitious names, characters, places, and incidents. Any public names are used solely for creative purposes. Any resemblance to actual people, living or dead, or to companies, institutions, or locales is entirely coincidental or accidental.

Line edited by Stephanie Ward

Proofread by Eliza Dee of Clio Editing Services

Cover Design © 2020 by Regina Wamba of MaeIDesign.com

Published by Phantom Heart, LLC

27702 Crown Valley Pkwy, Suite D4, #201

Ladera Ranch, CA 92694

Printed and bound in the United States of America

First printing December, 2020

Learn more about A.L. Hawke at www.alhawke.com

Correspondence: contact@alhawke.com

❀ Created with Vellum

1

———

ADDER

I'M WORRIED. ONE REASON IS REAL DUMB. I'VE PREPARED FOR this service all week, and even though these are my closest friends, I hate talking in front of people. I should never have become their leader. But there's a far greater reason for my troubles. A witch showed up at my doorstep last night and ruined what was supposed to be a romantic evening with my boyfriend, Bryce. As all my friends hug each other, with their hoods back, revealing smiling faces by flickering firelight, they're oblivious to my uninvited guest, hiding somewhere behind me in Alondra's dark nineteenth-century home.

Outside, I enjoy the smell of the burning embers of our bonfire as everyone sits in the circle of white plastic chairs. The crescent moon and stars shine brightly in the center of Alondra's backyard and I still can't get over how lovely the night sky is away from the city. The stars are so vivid and bright. You can even make out the river of light across the Milky Way.

After everyone sits, all smiles, we hold hands. My best friend, Maddie, sits on my left and the love of my life, Bryce, is on my right. I clear my throat and prepare to recite the words I rehearsed.

"Yatu," I say.

"Yatu," they all repeat with a nod. Yatu means "hello."

"We celebrate Lammas. Lammas recognizes hard times ahead. It is a turn of the season, like all holidays on the wheel. This afternoon was hot. Soon it will turn cold. Lammas is the first harvest. Mabon comes next, and finally, my favorite, Samhain." I face two new recruits across from me and smile. "Samhain is Halloween."

The newbies look nervous and out of place. I mean, they're the only ones not wearing black cloaks and thick witchy makeup.

I pause and gather my thoughts. It's quiet. The crickets chirp more loudly. The fire crackles.

"Lammas is a special harvest, as it represents the time when Apollo radiates his energy down upon Gaia, growing our first grain. As such, we celebrate the reaping by partaking in bread. And as we share the grain, we consume the Earth. Gaia is a part of you. You consume the Earth, and as you pass into the Summerland, you shed her. So as you partake, I ask that you reflect, deep inside, about your place among Earth and..." I raise my arms and feel the sleeves of my black cloak slide below my wrists. "The moon and the stars. One soul. Atman. Blessed be my coven under the gods Gaia, Selene, and Astraeus."

"Atman," says Bryce, nodding and closing his eyes with a smile.

"Atman," says everyone else.

"Blackbird, please hand me the bread."

Blackbird is the mystic name for my best friend, Maddie. Maddie jumps up and walks over to a white linen cloth behind us on the grass, where there's a chalice and a loaf of bread. She seems so happy. Everyone is. We're all loving the festival and seeing each other again.

"It's buttermilk bread, Katie," Frida explains in her beautiful Brazilian accent, reaching over and touching my hand.

She's next to Bryce. I can't wait to taste it; she always bakes the most amazing stuff. "And I brought pomegranate wine."

Maddie hands me the loaf. I tear off a piece and lay it on my lap. It smells fresh and sweet. I hand the loaf to Bryce, on my right. Bryce nods to me, breaks off a piece, and passes the rest to the witch beside him.

"Happy Lammas," I say with a big smile.

They all burst forth with "Happy Lammas!"

Then my friends jump up, saying the words over and over in greetings to one another. Hope hugs Mandy, and Helen leans down and kisses Maddie on the cheek. Tammy leans over and lays a white flower wreath around my neck. As I'm still technically officiating, I'm seated in the middle. I sit quietly, readjusting the sleeves of my cloak, just enjoying the warm, clear starry night in the company of my best friends.

"May you never thirst," Maddie says on my left.

May you never thirst.

Usually those words make me happy, but tonight I'm a little sad. I first heard the saying from my friend and mentor, Alondra, the owner of this house, who passed away last year. These words have many meanings, but to me, the most personal is love. A wish that the togetherness between me and my twelve closest friends, who are in this circle, will never dry up. That's sweet...but bitter. See, this is my last year at Hawthorne University, and my friends are leaving. Every event, starting with this one, takes me closer to the end.

"May you never thirst," I echo, feeling the bitterness. I try to hide my thoughts.

Hope, the only one still standing, walks behind me and grabs a fancy-looking gold chalice from the white lace cloth behind me. (Shh, don't tell anybody, but the cup's a brass trinket I bought with Maddie in Atlanta.) Hope hands it to me, and I hold the cup with both hands, drinking some of the tart pomegranate wine.

"Umm. This is really good, Frida."

"Thanks, Katie." We laugh.

I wait for Bryce to pass the cup to all the other witches in the circle. When everyone has sipped, I nod to Maddie.

"Thanks, Windstorm," Maddie says. "Hey, guys, have a nice summer? I want everybody to meet our two new recruits, Josie and Debra. They're considering joining us. Can you believe it? Crazy, right? Try not to scare them. They're terrified."

"We're not!" cries Josie.

"Yatu, Josie," says Bryce. "Debra."

"Yeah," Maddie continues with a chuckle. "Josie likes hiking. Not your enjoying-the-fresh-air type of hiking but mountain climbing. Like risking her life hiking in the mountains at Zion State Park. She's also a physics major, and that marks the first witch we've ever had in our coven that's a scientist. What is the world coming to, right, Katie?" I just nod. "And—my best of friends—Debra is a local girl, living close to Flintwood. I knew Debra in high school, guys. She's quiet but has more of a love for magic than anyone I know—except maybe Mira. In fact, she was practicing witchcraft even before I joined. She's also real scared."

"Yatu, Debra," says Tammy, who is sitting close to them. Tammy's a super-sweet bald black girl. "Relax, girls. The only one to be afraid of is Cadence over there."

"Stop," I say.

We laugh some more. It's fun. This is the part I love about our coven, just turning to friends and talking, you know.

"Thank you, Madison," I say. "Welcome, girls. This is just an introduction. If you're still interested, let us know and we can initiate you."

"Thank you, Windstorm," says Josie. Then Debra nods.

"Thank you for introducing them to the group, Madison."

"Don't mention it, Cadence Hawthorne." There's more laughter.

"Let us eat," I say. "And as we eat, be thankful for the food that the gods have gifted us."

And that's it for the ceremony, thank God. Like I said, I don't like talking in front of people. Alondra made me their leader last year, but I never asked to be.

"Are we going to make puppets tonight, Cadence?" asks Frida innocently.

"I've gathered the cornhusks in the kitchen," replies Maddie. "The newbies have already made some. If you guys want, later tonight we can do it with popcorn."

"And I brought beer," says my boyfriend.

"Hey, Bryce, how was last night at the house all alone with Cadence?" Tammy asks. But we weren't alone, and Bryce loses his smile.

"It was fun," he says after swallowing some bread. "We just got back from Atlanta, where Katie introduced me to her dad and brother."

"Oooh," says Tammy with a big smile. "Getting serious, guys."

"They're as amazing as she is," says Bryce, hugging me.

"Ah," I say, leaning into his arms.

Everyone's happy. But, you know, the minute I talk about the visitor, things will sour.

I glance back at Alondra's house. I left her in the bedroom upstairs, where a floor-to-ceiling window looks out into the backyard. But it's dark inside. Well, I don't want to do what I did last year. Last year I opened my mouth at our reunion gathering, and it was a total downer. But Bryce keeps looking at me. I'm guessing he expects me to say something. As Tammy talks about a date she had with a pilot in Savannah, Bryce grabs me by the arm and leans close to my ear. "You want me to tell them?" I shake my head. I think Maddie overhears, but she's busy stuffing her face with bread.

We go around the circle, and everyone talks about their summer, enjoying the freshly baked bread.

"Did you guys hear about Greg and me?" Frida asks, showing off a big diamond on her finger.

"Congratulations," I say. "I'm so happy for you. Maddie said he's cute."

"Duh," Maddie says. "Look at Frida."

"He asked me in Hawaii, Katie," Frida explains. "I'd just been having fun in the sand, and I was lying on a towel when I felt a hand on my belly. I tipped my shades and my Greg was on his knee." She laughs again. "He's so romantic. I said I dreamt once that I'd be asked for my hand in marriage on the beach. Greg had planned the whole Hawaii thing just for that moment, I think. He's wonderful."

"Cute," shy Helen says. Frida nods.

"Greg is really cute," Maddie says with a nod. "Wait till you guys meet him. But then why wouldn't such a swell guy be hanging with Frida?"

"I can't wait to introduce you," Frida says.

We talk about clothes. Then shopping. It's times like these that I feel like Bryce is left out. He's the only boy in our group. But that's tradition. One male High Wizard and twelve witches always make up a coven.

"I went with Don to Europe, guys," Tammy says. She's just as boisterous as Maddie. "England. The traditional home of witches, you know. Mother Shifton's Cave in Yorkshire and the Petrifying Well. It was cool. You know, maybe it was Mother Shifton's famous ugliness that made everybody think that we witches are ugly." We laugh and she tells us about all these petrified teddy bears and hats.

I feel more at ease. As my friends keep yapping, I glance over at the tall, thin trees in the shadows of Alondra's yard. The trees surround Alondra's backyard field. I love the woods.

I've wandered alone there many times. It's so peaceful. If

you venture down the hill from here, along some dirt paths, you'll be at my college. Hawthorne University is surrounded by trees too. And looking over the trees, if you gaze far enough, you can see the nearby mountains. But everything else is shadowed by the woods.

I have an urge to leave and wander right now. Besides the sound of crackling wood and my friends' laughter, there's a calmness in the air. The crickets are still chirping. Air brushes gently against my cheek. A squirrel darts up a tree trunk, running away from a deer whose hooves are crunching leaves. The deer looks right at me, but I know she can't see me. The deer is standing near a ditch, in a clearing in the forest, about a fifteen-minute walk from the backyard. I know because I've walked along the path many times before.

Then I feel something in my chest. Magic. I feel myself slipping into a trance, and that puts me on edge. It's bad because usually when I've slipped into a trance unknowingly, it's been for protection, with a spell.

Someone shrieks. Tammy stops midsentence with her mouth wide open. There's another gasp. Then another. Everyone is looking at the house behind me. I turn.

Beatrix—you know, the unwanted guest I still haven't told anyone about—walks slowly from the back porch to our bonfire. She's wearing the same brown leather jacket, jeans, and shirt she wore last night, with her long blond hair flowing around her pale face. But her makeup isn't running down her face from crying like it was last night. She's an uneasy young girl, only seventeen. And she's close enough for my friends to recognize her. How could they forget her? Last year she helped murder a professor and tried to hurt Bryce.

Maybe I should have told them?

Everyone except Bryce and the two new recruits jumps from their chair. The newbies have no idea who she is. My friends do. They remember her licking and sucking the blood off our murdered professor's arms last year.

"Yatu," Beatrix says with a shy wave.

No one's "Yatu-ing" anyone.

Bryce gets up and tries to shush everyone, but they're in a panic. I remain seated, but I turn my chair toward her and the house. I wait for everyone to calm the hell down. When they're quiet enough—

"Guys, I invited her," I say. "And if you all knew what she's going through, you would too."

That makes them go nuts again.

"Everyone, quiet!" shouts Bryce. "Let Katie explain."

"I didn't come for your service," Beatrix says to them. Then she looks down at me. "I'm here to warn you. Adder is coming. She'll be here any minute. She's coming for me, so...I have to go." But she pauses, looking very unsure about it. "I don't want any trouble for you. Thanks for everything, Cadence. All of you are so lucky to have Windstorm as your High Priestess. Remember what I told you about Raven. Adder's not only coming for me, she's coming for you. All of you. Don't trust her. She only wishes bad things for you."

"Go back to the house, Beatrix." I finally rise from my chair. "I won't let her touch you."

"You can't do that," Bryce says to me. "You need to let her go."

I stare at my boyfriend, dumbfounded. You have to understand that this is Bryce. Nice Bryce, the nicest guy in the world.

"She told us Enora has it in for us, Bryce," I say. "We're in danger whatever we do. Why wouldn't you want to protect her? Enora will kill her if I let her go."

"What's going on?" asks Josie.

"They're forbidden to come anywhere near us," Mandy says to the new recruit, pointing with hatred at Beatrix. "Everyone from the Abaddon coven has no right to step foot in Hawthorne. That was your own order last Christmas, Katie."

"Her life is threatened."

"So?" Mandy replies. "Ours is too if you let her in the circle."

The recruits look scared again, but now they have good reason to be. For them, this was just another visitor to our holiday festival. An excuse to meet new friends to help them make corn dollies.

"Maddie, please take Josie and Debra into the house," I say. Maddie nods and quickly corrals the two girls in her arms and rushes them back to the house.

I turn to Mandy, a witch with long blond hair who's in a perpetually bad mood. Well, she doesn't like me, anyway—especially as the coven's leader. She and Natasha have never accepted me. "I'm not letting her in our circle," I say.

"You're involving us if you let her stay," Mandy replies. "Weren't you here when Reardon was killed? Or what about Bryce? Weren't you there when she tied up your boyfriend? Tried to burn him alive?"

"Of course I was!"

The two recruits look back as they walk to the house. They heard that.

And now Beatrix is walking away. It looks like she's heading into the woods.

"Wait, Beatrix."

"Let her go!" Mandy snaps.

"If you heard what Enora asked her to do, you'd protect her too."

"What? What's so bad that you're willing to risk our lives for her?"

Beatrix stops. She begged me not to tell anyone. She made me swear. She turns and looks right into my eyes, reminding me.

"She was asked to have ceremonial sex with a stranger."

"So? They're a black witch cult."

"That's not all."

"No, Cadence!" Beatrix runs back, shaking her head desperately. "No!"

"She was to have sex until bearing a child," I continue. "Then in six months, the fetus was to be removed through ceremonial abortion and—"

"Cadence! You swore!" Beatrix violently shakes her head.

"They planned to drink her baby's blood."

"*I told you not to tell them!*" Beatrix is right up in my face, practically spitting on me. "*I told you!* How could you tell them? How could you do that!"

Everyone turns quiet. Some sit back down in the white chairs and stare at the fire.

"Why'd you tell them!" Beatrix shouts again in my face. "Why? You swore, Cadence! How could you do that!"

"They have to know why I'm protecting you."

"I don't need your protection!"

I laugh. Yeah, I actually laugh in the poor girl's face because, honestly, right now I hate her. I spent all night talking her down from killing herself when she threatened to slice her wrists in front of Bryce and me. I've lost all patience, and now she's destroyed our holiday. She's exhausting me. I don't want to protect her. I wish she had never come here.

"She's not a part of our circle," I explain to my friends, "but that doesn't mean she doesn't have a right to stay at Alondra's house. Alondra would have wanted us to help her."

"Keeping her here is the same thing," Mandy says quietly, shaking her head. But she doesn't seem to be in the mood to fight with me anymore. She doesn't say another word.

Beatrix turns to the house hesitantly, looking like she's going to leave again. It's too late. She screams instead.

Another witch, carrying a torch, is slowly walking toward

us from the side of the house. Her cloak is similar to ours, but it's scarlet. Under the fire, I recognize a face completely covered in black tattoos. Cordelia. Her mystic name is Adder. Last year, Cordelia and Beatrix were Enora's henchwomen— her favorite witches. Yeah, Cordelia tried to kill my boyfriend too.

Behind Cordelia, candles are flickering through the living room sliding glass door near the outdoor patio. The electricity doesn't work in the house. At least Maddie has the new recruits inside the house, hopefully trying to do something nice like make more corn dollies or prepare popcorn by the fireplace.

"Sit down," I say to my witches, staring at Cordelia as she makes her way over. The bitch has a large smile. "Do as I say." From my periphery, I see my friends obey.

"Yatu, Windstorm," Cordelia says with a fake smile. Then she lifts her left palm and shows us a red pentagram painted on her hand. She looks at Beatrix. "Yatu, Manthis. Sister. What are you doing here? Do you think witches you tried to kill can help you?"

"They have nothing to do with this." Beatrix shakes her head. "Just leave them alone."

"Then come back with me."

"If she wants to," I say.

Cordelia walks right up to me. Her black-tattooed face is right up against my nose, and I can feel the warmth from her torch on my chest. Bryce grabs Cordelia's arm, but she yanks it off, still staring at me.

"Happy Lammas," Cordelia says smugly, gazing down into my eyes.

"I told you to never come here."

Cordelia laughs. "Then why is she here?"

"I'm leaving," Beatrix says.

"It's sweet that you honor your teacher by holding your holiday parties on her sacred grounds," says Cordelia, finally backing away and looking around. "I hope her spirit won't come here to disturb your gathering again."

"She only comes when you and your friends are here."

"That was a neat trick. The power to summon a ghost is impressive. But I told Enora that you never really saved her life. I said you summoned your teacher and that all you did was not finish your kill. Enora understands. Ghosts don't have the power to throw people off cliffs, only people do. Only you did. Enora doesn't owe you a thing." Cordelia sighs. Then she looks at Bryce and smiles smugly. "Yatu, Bryce. Enora sends you a special greeting."

"Go to hell."

"My pleasure."

"I'll say it one more time," I say. "Get out."

But Cordelia nods and walks over to the bonfire. She touches the fire from her torch into the flames and then plants the torch firmly in the grass. With a fake smile, she sits down cross-legged in front of the fire. We're all standing over her.

"Tradition allows a witch from another coven to visit freely during Lammas," Cordelia says. "I send you greetings from Panthera and her Abaddon coven, as a representative of her circle. My master would love for me to join with you in partaking of bread."

"Get the hell out of here," I repeat.

"How rude. Enora warned me you'd be like this. She said you sent the same regards for Alondra's memorial." Then the bitch looks at Beatrix with contempt. "And how are you doing, Beatrix? Didn't you help me bind Bryce's wrists and try to burn him alive? I think it was you. It was you, wasn't it? I think Katie remembers."

I grab Cordelia by the arm. She's much bigger than I am and could normally bend me over her knee and break my back. She jumps up, flaunting her size. But I'm angry, and when I'm angry, I feel magic. I feel my trance growing and giving me confidence and power. And when she moves to grab Beatrix, I throw her to the ground.

"*Get out!*" I yell.

She laughs, lying on her side on the wild grass.

"Okay." She puts her hand up because I'm about to grab her and throw her again. "I'll leave. But I come with another message. My master told me that I better not find you actually helping our little harlot. For a year, she respected your wishes for saving her, but if you dare help Beatrix, you are threatening to break the peace."

"Where's Mira? Beatrix said you've taken her. You're the one who's breaking the peace."

"We didn't take her," Cordelia says. "She was bored. She wanted to practice real magic."

"I don't believe you."

"Ask her yourself."

"I can't reach her by phone."

"Raven is a real witch now." Cordelia laughs again. "She doesn't need a cell phone."

Beatrix starts wailing on her knees by the fire. We all look at her. This is what she did all last night. She just cried and cried and cried. She's a complete mess. It's really annoying. Cordelia looks at her with disgust, and I'm thinking she's probably spent hours consoling the witch too.

"You won't let me return with her?" Cordelia asks, still leaning on an elbow in the grass. "I told you the risk. I warned you, Windstorm."

My silence is my answer.

"Very well." Cordelia gets up with a nod. "I'll tell my master. But I don't think you're going to be happy with Enora's response."

"Wait, I'll go!" Beatrix yells, jumping up, still in tears. "I'll go! Please! Please leave them alone."

Of all people, Mandy grabs Beatrix's arm and pulls her close. Mandy looks at me and shakes her head.

Cordelia lets out what sounds almost like a growl. For a moment, I could almost swear her eyes flicker red. I reach for her torch, leaning beside the fire. The torch flies about twenty feet through the air and lands in my hand. Cordelia stares and shakes her head, and she looks afraid for the first time. I shove the torch against her chest.

"*Go!*" I shout. "*Get out of here! Get out!*"

Cordelia steps back from me, nearly falling over. "Talk...to Mira," she mutters. Then she forces a fake smile but steps far away from me. "We'd love to recruit you too."

2

───────

THINGS ON MY MIND AND, OH, SCHOOL

TODAY I'M NOT GOTH. THAT'S UNUSUAL FOR ME, BUT THIS morning's different. My usual look on campus is thick black lipstick and mascara, a black dress, and black boots, matching my long wavy black hair. Instead, today I'm dressed like a *normal* girl, with a sharply pressed navy-blue dress, my hair in a ponytail, and red lipstick. And I'm sitting stiffly in a black leather chair across from the dean of the history department, Dr. Bainer. Dr. Bainer's a short baldheaded man who's holding spectacles while staring at papers behind his large dark-mahogany desk. He's been doing that since I walked into his office five minutes ago. Behind him, through the window, is a gorgeous view of Hawthorne Forest.

I already waited thirty minutes in the history department's administration office, and now I'm waiting again. That gives me time to think. I really don't want to think.

I've got so much stuff on my mind. My friends. Mira. And... Beatrix. I left Beatrix alone at Alondra's house. What if she burns the house down? And Damien. I'm supposed to meet my brother, Damie, by ten to help him move into his dorm room at Krunner Hall. Yeah, my brother's going to Hawthorne this year.

Can you believe that? That's after I warned him and Dad against it like a zillion times.

Dr. Bainer sighs and sifts through more papers. I pull out my cell phone to look at the time. I bite my lip. My brother's waiting for me. It's ten thirty.

I take a deep breath, hoping it will elicit a response from my interviewer. It doesn't.

Mira. I thought Mira was still in Florida with her folks, looking for work after she graduated. She wanted to land a teaching job. But Beatrix told me she'd moved to Atlanta with Enora's sick satanic sex cult. I entertained the idea of driving downtown last night to visit her, but Bryce convinced me not to. Apparently, I have an interview I'm not having.

I wiggle loose a nail jutting under the armrest of my chair. Dr. Bainer's oblivious, still staring at whatever the hell he's staring at. I wiggle and wiggle until the nail comes out and falls into my right palm. I put the nail on the leather armrest. Then I play with it a little more, looking down and rubbing the silver metal thingy between my black-polished fingernails. It moves very easily. It spins like a top.

Bryce. I just have to get into graduate school at Hawthorne next year. If I do well in this interview, my boyfriend and I are set. Bryce is finishing his dissertation and plans to teach history here next year. But...what if I don't? What if I go somewhere else, like another state? You've heard about what happens in long-distance relationships, right?

That was the wrong thing to think about. My heart races and I suddenly feel sick—like I have to move my bowels or throw up. But I'm supposed to be nervous, right? I am in an interview, aren't I?

"Hmm," Dr. Bainer finally says. But then he's back to staring at the paperwork.

Fuck.

It smells like books in here. Or is it old musty carpet?

My metal nail is spinning by itself now, but the dean doesn't notice. He doesn't notice me either. I hold my hand about three inches over the nail and jerk my palm every few seconds to keep it turning.

Maddie calls him Dr. *Brainer*. I know that's real corny, but it's also funny. He really doesn't talk much to students. Bryce says he's a little rough around the edges.

His office is a mess. I'm surrounded by boxes, books, and papers. The dean's Indian, which is cool. I see a book from ancient India, the *Bhagavad Gita*, that I've always admired on his bookshelf. The *Bhagavad Gita* says that we should just act and not worry about consequences. I wish I could do that. Especially now. Then he's got books I don't care for as much—modern history books on the Cold War, the space race, and the Vietnam War. I don't really like modern history. There's a very nice old picture of a wedding on a matching mahogany bookcase. He had hair back then, and he and his wife were wearing lovely multicolored robes. It looks like a traditional Indian wedding. It sits beside a picture of two kids next to a roller coaster. The boy is carrying messy vanilla ice cream, and the girl has cotton candy.

"Is that Disney World?" I ask, just to say anything.

He glances at me in irritation, leans back in his reclining leather office chair, and thumbs through more papers on his desk.

Fuck!

I look behind Dr. Bainer at the gorgeous view of the dense forest. It's so lovely. I wonder if he appreciates just how lovely his view of Hawthorne Forest is.

"You've had a tough time," he finally says, wrinkling his brow and staring at one particular page. "What happened?"

"What do you mean?"

He looks up at me and raises his eyebrows. "What

happened, Ms. Hawthorne, to the fall semesters in your sophomore and junior years?"

"Well, my mother—"

"Died. That was in your sophomore year."

"And last year, Alondra—"

"Dr. Johansen died last year." He puts one stem of his glasses in his mouth and squints his eyes. "So? Ms. Hawthorne, this is Hawthorne University."

I'm kind of hoping he notices what he just said. Like maybe the fact that my family founded the city could help me get in? No, I don't think so. This interview is not going so—

"Hawthorne University's history program has the top reputation of all the liberal arts colleges in the United States. I can't accept slips every time something bad happens. We've all lost loved ones. You can't fail your semester because of it."

"I didn't fail. I passed after making everything up."

"Well, I'm not sure why the provost allowed you to remediate. You remediated twice. And you passed, you didn't excel." He chuckles, but I don't think it's very funny. "You did do well on testing. Every test was nearly a hundred percent—or a complete fail due to absence. A peculiar record. Then there are notes by your teachers. Everyone liked you. Especially Dr. Alondra Johansen. Dr. Johansen recommended you with high marks in her honors program, even though you only received a C in her class."

Yeah, Alondra's "honors" program was supposed to ensure that I could get into the graduate program here—or anywhere in the country, for that matter. And if Alondra were still alive, I know she would have vouched for me and I'd be in. Maybe even Maddie, with her miserable grades, could have gotten in.

"Then there was Dr. Riker." He raises a finger. "He's the only teacher who failed you." He looks down at the note he was studying before and laughs. "You had Mr. Wallace teaching you then, right?"

I'm getting angry. This guy seems mean. First, he makes me wait half an hour; then he says nothing for what feels like another. Now he's belligerent over my grades. Why even interview me? I've got so much shit on my mind right now. I don't think this guy could even imagine my stress.

But I have to calm down. Maybe he's just testing my nerves. You know, I have an anger problem.

My "top" is spinning like crazy, on its own, under my palm.

"Mr. Wallace actually had good things to say," he continues. That's *Bryce* Wallace, my scrumptious boyfriend and TA for two of my classes. "He wrote a note in your file. Would you care for me to read it?"

No. Not really.

He reads:

Dr. Riker does not believe in remediation. Therefore, unfortunately, Cadence Hawthorne must fail her art history class. But we want it to be noted on record that she is an outstanding student. Dr. Riker believes that her final essay was one of the best student essays he's read in his twenty years of teaching. As for my observations as her teaching assistant, for the second time, I can vouch for Cadence's outstanding work. It also should be noted that she fell ill during the month of December of her junior year. She approached the provost, who allowed her to remediate. I hope her illness will be considered when looking at her fall semester grades in her junior year.

Signed, Bryce Wallace.

"Everyone likes you," he says with a very long sigh and an open-armed gesture. "Especially your boyfriend."

Why, you patronizing fuck!

"Look ..." I stammer because my word sounds like a shout. "I...I don't like what happened. I really don't. If I could go back and change it, I would. But I know I can give it my all. I love history. And I love this school. I love studying here. Near the forest and the trees. There isn't a better school in the world than Hawthorne. And everybody, all the teachers, are so nice. It's the perfect place. I really like studying history and—"

"What do you like about history?"

"It's like a story, you know."

"It is a story. It's the most important of stories, because it allows us to learn from our past. But why do you want to study here?"

Because my boyfriend is going to be a professor here next year. Instead I stupidly repeat, "Everyone's just so nice and friendly and it's so beautiful, you know."

My "top" is spinning super-fast on the armrest now. It's as desperate as I am to get his attention.

"Dr. Brainer...I mean—" *Idiot, Cadence!* "Dr. Bainer, I had so much trouble because I love it here. Alondra was family. So when she died, I lost it. It was like my mom died all over again. Because when my mom died, Alondra was there for me."

"I thought you were sick," he says, lifting his eyebrows suspiciously.

"I was. I know it doesn't excuse my actions. I know I should have done better."

"What are you going to do if something like that happens during our doctoral program?"

"I don't plan on anyone dying."

And that does it. It sounds really sarcastic. He squints and looks angry. But it's so unfair. If anyone should be angry, it's me. I think this guy's really mean.

He shakes his head and jumps up.

"Well, good day, Ms. Hawthorne. This program is very selective. The problem is your GPA dropped because of the fall semesters in your sophomore and junior years. You're a good student, but your grades are not typically acceptable for our graduate program. I agreed to the interview because of how well liked you are and because you went here for undergrad. I will notify you of my decision in a few weeks."

I think you just did.

He sticks his hand out for me to shake.

"But, Dr. Bainer," I say, standing up and handing him a limp handshake. "Isn't there anything I can do to bring up my GPA? If that's all that you're concerned with, can't I do something to make up my grades? You saw how well I did other than those two semesters. And on testing—I ranked at the top in the country. And you said everybody likes me."

"I read you that note because I found it inappropriate," he replies, shaking his head, "I don't approve of favoritism, Ms. Hawthorne."

"Then just ignore it."

"Good day. I can't change your past. I'd love to erase it, but I can't change what happened to you."

And that hits a nerve. *Erase?* That's what Enora tried to do last Christmas when she tried to burn my Book of Shadows along with my boyfriend.

"No one can erase the past!" I snap.

Shit. Apparently, my thoughts are directly connected to my lips because I'm so angry. Now he knows I don't like him. His eyes open wide, and he moves back a little. Or is it a sudden gust of air that I feel rushing through the room? I'm not sure. Boy, I really hate him.

"I...I...I..." I do everything in my power to force a smile. "I'd be willing to do any extra projects or any testing that could raise—"

He shakes his head.

"Isn't there anything I can do?"

"No."

"But—"

"I'm sorry."

"There must be something I can do to—"

"No. Good day, Ms. Hawthorne."

FUCK YOU!

The nail flies from my armrest into the window. There's a loud crack. Dr. Bainer whirls around in surprise to see a crack at the side of his window. He jumps up to look outside, thinking someone hit it with a ball or something.

I'm running out the door. I might have nodded a goodbye to him, or maybe I didn't. I don't know. I don't care. All I know is it was a horrible interview—the worst interview of my life. Of course, the office assistant gives me a really big smile as I rush out of the room.

In my high heels, enduring blistering summer heat, I rush to the dorms to catch up with my brother. I'm late. I'm going to help him move into the school I begged him not to go to. At least *he* will be coming to Hawthorne University next year.

3

THE BILLINGTON HOUSE

I'M SUNK IN A VERY UNCOMFORTABLE BROWN LEATHER BEANBAG chair, staring toward a big central window in the Billington House, as a bunch of freshman kids are getting drunk and talking up a storm around me. I don't mind their noise. I like that others are happy.

The Billington House is a large haunted house, the oldest house in Georgia. Even older than Alondra's. It's a brick building with sash windows and a broken-down white fence, sitting on a grassy hill surrounded by the woods. The large central window—the one I'm staring at now—is where a ghost is sometimes spotted after midnight, holding a candle or knife and facing our campus below. Meanwhile, the inside of the mansion has been transformed into the Psi Kappa Psi Greek frat house with the usual cheap, ratty furniture, holes in the walls, pool and ping-pong tables, paper murals announcing events, and bikini-clad, beer-holding girl posters.

Maddie's leaning on the wall beside a door, holding a red plastic cup, talking to my brother. She tosses her hair back a few times between guffaws. She's having a great time with him. Damie brushes back his long hair, which is longer on one side with this surfer look. They're happy together. That's nice. But I'm still pissed that my brother's even going here.

Bryce is only a few feet from me, laughing with a bunch of his old friends. Bryce loves the Billington parties. He used to live here, you know.

My phone vibrates in my jeans pocket. With my free hand —the other is holding a beer bottle—I answer it.

"Hi, Cadence," says a real depressing voice. It's Beatrix. I have to press the phone close to my ear since country music is blaring.

"How you holding up?"

"All right." She doesn't sound all right. "I wanted to ask if I can keep a cat here?"

"Sure. Alondra used to love cats. As long as you take care of it."

"Oh, great. And I want you to know, I've been cleaning up the place. It's the least I can do. But the AC keeps turning on around sundown. It gets really cold at night."

That's super weird. Bryce had an electrician come by to take a look at the place after our weekend stay. The man looked at my boyfriend like he was nuts when Bryce told him about the air conditioner turning on by itself. He said that there was no way it had turned on because he had removed the power grid last month, to prevent fires, after our complaints of flickering lights. When I heard that, I became convinced that Alondra's house is haunted. So now there are two haunted houses in Hawthorne.

Bryce reaches down and touches my knee and winks at me. He's in such a good mood. Of course I haven't told him about Dr. Fucker yet. I just nod and point to the cell phone. Then I make a gesture circling my finger around my ear. He nods. I'm sure he can guess who I'm talking to.

"It's the least I can do," Beatrix says in my ear. "You've been so nice, Cadence."

"Are you feeling any better?"

"I guess."

She's so odd, you know. She keeps telling me how she misses everyone in her coven terribly, even though they all want to kill her.

"So the cat's okay, right? Are you sure?"

"Yes, Beatrix."

Bryce nods when he hears her name. He sips his beer. A short, overweight, dark-skinned guy with a beard is standing beside him, looking around the room, drinking. I think Bryce wants to introduce me to him.

"Thanks," Beatrix says. And she sounds happier. "Talk to you later, Cadence."

"Bye, Beatrix."

I hang up the phone.

Bryce leans on a knee beside me. There are no more chairs or beanbags to sit on.

"Katie, this is Mason. Remember Mason? You guys said hello on the phone a while ago. He's down for the weekend. We used to be roommates."

"Hi, Cadence." Mason takes my hand. "Great to finally see you. Bryce said so much about you."

"Oh, yeah? Good stuff, I hope?"

"Very. You're a grad student too?"

"I'm a senior."

"Oh. So you didn't know Bryce back in the days when he used to live here?" And he has this really big smirk. Well, I know the crazy things he did in my coven. I can just imagine the "normal" party animal things Bryce did. Not to mention he used to go out with Enora back then. Yeah, really. His girlfriend was Enora. Can you believe that?

Then Mason adds, "He was *quite* the roommate."

"Oh, really?"

The sweetest thing is Bryce's reaction. He blushes. "Mason was quite the frat boy himself," Bryce quickly says.

"*Oh no*," I say with a big grin. "You don't get off that easy, babe. Don't try to put the blame on him. Tell me more, Mason. Please. Tell me. I want to know all the specifics."

"Cadence," says Bryce.

Mason smiles again, but he just shakes his head and says, "They were great times. I remember lots of beer."

"And girls?" I ask.

He nods. Bryce sighs and I laugh.

"Boys will be boys," I say, reciting the old adage. "As long as he doesn't go back to being *quite the roommate* now."

"I wouldn't dream of it, Katie."

"Where are you living, Mason?" I ask. I want to get up, but I'm sunk in the beanbag and he's standing in my way.

"I'm a gamer," Mason says. "I work near Columbus. I couldn't resist coming to the back-to-school party." Bryce is still leaning on a knee, and Mason puts a hand on his shoulder. "And I had to see my old buddy."

"What sort of games?"

"Mainly role-playing and adventure games. I love it. It's fun programming the details of characters. A lot of fun. Bryce and I used to play a lot on the computer back then."

"Among other things," I say with a sly smile.

Bryce puts an arm around me and says, "Just lots of gaming, Katie."

"Aha." I laugh.

"Listen, I've gotta catch up with some of the others," says Mason. "Fantastic meeting you, Cadence. You're as attractive as he said you were." I try to get up to hug him, but he's still standing right in front of me and I'm deep in the beanbag.

Bryce jumps up and grabs his hand. "Come by later, man. We have to go out while you're in town."

He nods.

Then Bryce kneels beside me.

"*Quite a roommate*, huh?" I ask, running my fingers through his short, feathery hair.

"Stop, Katie," he says with a laugh. "Listen…I was hoping we could go on one of our dates this Monday?"

I look at him funny because he looks nervous. That's super weird being that we're living together.

"Love to."

Then he furrows his brow and examines me. "What's wrong, babe? Why are you so blue?"

"Just got a lot on my mind."

"That was Beatrix on the phone, right? She's okay?"

"She sounded okay, but I'm not sure."

"She's lucky to have you. You've been so nice to take her in."

"That's not what you said when she first came to the house."

"I know. She's disturbing." But he winks again. He's being cute. I smile in spite of my sour self. He's in such a good mood. "It was such a nice thing to do," he says.

"Must be learning from you."

He reaches over and kisses me on the lips.

When I unlock my lips from his and stare into his blues, I say, "Is this what being *quite the roommate* is?"

"Stop it, Katie."

"Hey, guys, get a room," says a young boy's voice. I'd recognize that voice anywhere. It's my tall brother, Damie. Maddie's trailing right behind him. Maddie looks funny standing next to my surfer brother. She's got on a black skirt and dark makeup, but nothing would stop her from looking beautiful.

"Showing my kid brother around, Maddie?" I ask.

"Sure am. He loves this house. He's freaky and weird like you."

"I don't like being freaky."

"Any drinking games 'round here, guys?" asks Damie.

"Not after what happened last year," Bryce says, lifting his eyebrows.

I elbow Bryce hard in the shoulder and look at him crossly. Last year, I nearly tore down the house on Halloween during a drinking game. Enora was using a spell to show me her and Bryce together. I got so mad that I nearly took the house down. But I don't want him telling Damie. I don't want Damie involved in any of our witch stuff.

"Hey, man!" says another tall dark-haired boy. It's Harvey, Damie's best friend. He hugs my brother and they clink beer bottles together. Damie looks like a surfer, but Harvey's more preppy looking, like my boyfriend.

"I heard this place is haunted by your family." Harvey smiles at Damien. "Escoba and Maverick Hawthorne." Then Harvey turns to us. "Hi, Cadence. Bryce. Maddie."

"You see that window over there?" Maddie says to Harvey— pointing, with her red cup in her hand, at the window I've been staring at. "The ghost of Abigail supposedly haunts the window, looking down at Hawthorne every night. Abigail knifed Escoba, a voodoo witch..." She points at me with a wink. "Katie and Damie's relative. Or people think Escoba was knifed by Abigail. It was never proven. Abigail's killing was revenge for Escoba's curse. Abigail's ghost appears by that window every night holding a knife."

It's an awful tale, but it's told to all the freshmen who come to Hawthorne, especially during the orientation party. When Maddie finishes, Damie looks at me and says, "Witches, huh. Interesting."

The little shit. He's said other things, over the past two weeks, hinting that he knows I'm a witch. I hate that. I mean, my makeup is suspicious, but I keep telling him I just like looking goth.

"Babe," Maddie says to me, touching my hand, "how'd your interview go?"

Shit.

"Yeah, sis?" asks Damie. "How'd it go?"

Bryce looks at me but doesn't say anything. I think he's tired of prodding.

"Excuse me," I say to all of them, finally climbing out of my sunken beanbag. "I have to use the little ladies' room."

I don't, of course, but you know I don't want to talk about my interview. I haven't talked about it in days. And as I walk away from my friends, dodging more bodies, I could swear I see Maddie and Bryce talking behind my back, looking concerned. They're on to my failure. I just know it.

When I return to my beanbag a few minutes later, all my friends are off to the side, enjoying getting inebriated together. I don't mind. Like I said, I like that everyone's having a good time.

Then I recognize my dear, sweet friend Frida. I'm so happy to see her, but she startles me with her expression. She runs over, so scared.

"Katie!" Frida says. "Katie! She's here. Did you see her? She's here."

"Who? Who's here?"

"Enora."

I open my eyes wide. "Here?"

Frida nods.

That's when two girls wearing tight pitch-black dresses and thick, dark makeup walk into the living room. Accompanying them is a tall, blond man; he's shirtless, flaunting his buff physique. They get a lot of attention. A crowd forms around them. It's Enora and Cordelia. I don't know the bare-chested man.

Many older students say hi to Enora because she used to visit the fraternity house when she was Bryce's girlfriend. She's also very pretty. Like model pretty. Everyone's looking at her face and tight black lace dress. She's got tanned skin and a perfect figure, but her dress is indecent—it's just nasty. She keeps staring over at me with her bright blue eyes. She's always done that. She's so fascinated by me. I hate her. They're socializing as if they're just visiting the orientation party, but Enora keeps glaring at me.

The guy standing with them is really odd looking. He's got pale skin, a goatee, and a rippling muscular chest, and he stands like two feet taller than the girls. Actually, he towers over everyone. He also snarls and glares at everybody. He reminds me more of an animal than a human. Enora pulls at his elbow as if it's a leash for a pet dog.

Bryce approaches them, and that lures me out of my beanbag. I swear if Enora or that meathead even lays a fingernail on him, I'm gonna go berserko.

"Bryce," Enora says, all fake and cheery. "How are you?" Like she cares. Last time they saw each other, the witch tried to burn him alive.

Then Damie walks over with Harvey. Enora sees my brother. My hands grip into tight fists, and for a moment the lights in the room flicker. Most people don't notice, because it's not that uncommon for the lights to do weird stuff in this old house. But Cordelia does. She flashes an infuriating sly grin at me.

"Aren't you?" Enora asks, wagging a finger at Damie. The bitch giggles. "Why, aren't you? You even look like her. You're little Katie's younger brother, aren't you? I can see the resemblance."

Don't you dare touch him!

Damie nods. He seems enchanted. Like I said, Enora's strikingly beautiful. But when she talks to Damie, I've had enough. I rush over.

"What are you doing here?" I snap.

"Katie?" Enora says in fake surprise. "Oh, hi, Katie. I didn't know you were here." Then she lifts her left hand, flashing me a red painted pentagram. "I should have guessed after seeing Bryce. So very nice to see you again."

"She's rude, master," says Cordelia, looking at me with disgust.

Her tall dog-man snarls at me. I lurch back when he opens his mouth. His teeth are filed down and he has two fangs. (Seriously, I'm not making this up.)

"Adder," says Enora, "this is our reunion, dear. It's so great to see little Katie with her boyfriend and family." Then she looks around the room in wonder and seems to address the crowd. "Family." Enora gestures at the living room with open arms. She rubs her black-lace-gloved hands together. "Ah, why, you can just feel the paranormal energy run through the walls." Then she looks at me with full-on bitch-smugness. "Even the lights flicker. Almost, one could guess, a witch's magic? Your ancestors still roam here, Cadence? How are they? You been talking to them lately?"

"Where's Mira?"

"Nuh, uh, uh. You first, Cadence. Where's Beatrix?"

"Who is this ape?" I ask.

"Gus," he says, turning to me. "My name's Gus. And you better watch your mouth, girl."

There are some oohs and aahs from bystanders. I reason that this must be a lot of entertainment for the party. Even though few know what the hell's going on, it must be obvious that there's some kind of commotion. In fact, all my witches who attended this party are now standing behind me.

Enora runs her hand lasciviously along Gus's naked arm. "Careful, Gus. Little Katie might look like you can squash her, but looks can be deceiving."

"She seems like an ordinary little girl," Gus says, looking me up and down.

"Yeah?" asks Bryce. "Well, Katie's right. You look like a gorilla."

But then he freaks Bryce out by opening his mouth, showing his fangs.

"Shut your mouth, Gus," Enora says, waving an arm at him with a chuckle. Then she turns to me. "Adder and I want to know where my sister Beatrix is. Can you please tell us?"

"She's with me."

"Where? I don't see her. You know, it's a real long, boring drive from Atlanta." Then Enora looks around at all the students swarming us. She puts a hand up. "No offense, everyone. The forests at your school are very pretty. I miss the trees. But the drive's shit. I was hoping you'd be more welcoming, Cadence."

"How can you expect anything else from us!" snaps Frida in her Brazilian accent. I've never seen Frida look so angry. Those who know her are shocked. Frida's the sweetest, shyest girl in the world.

"Shh," Enora says to Frida. She runs a lace-gloved finger over Frida's lips, and Frida knocks her hand off. "This is a talk between *real* witches, señorita."

When she touches Frida, the witches in my coven go crazy. No one touches our dear Frida. There's Tammy, Hope, Helen, and Mandy. They shout profanities and yell at Enora and Cordelia. The other students at the party have no idea what the hell's going on, but everybody in the house is now gathered in the living room. I glance at my brother. He and Harvey are completely dumbfounded. I gesture for Bryce to do something, anything, to get my brother the hell out of here.

"Let's talk away from the party," I say to Enora when it's quiet enough to get a word in.

"But I always liked the Billington House back-to-school party. I miss it here. Bryce and I had really good times together. Remember, Bryce?"

"Outside," I repeat.

Gus grabs my arm and I angrily shrug it off. I think if he touches me again, I might light his hand on fire.

"Suit yourself, Windstorm. *Et nos unum sumus.*" Enora chuckles. Then she turns to her crowd. "Don't fret, dears, I'll be right back. Apparently, Katie Hawthorne and I have some catching up to do."

She laughs at her own words, which aren't funny. Then she gestures with a black-gloved finger for us to walk outside all snooty, as if I'm deigning to be in her presence.

All my friends and Enora's two companions walk together into the front yard. There are still partygoers watching us. Bryce doesn't accompany us. At first, out of curiosity, Harvey and my brother were going to join, but Bryce grabbed them to keep them inside. I signal to my other witches to stay in the house also. Everyone but Maddie. I need some support. Anyway, Cordelia's by Enora's side and has always been like Enora's best friend, so why can't I have mine? Gus remains by the front of the house, leaning against a wall with folded arms, staring at us.

We walk down the hill to a dirt path near the forest, where Enora finally stops and turns. She's not smiling anymore. She looks dangerous.

"Enough playing around," I say.

"Agreed. You have Beatrix. I want her back. She will accompany me and Cordelia back to my Abaddon coven. *Now.* Either have her leave Alondra's house or have her accompany us. I wasn't joking about not enjoying the drive here."

"What are you going to do to her?"

"That's none of your fucking business," Cordelia snaps.

"I told you to never return here," I warn.

"I had to come to take back what's mine," Enora says. "I respected your wishes, but then one of my witches left and came to you. She's *my* witch. From *my* coven. *My* circle. Give her back to me and I'll leave." Then she looks around at the forest. "Honestly, I don't really care for Hawthorne. I lied about the trees. They're really boring."

"Beatrix told us what you were planning to do to her," Maddie says.

"Why are *you* here?" Enora asks.

"She said that you were planning on getting her pregnant," Maddie continues, ignoring the insult, "so that you could drink blood from her dead aborted baby."

Cordelia bursts out laughing. I don't think it's very funny. Enora develops a big grin. Then she shuts Cordelia up by showing her hand—the hand with the pentagram.

"Beatrix is mentally ill, Madison," says Enora. "I already visited her before I came here. I knocked on Alondra's door but, of course, the little whore didn't answer. She's hiding. And lying. And you're helping her. She did the same to us, but we still love her. She's a part of my coven, crazy or not. Release her from your house, Cadence."

"She can go if she wants," I say. "But if she's unsafe, I'm allowing her to stay."

"Then you're minding my business," Enora says, infuriatingly wagging a finger at me. She raises her eyebrows. "You know a witch that harbors another witch is calling her one of her own. You're taking one of my sisters. Or must I teach you again about our arts?"

"How do we know you didn't send her?" asks Maddie.

"Why would I do that?" Then she looks up and down at Maddie as if amazed that she's daring to speak again. "You're an interesting witch. Are you one? What exactly do you do? I've never heard of you casting a single spell. Do you just follow your High Priestess around like a dog?"

"Like her?" Maddie points at Cordelia.

Cordelia's eyes open wide, and I could swear there's a flash of red circling the whites of her eyes.

"Uh, uh, uh," says Enora. But she chuckles, amused. "Careful. Adder is a powerful witch, Madison. Unlike yourself."

"Maddie's a lot better witch than any of you," I say.

"Fine," Enora says, rolling her eyes. "Whatever. Look, you saved me, Cadence. I haven't forgotten that. I respected your wishes and kept away. But taking one of my sisters from my coven is not acceptable. All I ask is that you let me take her home."

"Why do you have Mira?"

"I already told you," Cordelia answers.

"I want her to tell me."

"She loves our spell casting," Enora says with a shrug. "It's her life. I offered her an opportunity to practice magic. You never did. She was willing to move to Atlanta with me. As you know, our coven just moved, so I invited her. She enjoyed it so much that she wants to stay."

"I don't believe that. Mira never liked you. Maybe if you release Mira, I'll give you Beatrix."

"I don't have Mira to release, you fuck!" snaps Enora, suddenly enraged. Then she looks down and shakes. But she tries to laugh it off. "She's free to go if she pleases. That's more than I can say about that harlot you're harboring."

"I'll talk to Beatrix. If she feels safe, I don't care if she leaves."

"No." Enora walks right up to my nose. Then she shakes her head. "I didn't travel to the middle of nowhere for nothing. You will release her now, whether she wants to or not. You will tell her to leave, or I will take her. I warn you. The choice is yours. Do not test me. I was very happy to leave you and Bryce alone after I killed the High Wizard, but if you get in the way of my coven's business, I will have to move into yours. And if you don't release her, I'll take her my way—very possibly in a fashion you won't like. Mind your own business, or I'll mind yours. Like that of your boyfriend or...your brother."

"Don't you dare touch him!"

A wind develops from clear skies. Clouds cover the moon and it becomes dark. Cordelia looks around nervously as our long hair blows in the wind.

"Always a pleasure, Cadence." Enora looks at the sky and feigns a smile. "You don't have to conjure a windstorm to remind me who you are. This is about you trespassing on me, not the other way around. Tell Beatrix to leave. Tell her I'm giving her a week. After a week, if she doesn't return, I'll take her. My way."

And that's enough. The bitch twirls her dress and walks away with Cordelia.

"Forget the party," Enora says to Cordelia. "We've seen all we wanted." Then she signals toward the house, claps her hands together, and hollers, "Come, come, Gus. We're going home now. I have a special treat for you."

And all three of them briskly walk down a side path to an adjoining road, away from the Billington House.

"You have to get rid of Beatrix, Katie," says Maddie, watching them.

I turn and look at my friend. Maddie forces a smile, but she looks really scared.

"I hate her," I say.

"Let's just go back to the party," Maddie says with a nod and takes my hand.

4

____

DARKNESS

"BEATRIX?" I SHOUT.

I'm in the foyer, yelling up the stairs to Alondra's bedroom. That's where Beatrix usually is. Standing in the entryway of Alondra's house is terrible because the house is super creepy at night without electricity. Bryce drove me here from the Billington House after the back-to-school party. He wanted us to go home and go to bed, but after seeing Enora, I had to check on Beatrix. He was going to join me in the house, but his old car was vibrating on our way over. Right now, he's checking his engine.

I wish I weren't here. It's so dark. Well, at least the AC isn't on. That would be too creepy. But it's warm inside after another hot summer day.

"Beatrix?" I holler again. "Are you up there?" She wouldn't answer her phone either.

So I do what I really don't want to do. I light a candle from the small table by the front door and walk up the shadowy stairway.

"Beatrix?"

Damn it. Where is she?

At the top of the stairs, I turn left down the hall to the main bedroom. I hate going in there. I still see images in my mind of a sick Alondra groaning in bed. But her ghost isn't here. At least I've never seen her ghost here.

The main bedroom is brighter. The drapes on the large window are open. This view looks over the grassy field behind the house; in the center is a pile of logs where we light our bonfires. Shadows of trees in the distance surround the yard.

The master bed is a complete mess. There's trash strewn all over the floor—paper bags from fast-food restaurants with left-over food, magazines, books. I take out my cell phone and call her again. I jump when the phone rings under the bedsheets. Then I jump again when my phone vibrates in my hand. Bryce is calling.

"Hey, babe," he says. "Did the ghost get you?"

"Shit. You really scared me. Not funny. What's the matter with the car?"

"I don't know. Maybe the spark plugs or engine mounts."

"Wow. Sounds like you really know your stuff."

"I just looked it up on my phone."

I laugh.

"The car can wait till tomorrow. I'll take it to a mechanic. Look, can we go? Is she okay?"

"I don't know where the hell she is. The room's a complete mess. And I can see why she's not answering her calls. Her phone's on the bed. I'll look around the house."

"You need me there?"

"No. No. I'm okay. I'll be outside soon."

I hang up my phone and make my way down the stairs with my candle.

"Beatrix?"

I pass my favorite dining room. It's really dark. It's brighter outside, and I can make out the lovely forest through the floor-to-ceiling window. Then I check the living room. It looks chic when it's brightly lit, but in the shadows, it's just another dark, creepy room. I walk back to the entrance to the house and head down another hall toward the guest room.

That's when I really get the heebie-jeebies. A light flickers near the end of the hall—right where Bryce and I slept a few weeks ago. The guest room.

I walk down the hall. By the door, I gasp. There's a black cloak curled up in a ball in the center of the room. The cloak is circled by flickering candles, which are surrounded by a pile of white chalk. And in front of the cloak is a book. My book. *Broomstick.* I'm thinking maybe it's Alondra's ghost. With a hood over the witch's head, I can't tell. But then—

"Hi, Cadence."

"Shit!" I exclaim. "You scared the hell out of me, Beatrix."

Why she's curled into a ball in the middle of my guest room, with candles and my book, is beyond me. Last year, Alondra sat like this when she was dying. It's similar to a yoga pose.

Beatrix breaks all the spookiness when she lifts her head, revealing her girlish features, long blond hair, and chubby cheeks. But her makeup is smeared. She's been crying again.

"What are you doing?" I snap.

"Meditating on death. I'm trying to cast a protective shield spell with your book. I'm drawing power from Gaia by our feet and energy from Alondra and your Book of Shadows."

"Well, can you stop and answer me next time I call out your name? You're really freaking me out."

"Sure, Katie," she says with a sweet smile. "Sorry." For a second, it makes me let go of my anger.

"You okay?" I ask.

"Sure. How come you're here so late?"

"I saw Enora at the party."

"She came by here too." Beatrix nods. "But I didn't let her in."

"She told me that. She's asking for you back."

Beatrix turns her head, fighting back tears.

"You can stay here," I say. "You don't have to return to her if you don't want to. I told you, you have a home here."

Beatrix nods again. But then she starts to cry.

"What's the matter? I said you can stay."

"That's not it." She shook her head. "The cat died."

"What?"

"The cat I asked you for. She died."

"You asked for her only a couple hours ago. What are you talking about?"

Beatrix wipes her arm across her nose and flashes a fake grin. She shrugs. "I took her in from outside. She was wandering the woods. She didn't look good. Her back had hairless patches and she limped. I could tell she was sick. That's why I wanted to help her. I felt so bad for her. Alondra used to love cats, you said, right? You think it was one of hers?"

I shake my head. I personally gave Alondra's cats away a year ago.

"Then..." Beatrix shrugs again. "She just died in my arms. God, it was so terrible, Cadence." And Beatrix starts crying again. She's so depressing.

"It's okay, Beatrix. We can get you another cat that's not a stray."

Beatrix shakes her head and her eyes bulge. "It's a sign, Windstorm. It means I'm going to die. I just know it. And you know what else, Cadence? I'm going to hell. Damnation for all my sins. For all the sins Enora had me do. I just know that too. See, the cat is me. One of Panthera's cats. It's like a prophecy. It was sent by Panthera. I saw the cat in the forest and it ran right into my arms, but it was hurt. It was so hungry. Just like me. And, I don't know, maybe I overfed it, but it just wasn't going to make it. So I took it into my arms. And then...and then you were nice enough to let me keep her. So I got her some milk and fed her. But she drank so weakly. Its fur was shedding all over the patio. And its nose was full of mucus. I tried desperately to care for it, rocking it in my arms." She looks right into my eyes. She's so awfully sad. It's horrible. "She just died in my arms. On the patio. She's gone! She's dead!"

She loses it and starts bawling again.

I sigh and put a hand on her shoulder, but she shakes her head and jerks from me.

"Stay away from me! I'm cursed. Damned! Stay outside the circle." She points at the chalk surrounding her. "Enora is Panthera, right? Think about it. She sent her animal totem. A cat. To send me the message. She warned me that I'd die if I didn't return, but if I go back, I'm going to die anyway. So I set this magic circle to prepare my passing into the Summerland. To meditate on death. But I don't want the curse to spread to you. No, not you of all people. You're so nice."

"Oh, come on, Beatrix. You're being ridiculous."

"It's a sign," she says, nodding, her eyes bulging again. "It's a sign that I don't have much longer to live. Enora is coming for me. I even...saw a flock of crows overhead right after the cat died!"

They probably smelled the dead animal, but I don't tell Beatrix that. I don't think logic will make her feel any better right now.

Beatrix is scared because Enora's mystical name, Panthera, represents cats, although all last year she used her magic to shapeshift into a blackbird. In fact, last year Enora deceived me by becoming my "friend" after transforming into a raven. I have to admit, when you put all these signs together, it certainly looks like Enora could be behind it. But it could just be a coincidence.

"I'll get you another cat," I say.

"And then you can get yourself a new Beatrix."

"Oh, Beatrix, stop. You've got to get a hold of yourself."

"Did you know, Katie, that my father is a Catholic priest? Did I tell you that? I ran from him too. I will never have a home again. Last time I came by his house, he said, 'Get back, devil.' He said that to his own daughter. He knows I'm a witch. A satanic witch. He doesn't want my sins to rub off on him. He doesn't want to be damned like me. Same thing happened when I went into a church a few months ago. I went to ask for forgiveness. The priest chased me out of there too. I will never have a home under God, because I'm damned. All because of what I've done. Do you understand?"

She completely loses it again.

"*Fallen like God's fallen angel!*" she screams. "*To the depths of hell under Lucifer's wing! When I die, I join Satan down in the depths of the Earth to suffer from pain and burn for an eternity in hellfire!*"

And she weeps again.

My phone buzzes in my pants pocket, and it's a welcome distraction. It's Bryce again. I don't have to look. I know he's asking me if I'm almost done. Done with what? No professional psychiatrist could help this girl.

"I just came by to make sure you're safe," I say with a sigh. "And to make sure you're not doing something stupid."

"Like kill myself? I wouldn't do that. You...you know why, Cadence?" She looks at me with watery, bloodshot eyes. I just shake my head. "Because that's a sin." She chuckles. "That would be proof to the Lord above of my evil. It would seal my fate and bring me down even faster to damnation. But...I suppose it doesn't really matter anyway." Then she bursts into laughter.

"Look, I have to go. Bryce is waiting for me in the car. I told you, I'll get you a new cat. Okay? I think Alondra would like a cat roaming these halls again."

"I wish Alondra were here. Falconsong was such a powerful witch." Then she puts her hand out to me and shakes her head.

"But, of course, you are too, Windstorm. I need all the protection I can get."

"You're safe, Beatrix. But it's really late. I'm going to go."

She nods.

"Can you get up off the floor?"

"I won't leave this circle tonight. Can you say an incantation to protect me? I set up the candles, Windstorm. And I poured white dust around the light to make a sacred shield. I thought of painting a pentagram in the center of the carpet, but then I thought it would make you mad. Enora used to give me a spell to protect me when I felt like this. I tried to use your book, but I'm not sure it has enough energy alone. Can you utter a quick incantation to protect me?"

Enora used to give her a spell when she felt like this? So she's felt like this before?

Her request for an incantation sends shivers down my spine. It reminds me of a child asking their mother for a bedtime story. I'm beginning to be more creeped out by Beatrix than by Enora.

"I have to go," I say with a sigh. "Just go upstairs and go to bed."

I walk to the door, but before I can leave, she begs, "Please? Oh, please, Cadence! Please, say an incantation for me. I know it will protect me tonight."

"An incantation?"

She gestures to the circle of candles around her and nods.

I roll my eyes. "What do you want...?" I look at her. She's so scared. So I take a deep breath and cross the room to stand beside her, flick my fingers over her head, and say the first words that come to my mind: "May the witch inside this holy circle be protected."

"Oh, thank you, Windstorm! Thank you! I just know any magic from you will work."

I nod. Then I head to the door again.

"Wait. Before you go, I have to tell you something else."

"What?" I snap. I don't mean to sound mad, but she's so difficult!

"I lied to you."

"What?"

She sits up straighter and looks really guilty. She fights back tears again and averts her eyes. "Enora sent me. She sent me on purpose to break the peace."

"What?"

"You've been so nice. I wasn't going to tell you. I wasn't ever going to tell you, but I owe you. I like you and your friends so much. I owed you the truth. Enora said that if you took me in, she'd have an excuse to go after the Hawthorne coven again. I told you, she still hates you. She just needed an excuse. Right after we came to Atlanta, she said she had to cleanse the lands under Hecate and take care of Hawthorne."

"Beatrix, explain quick. I'm getting mad. What exactly do you mean?"

"I told you Enora gave me two choices, right? It wasn't two, it was three. There were the two terrible blood sacrifices—the blood of my unborn child or the death of me. But there was a third choice involving you. Of course I didn't know you well enough, so I didn't really care. But you've been so nice, and I don't think there's much hope for me now anyway, so I wish I had chosen one of the two blood sacrifices instead. I'm doomed anyway. I don't really want anything bad to happen to you. The thing is, maybe I should have just accepted the blood sacrifice of my unborn baby. I think then she would have rejected Mira and kept me. I could have gotten pregnant again and then, you know, we usually get a doctor to do the procedure. Enora makes sure we're safe. I did it once before."

You did it before!

"The thing I was worried about was that she could ask me to do it again. And again. And again. I just thought it was the height of sin to do it again. Maybe it's because my father is an ordained Catholic priest? I don't know. But maybe I should have accepted her—"

"Beatrix!" I put my head in my hands. I take a deep breath. Why am I helping her? How can I help her? I don't think anyone can help her. And now she's endangered me and my friends.

"Look, the stuff you're saying is horrible," I say. "You've done it before? What do you mean you've done it before? Are you serious?"

She almost starts crying again and, for a flash, the lights in the room turn on. This is, of course, impossible as the house has been disconnected from city power. But my hands are clenched tightly. It's me. I'm furious. Beatrix opens her eyes wide. Then she quickly crouches into her ball again, terrified of me. She is shaking and whimpering again.

Shit.

"Stop crying!" I shout.

She nods with her head still buried.

"Beatrix...you lied? You weren't in danger of being forced to do something you hadn't done before?"

"*But I didn't want to do it again!*" she yells, shaking her head. "Don't you see? *I didn't want to do it again!*" She's screaming between sobs. "I didn't want to do it again, because I knew she would keep having me do it over and over and over. *Again and again and again!* It would never end, Cadence! That's another reason why I came here. I couldn't do it anymore! I thought following her and coming to see you would get her off my back."

"All right," I say as calmly as I can. "Okay. Just calm down. Stop crying. It's okay."

She shakes her head. And then...she laughs. That sends another shiver down my spine. I think laughter is the last thing I'm feeling right now.

"You don't know us," she says, shaking her head. "You don't know our ways. There are many secret witch gatherings like ours all over the world. There isn't just Wicca. Many other witches worship evil. The devil. Under Baphomet. Against the Christians and any god you would consider good and holy. What you're so disgusted by isn't as bad as other things I've seen. Or done." She shakes her head and leans over the carpet outside the circle. She dry heaves for a moment. I'm expecting her to throw up, but she doesn't. "I've partaken in eating flesh too."

What monster did I let into Alondra's house?

I step back. She's still crouched like a black onyx stone, wearing her black cloak, curled up in a ball. That angers me because it reminds me of my teacher. How dare this girl pretend to be anything like Alondra. I reach down in front of her and snatch my book. It seems random, but suddenly I really don't like her being anywhere near my book.

She laughs again with her head still buried. That only makes me hate her more.

"I'm damned. But so are you, Cadence. Alondra's husband worshipped Baphomet to increase the power of Hawthorne, and whether you're a devil worshipper or not, Cadence, you were initiated into the Hawthorne coven under Baphomet's rule. Your power stems from Satan. And Enora hates Hawthorne more than anything in the world. Last year, she tried to take control of your coven, but you stopped her. So now—"

"Beatrix, stop for a second. What do you mean, you ate flesh? You mean like human flesh? Like cannibalism?" I mean, can we step back and revisit this for a moment? I can't believe this.

"Well," she says, lifting her head and finally looking at me with her bloodshot eyes. "I mean, I didn't kill them. It was fed to me."

Ah. That makes it much better.

Beatrix looks down and practically talks to herself. "My hope was that if I did what Enora asked, she'd take me back. I could come back home, and things would be the way they were before Mira joined. And then Enora wouldn't hurt me anymore. But any love she once had for me is gone. I could tell when I talked to her today. She just wants to finish you. You and Mira. And Hawthorne. And Bryce. She wants you all gone. But Mira's too lovestruck to see it."

"I'm going to go."

"There are no more lies," she says, raising her head. "I'm sorry. I know how much you value the truth. I won't lie to you anymore. I promise."

"Okay." But how can I trust anything she says after she told me all those things? Then again, I don't think I ever really trusted her.

"I see the way you're looking at me," she says with a nod. "I get it. Now you know I'm a monster."

No, I think you're insane.

"Well, so is my master. So is my coven. But after I leave tomorrow, I won't blame you. I will only feel grateful to you for letting me stay here when you did."

"You're not leaving tomorrow."

She looks at me like I'm nuts. In another circumstance, perhaps that would be funny.

"You don't want me to leave tomorrow? After I lied to you? After Enora threatened you? I..." She looks at her candlelit circle and trembles. "I understand. I'll leave tonight if that's what you want, Windstorm. That's okay. I will."

"No." But half of me is thinking, *yes.* "You're in danger, whether she sent you here or not. And even with all those things she made you do, you need protection. Right?"

She nods.

"Then it's up to you. My invitation stands. You can stay here as long as you have to."

"You're such a white light!" she says with a big grin, almost breathless. "Such a bright white light! You remind me of your teacher, Alondra. No, better. I... thank you so much, Cadence. Thank you!"

"You'll be all right, Beatrix," I say. "I'm going to get you a cat, okay? A healthy one."

"You're so nice," she says with a chuckle. Then she looks down and shakes her head. "But you know, Katie, I really think we're damned and going to go to hell anyway."

5

BY CANDLELIGHT, MY DREAM

Lacey's is always a romantic dining experience, with candles, large comfy booths, and darkness. You can't see much except your date. I think that's why Bryce loves it so much. It's really romantic. And in Hawthorne, it's the only fancy romantic steak house for a hundred miles. Bryce and I come here now and then. Our first real "date" was here. I signed a confidentiality agreement to join the coven. Back then, unlike now, there were good reasons to be secretive. Even now, my witches are still secretive, and we don't talk about our coven in school, but we don't do anything crazy that warrants confidentiality agreements anymore.

Anyway, we're here again and Bryce is looking through a menu, even though he probably already knows what he wants. I'm not. I'm sipping water, staring at an empty table across the room, thinking about Beatrix. And that makes me think of Mira. And then...my interview.

"They have a new special for lobster bisque tonight, babe," Bryce says.

"Sure," I say with a slight grin.

"We could order something different?"

"No. No. I don't mind either way. Just happy to be here with you." I force a smile.

Bryce puts the menu down. He's about to say something when our waitress comes to the table.

"Welcome," the waitress says, lighting a candle in the center of our table. She's an older woman, with her curly dark hair in a bun, wearing a bow tie and a black-and-white suit. "Is this a special occasion?"

"Just celebrating the new school year," Bryce says. "We'd like a bottle of wine. Your house merlot." Then he looks at me. "Merlot's okay, Katie?"

Sure. But a whole bottle?

"Can I see your IDs?"

Why do they always ask that? I don't look that young. And Bryce, he has a beard, for goodness' sake. Then again, his beard is pretty thin.

When she leaves, Bryce turns back to me and says, "What's the matter? Still upset about Beatrix?"

"Of course. Sorry. She's so odd. She asks me if she can keep a cat, and then three hours later the cat's dead. For all I know she killed it. We've been helping a total wacko."

"Well, how about I take your mind off of it and we talk about something else?"

"Okay, like what?"

"Us."

I lift my eyebrows. *Sure.* And he scoots closer to me on the booth. *Cute.* We're sitting side by side.

"How's your classes?" He's close enough for me to smell his lovely spearmint-laden breath and Bryce-cologne.

"I thought we were going to talk about *us*?" I ask, blinking my eyes stupidly.

He kisses my lips. Then he shrugs. "What's there to talk about? I'm madly in love with you."

I laugh, but then I feel a little sour. "Classes aren't great."

"Jesus, Katie, what's the matter? I can't believe how down you are."

I brush my fingers along his short hair and then his cheek, over his thin beard. "You're not. I like that. You're in a good mood."

"I'm not happy if you're not. What's wrong with your classes?"

"You're not teaching them," I say with a shrug. "And Maddie's not in them."

He laughs again and puts an arm around me.

"I like my Eastern religion history class, I guess. We're studying Buddha."

"Dr. Grange kinda looks like the Buddha."

"Aha. He's the sweetest guy in the world. Everybody loves him, and the class is always packed. I mean, sometimes I feel like I'm meditating just listening to him. And it's neat, Bryce, 'cause the religion reminds me of ours in a way."

"Ours? We don't have a religion, Katie."

I shake my head. I'm about to reply, but we're interrupted by the waitress again. I love the wineglasses she places in front of us. They're giant, like twice the size of normal wineglasses. She serves the wine and leaves us again.

"To us, Bryce," I toast and we clink glasses.

"It is a religion," I say after swallowing some wine. The wine's good. Smooth. "All of our witches believe in the magic and power of nature. Nature is our religion. Buddhism isn't all that different. Dr. Grange teaches us that the goal of Buddhism is thoughtlessness. This is so similar to what Alondra talked about with meditation. She always told us to center ourselves, concentrating on our oneness with nature. And it's not that different from Hinduism either, with the belief in one thought, one soul, or Atman. I mean, Alondra even adopted the word Atman, meaning *the soul*, for our circle."

"You seem to really like this stuff."

"It's interesting," I say with a shrug. "Yeah, I really do."

"But it's not really history."

"Well, you taught art last year. Dr. Riker's class was more like an art class than history. And I've got to tell you, I don't think Riker was as nice as I thought."

"Why?"

I don't want to answer that. If I answer that, I'm going to talk about my interview. And if I talk about my interview, I'm going to bring up how I may never see my gorge boyfriend, who's peering at me right now with his irresistible bright blue eyes. And if I do that, it's going to be another thing, along with my schizophrenic houseguest and magical witch-bitch archenemy, to be concerned with instead of focusing on this lovely candlelit dinner date and smooth, yummy wine. So I fall silent.

"Dr. Riker liked you," Bryce says after some silence.

"He failed me."

"I know, but that's his way. He doesn't believe in remediation. It wasn't personal."

"You know, Satanism is a religion too."

Bryce lifts his eyebrows.

"Christianity is a religion of dichotomy, right? Good versus evil. A religion, like Judaism and Islam, against sin. Well, Satanism takes the evil side and just mimics these three religions, worshipping everything antithetical to them. But that's still worship. It's still a religion, Bryce."

"This is coming from someone who hates Satanism more than anyone I know."

"I didn't say I like it. I said it was a religion. They worship the opposite of Jesus's teachings. They worship the body because Jesus worshipped the spirit. They worship sin, arguing that there is no afterlife, no heaven. And they worship ceremonial sex because the Bible tells us to refrain until marriage."

Bryce raises his eyebrows. Yeah, well, we've kind of failed that one.

"Satanism worships everything antithetical to the church. But see, they worship. William Reardon worshipped the devil. It is a religion."

"You're smart, babe," Bryce quips, sipping more wine.

"Shut up," I say with a smile. "Anyway…" I sip more wine; it is really good. "That's why I took a religious history class. I like this stuff."

"So that's your favorite class?"

"Yeah. I guess. How 'bout you?"

"I like teaching Dr. Riker's class. I like art."

"But how boring. I don't get why they made you teach the same class this year."

"They didn't make me, I chose to," he says with a shrug. "You know, I'm so busy working on my dissertation. Of course, Alondra was supposed to have been my dissertation advisor. Now, who knows. I'm not even sure they'll graduate me this year."

"Come on. The department loves you."

"Hmm."

The waitress walks over. "You guys decide on what you want?"

We already talked it over during lunch today. It's kind of silly, in a way. Bryce and I have our "date" tonight, but I'm living with him. But coming here, making it a date, makes us concentrate on us. And that's nice. But we're talking about school instead. Maybe that's what Bryce is doing? Maybe his plan was to join me in a romantic dinner to sneakily bring up my failed interview?

We order and then Bryce looks nervous. Why? That's weird. He's looking all over the candlelit room. He's in a good mood, but he's nervous.

Well, I'm nervous too. I want to talk about the interview so badly, but I don't. He takes my hand and smiles, and I bring his hand up to my lips and kiss it. Then we just hold hands and fall silent. I scoot as close to him as I can and just enjoy his warmth, sipping wine.

"Speaking of religion," I finally say, "you know, when I visited Beatrix, she really affected me. I haven't been sleeping well."

"She's creepy."

"She said I was damned."

"Is that it?" He looks right at me, searching my eyes. Then he shakes his head. "She's the one damned, Katie. Not you."

"But Reardon was practicing Satanism when you initiated me. She's right about that. Doesn't that mean that I became a witch under the devil? Doesn't that—"

"Oh, Cadence," he says, shaking his head again, "are you joking? You pulled me through crazy talk like this last year. And you know, if anyone is damned, it's me. So you took mandrake? You didn't do a blood sacrifice."

"She cut my arm."

"You never bowed under a pentagram," he says, getting angry. "Or...Jesus, had sex on one." He runs his hand through his short hair. "If there's anybody going to hell, it's me."

"So? So we can go to hell together."

"Is this why you're so unhappy?"

No.

He shakes his head vigorously as if trying to shake off these thoughts. "Don't you remember what you said to me when we lit candles for Alondra and your mother? You said there's no such thing as pure evil. Just like there's no such thing as pure good. Alondra believed that. Your love saved me. Don't you think if there's a God, he or she judges us by all the good we do? You said yourself we're judged by who and what we love. Even if a rite damned you—and it didn't—don't you think God will forgive you? I mean, you're an angel for taking Beatrix into your home in the first place."

"She needed me."

"But you risked so much for her. And after she lied to you and told you all the crazy stuff she's been involved with, you still want to keep her safe. That's goodness. That's angelic. That's love. If it's not, I don't know what is." He snatches up his wine and swallows a little. "I don't like Beatrix. She's messing with your head, and that makes me really mad. Especially after everything we're doing for her."

"Sorry, Bryce. Now I'm bringing you down."

"It's okay. I just don't like you saying stuff like this. If there's anyone in the world who's going to heaven, it's you, Cadence."

"Well, anyway, that's not the reason I'm down. There's something I need to tell you."

"What, babe?"

Yeah, what?

"I...I..." I want to tell him so badly about my interview, but I just can't.

"What?"

Shit, I don't want to tell him. But now, with the "date," I feel like I have to. Because it's about us and...about us never seeing each other again!

I clam up and my chest feels tight. He squeezes my hand more tightly.

"Bryce, I didn't just *feel* like the interview went badly, it did go badly. I, sort of, lied to you. The interview...he told me. I don't know, I—"

"It's okay, Katie. Forget it."

"Hmm?"

"I get it about the interview, Cadence."

I furrow my brow and look right into his eyes, and he gives me that lovely reassuring Bryce smile.

"What do you get?"

"That it went badly. It's obvious."

"It was horrible," I say, shaking my head. "Dr. Bainer's a total jerk."

"He is," Bryce says with a nod. "No one likes him."

"You hinted that."

"I didn't want you to worry." Then he forces a smile and brushes the bangs from my eyes. "I think you're unhappy because you're worrying too much. Stop worrying, babe. Whatever happens, things will work out. I know they will."

"But how? He said he's not accepting me, Bryce. That's what I didn't tell you. What does that mean for us? I want to stay with you next year. I can't if I have to go to some other school. God, some other state? Can you imagine? Dad's going to want me to go wherever I can to study history. He's not going to settle for me not moving on in school. What am I going to do? I've got to go here next year. I just have to. But now I feel like I blew it."

He shakes his head. "Everything will be okay."

"No, it won't."

He loses his smile and becomes very serious all of a sudden. For a moment, I feel this sinking feeling that he agrees with me. But then he lifts a single finger to gesture *just a minute*. He lets go of my hand and digs into his pocket. I'm looking at him like he's crazy.

He takes out a small jewelry box and puts it on the table, sliding it over to me. The box is teal and velvety. I pick it up. It looks like a ring box.

Can this be what I think it is?

"What's going on, Bryce?" I ask suspiciously with a smile.

"You asked why I wanted to take you out to dinner tonight."

I open the box. Inside is a sparkly diamond ring that glistens in the candlelight. I carefully take it out of the box and lift it toward the flickering light. It's a large single diamond on a silvery ring. Exquisite.

"Well, what do you say?" he asks.

"What...what do you mean?"

"Will you marry me, Cadence Hawthorne?"

What...? "Are you serious?"

He's looking at me with a smile, but he looks nervous. I put out my left hand to try it on, and he grabs my hand to help me. But I still haven't said yes. Should I say yes? Do I love this man?

Yes, I love him. I adore him more than anyone. But I don't feel ready for this. There's so much going on. How can I get married *now*?

I look into his eyes. And I feel his fingers putting an engagement ring on my hand. He's putting it on whether I say yes or no. Wait, did I nod? Did I say yes?

Of course it's yes. I mean, God, I love him. I love Bryce so much. But I'm scared. I'm so frightened by everything that's happening.

"Is this a yes?" he asks as he's about to slide it all the way onto my ring finger.

I feel a tear fall from my eye, and that is definitely not the response my boyfriend was expecting. It makes me feel stupid, like I'm a crybaby like Beatrix.

"Now?" I mutter, almost to myself. "Oh...Bryce. I..."

"Babe," he says, looking into my eyes. He gently puts the ring back in the box. From the corner of my eye, I see our waitress coming over with bread, but I think she sees the ring and me rubbing my eyes, and she quickly walks the other way. "Don't you see? I love you. I want to spend my life with you. And, well, you've been so worked up with your interview this week, but I felt like it wasn't because you wanted to study at Hawthorne. I'm thinking it was for me. Us. I don't think it's Hawthorne. Sometimes I think you hate it here. I think it's because you were so worried you'd never get in and be with me. But, Katie, I'm telling you now that whatever happens to us, if you don't get into Hawthorne and get in somewhere else, it's okay, because I want to be with you. I'll leave the state if I have to. And if I land a teaching job somewhere else and you can arrange to do a graduate program there, I hope you'll follow me. Because we have to make it work for us. Together. We need to stay together, no matter what happens."

He pauses and smiles, but he looks really worried. I'm looking at his thin beard and perfectly groomed hair, his bright blue eyes, and his perfect smile. He's so gorgeous. Like, *too* gorgeous. Why does he want me? Then I'm thinking of his heart. Bryce is the nicest man I've ever known. Maybe my dad comes close, but Bryce is definitely at the tippy-top. And he's asking *me* if I'll marry him? Seriously? I don't deserve him.

"I love you," he says, looking into my eyes. "I want to spend the rest of my life with you. The interview, your last year, my last year in graduate school, made me think of all this, Cadence. So I decided to get you this ring to tell you that... but what about you? Do you want to be with me too?"

"Oh God, Bryce. Yes. Yes, I do!"

And I fall into his arms, sobbing like a baby. But my tears aren't tears of sadness; they're tears of joy.

"You make me so happy," he whispers in my ear, rubbing my back.

After Bryce finally puts the ring on my finger, the waitress comes over with our basket of bread.

"We're getting married," I say to her. It seems so weird to say it, but it feels wonderful.

6

____

ENLIGHTENMENT

I'm flying among the clouds. And it's not only that I'm marrying a man I'm madly in love with. That helps, of course. I realize the source of most of my anxiety has been leaving school after this year. Bryce being Bryce, once again, is helping me through it all. Will I marry him? He really needs to ask me that?

I'm surprised when I get up at seven in the morning for my lecture that isn't until ten. I'm never an early riser. On the other side of the bed, Bryce is facing me with his eyelashes delicately closed over his chiseled cheeks and with those soft lips. He's so cute. He's fast asleep and I don't want to wake him.

I grab a green tea latte, my favorite, from the university coffee shop and ramble along cement walkways, people watching, for an hour. So many students are making their way around campus right now. Even the grassy hill by the campus coffee shop is full of students, sitting on the grass, studying. The temperature fits my mood. It's a perfect seventy-two degrees without a cloud in the sky.

I decide to sit down on the lawn. I take out my black backpack and thumb through some folders I got last week, at the start of classes. But then I put my work down, lean back on my hands, and just look around. Down the grassy hill is the wide walkway that crosses the main campus, and behind me is the library. The main drag is full of students walking to and fro, in and out of the many brick buildings, heading to class. Some are riding bikes. Bikes are only allowed on certain paths, not near the lecture halls, but the riders are probably freshmen that don't know any better. Everything finally feels right. Perfect.

My phone rings.

"Hello?"

"Hey, sis." It's Damien. He sounds like he's in a great mood too.

"How are you doing, Damie?"

"Great! Orientation's been a blast. Maddie was right. I went around with Harvey and, just like Maddie said, it was so fun with him. Having my best friend with me made it awesome—like it was for you and Maddie. Did you hear that Dad might want to meet us down here for Thanksgiving instead of us heading back home? He figures since we're both down here, he can just come to us."

"I can head up."

"I know, but Dad thought it'd be better for me to settle in."

"Whatever, Damie. That's still a ways away. How are your classes?"

"Tough. It's not that the classes themselves are hard. It's just that I have to get As to get into med school. Physics and general chemistry are boring. I already had most of these classes in high school. I never liked physics. I love my biology class, though. It's with Dr. Rogers. You know him?"

"No, Damie. I've never taken a science class here."

"He's a lot of fun. Maddie recommended him at the Billington House party. Hey, what was with you and that older graduate...Enora? It looked like the two of you went outside to fist-fight or something."

Yeah, something like that.

"She used to go out with Bryce. I was suspicious when she came over."

"Maddie said something about that." *Maddie better not have told him anything else.* "You two caused quite a stir."

"Yeah, well, don't worry about it, Damie. So, Maddie recommended a science teacher? She's a history major. How does she know?"

"She said she used to have a friend who attended his lectures. She recommended choosing him instead of another teacher and, boy, was she right. You know I have that scholarship where I get first pick of classes. But how are yours?"

"I love my religious history class. I'm heading there in another two hours."

A girl wearing sunglasses and a large backpack nearly steps on my backpack. "Sorry," she says. It's so busy today.

"Must suck that Bryce isn't teaching you this year," he says with a snicker.

"Yeah, well... look, Damie, can you keep a secret?"

"Sure."

"Like a major secret? Like something you can't tell anyone."

"What?"

"You won't tell? You promise? This is a really, really big secret."

He pauses. Probably because he thinks I'm crazy. But why am I about to tell him when I haven't told anyone yet? Well, why not? I am crazy.

"I promise, sis. What is it?"

"Bryce proposed to me."

"Are you fucking kidding me! Really?"

"Yeah," I say, laughing. "I'm so happy. But..." I bite my lip. "I'm a little nervous about Dad."

"Dad loves Bryce. I think he'll like the news."

"I hope so. Look, just don't tell him yet, okay? You promised."

"Of course."

"Don't tell anybody. Word spreads fast around here. You'll find that out soon."

"Okay, I won't. I just—"

I have to move my backpack closer to me. It's so crowded that another student nearly tripped over it. "Huh?"

"I'm just congratulating you, Katie."

"I'm so excited." I giggle stupidly again.

"When are you getting married?"

"Huh? Oh, I don't know. Who cares? I just know he's going to marry me."

"Okay, sis," he says, laughing.

"We haven't planned anything yet."

"I won't tell Dad. Just like I won't tell Dad that you've been sleeping over at Bryce's."

"Hey, how did you know I've been sleeping over at Bryce's?"

Sleeping over? Well, I'm not just sleeping over—I'm *staying* over. But he doesn't know that, and I'm not about to tell him.

"Maddie told me."

"That snitch!"

"Or I kinda guessed when I visited her. Your bed was made, and a lot of your stuff wasn't there."

"Oh... hey, what were you doing in my dorm room?"

"Maddie had an American history book I'm borrowing."

Maddie and I took that class together in our freshman year. American History 101. There were non-history majors in the class too—people who needed to take the class as a general college requirement.

"She still has the book?"

"Yeah. It's one of her favorites. I'm just borrowing it."

"Damie, how is it—"

"Got to go, sis. I'll call you later. Love you."

"Love you."

"Oh, and congratulations again, Katie."

Yeah. I put my phone back in my shorts pocket and lean back on my hands, looking up at the sky. Cloud nine. Like I'm up there. I told you. I'm in love.

* * *

Dr. Grange holds his Eastern religious history class in the same lecture hall where Dr. Riker teaches his art history class. It's a large lecture hall, big enough to hold up to two hundred students. Both teachers pack the room, even at unusual times like midsemester. I loved Dr. Riker's class, even though I got my only F at Hawthorne University in it. And I love Dr. Grange's class too.

Dr. Grange is a tiny man with short hair, always wearing colorful clothes. Today he's in an orange turtleneck and brown pants. And, just as Bryce said, it makes me think the Buddha himself is visiting. He's Indian and has an Indian accent I love.

"No one knows for sure, it was such a long time ago," he says with a cough, talking into the microphone on his shirt collar, "but the dates and facts our history majors will be eating up this morning are about Buddha's life. Siddhartha Gautama lived until the age of around eighty years old, dying in around 500 BC. He lived in the northern regions of India, growing up in the city of Kapilavastu." A map of India pops up behind him. "That's *Kap-il-av-astu* and, no, you do not have to know that word for the test." Everyone laughs. "He was born into a rich royal family, and legend says that he was sheltered because it had been foreseen that he would achieve enlightenment if exposed to the world. *That* you need to know for the test." More people laugh and he chuckles. "One day Gautama ventured out of the royal palace and saw old age. Then he saw poverty. It pained him so much that he left his home and family, even his wife and child, and set out on a journey to find enlightenment."

Everyone is listening carefully to Dr. Grange because he's just that entertaining. I'm sitting in the middle of the lecture hall, near an aisle, feeling more content than I have in a long time. The cherry on top of my absolute bliss is my best friend, Maddie, is here. She's sitting beside me. You see, last week I complained to her about how bored I was in all my classes because none of my friends were in them this year. She picked this lecture to pay me a surprise visit, even though she's not enrolled. She just came to keep me company. She loves me, you know.

But having her here is a mistake. She won't stop yapping.

"I'm really worried, Katie," she whispers in my ear. "Do you think Enora's gonna do something crazy? We should meet and talk about it on the Sabbath. Maybe you should have just let her take Beatrix and—"

"Shh," I say. A few of the students in the row in front of us turn around, annoyed.

"Oh, sorry."

But I can't resist asking a question I've been wondering about. "What happened to Josie and Debra?" I whisper. "Are they totally freaked out about our coven? I feel like we ruined their night."

"No." Maddie shakes her head with a large grimace. "They're dying in anticipation to see what you're gonna do next. They saw that little trick with the torch. There's no stopping them from joining our coven now."

"Maddie!" I exclaim in a hushed whisper. She laughs.

"We were watching from the window. Sorry. But they're in for sure now."

This large guy to my left pokes my shoulder. He smiles sweetly. "Can you two keep it down, please?"

"Sorry." I turn to Maddie with a finger to my lips and look

back at the stage. There's a large picture of a tree behind Dr. Grange.

"It's significant," Dr. Grange continues, "that Gautama believed in the middle path. At his time, there were many who believed in starvation, even bodily torture, in order to achieve a different state of consciousness. And the Buddha tried these techniques too before his enlightenment. He sat under the Bodhi tree and starved himself. It wasn't until a girl came to him and offered him food and drink that he had enough strength to prepare for his enlightenment. And that was what he discovered. After years of following harsh techniques, he realized that it was only through strength, the middle path, that enlightenment could be achieved."

I turn to Maddie and whisper in her ear, "Why did you lend my brother your history book?"

She was listening to Dr. Grange. She turns and furrows her brow. Then she leans into my ear. "He told me he was taking American History 101. I told him I took that course and that I still had my book."

"Yeah, but how did he get to talking to you about all that?"

"We had time waiting in line at administration on his first day. Remember? When you fucked up your interview."

"Thanks, Maddie."

Maddie chuckles. Then she sees the guy to my left. She puts a finger on her lips to shush me.

"So what did Gautama discover under the Bodhi tree?" asks Dr. Grange. "This." He points to the screen behind him, and there are four sentences. "The four noble truths. Know this. It is fundamental to the Buddhist religion. The first noble truth is the realization that life is suffering."

"Maddie," I whisper really quietly in her ear. She nods, still staring at Dr. Grange with interest. "The interview doesn't matter anymore."

"What?" She furrows her brow. "Why not?"

"The second noble truth is that suffering is caused by desire," says Dr. Grange.

I point to my ring finger. I had been covering it with my book since she arrived.

"And the way to end suffering," Dr. Grange says, "is to end desire."

"*No fucking way!*" Maddie shouts and like half the class turns.

I sink in my chair with my head in my hand, completely humiliated. She has her hand over her mouth, apologizing profusely to everyone. Dr. Grange is squinting, searching the room and looking toward us, trying to see what all the fuss is about. It's like she just performed a sacrilege or something. I mean, I know we're in a lecture hall, but Dr. Grange's lectures are so good that they feel like something sacred. I feel ashamed. Like Maddie's insulting the Buddhist religion. So does Maddie. She feels awful. But as everyone in the room is shouting at her, she keeps looking down at my ring with a huge smile.

We get out of there. And I'm really mad. But when we're outside in the sunlight and I turn to my best friend, I just can't yell at her. I'm so happy that she came to see me that I can't reprimand her. I'm in too good a mood.

"Sorry," she says.

"I really like that class, Maddie. Why couldn't you just keep it down?"

"Keep centered, Cadence," she jokes. She's trying not to smile, but she can't help it.

"Are you making fun of—"

"Yeah. It's a history class, Kate. That guy runs it like a temple. But I am really sorry. And..." She looks at my left hand again and jumps into my arms. "Whatever, I'm so happy for you, babe!" Her voice is cracking, and she's trying not to cry. "Anyway, you're the one who flashed your ring. I was finally starting to enjoy the lecture. How did he ask you? I'm so happy for you."

"He asked me at Lacey's."

"Lacey's?" She puts her hands on her hips and frowns. "Lacey's! You're joking. Couldn't he have announced it to everybody at a Braves game or something? Jeez. Like, are you kidding me?"

"I don't care, Maddie. It's Bryce. He's vanilla, we know that, but he's...delicious, you know. I'm just so happy he asked at all."

She hugs me again.

"He said he saw how worried I was that we might be apart. He said he never wants to be apart. He said this was his way of telling me. To relax me, you know. To tell me that no matter what happens we'll be together."

She nods and rubs my shoulder. "I'm so happy for you, Cadence."

I nod.

She looks back at the lecture hall, worried. "Sorry I screwed up your class, babe."

"That's okay. I'm just happy you came."

"He's really good," she says with a nod. "Just like everybody says. He makes you want to convert."

"I've thought about converting."

Maddie laughs. I don't know what's so funny. I think it's because I said that really seriously.

"I've thought of moving to Sri Lanka to a Buddhist temple. It would put me at ease. I need that. I worry so much here in Hawthorne, Maddie."

"Just stop." She won't stop laughing. "Really."

"What? I'm serious."

"I know," Maddie says with a laugh. "You're the only girl I know crazy enough to do it."

"Yeah." I look up pensively. "A Theravada Buddhist temple. Like the original temple. To reach Nirvana."

"Just please stop, okay."

"I'm serious," I say with a shrug.

I stop. But I am serious. And why not? If there's one thing I need in my life, it's peace. Dr. Grange told us that he's had students that have done it before.

We're both silent at the moment. But I'm happy, despite my friend humiliating me. And Maddie has a grin splashed over her face. She's so excited.

"Maddie, you want to go to lunch?"

"Thought you'd never ask."

"And...tonight, I was hoping you could help me with something."

"What's up, Mrs. Wallace?"

"Stop."

"What?" she asks snickering.

"Can you come with me to Alondra's? I'm checking up on Beatrix, but Alondra's house is still creepy as hell at night. Bryce is pulling an all-nighter working on his dissertation. He usually checks on her with me."

"Sure. I'd love to." Then she smiles ruefully. "Oh, Kate, I miss you so much. I'm so happy you found Bryce, but I'm so lonely, you know."

"I'm right here," I say, hugging her. "Let's go do lunch."

"You're not mad about class?"

"I am," I say, but I can't hold back a smile. "But I'm so happy you came."

7

———

LIGHT

By nightfall, I'm walking with my best friend up the familiar creepy weed path, once a lovely garden, into Alondra's house. I used to adore her front yard. The flowers and freshly cut grass, surrounded by the tall, thin trees of Georgia, make the mansion look iconic, like some kind of Civil War historical landmark. Now the flowers are withered, the grass is brown, the one-hundred-year-old red carriage in the driveway—that used to be such a cute decoration—looks more like a creepy gateway into the supernatural. With Beatrix staying over, Bryce hasn't gotten much gardening done. I was supposed to help him, but Beatrix foiled that too, because I was busy consoling her. Now I'm dreading visiting her, because she's probably going to bawl her eyes out. Well, at least I have Maddie beside me.

Maddie's carrying a fat gray cat in her arms. I can't wait to give Beatrix the present. I think she'll love it.

Even though the grounds are creepy, what's really strange is all the outside lights are on. Everywhere, along the driveway and in front of the house. So much light makes it even creepier. And I thought the electricity wasn't working.

"Ah, can't we keep him, Kates?" asks Maddie, bringing the cat up to her lips for a kiss. "He's so cute."

"No. He's for Beatrix."

"What should we name him?"

"I was thinking we can name him Pete, Whiskers, or George. We should never have gotten rid of her cats."

"Well, who was going to take care of them—you?"

"Sure, why not?"

"You're not good with pets, Cadence."

That's true. Maddie and I once had a pet fish, and I was supposed to take care of it but I forgot to feed it. Then I bought another. That one died too. I like dogs and cats, though.

Maddie pets him. She's in a great mood as always. "I think Whiskers sounds good."

"We'll leave it up to her. Listen, why are all the lights on? Did the electrician come back to fix the place?"

"Sure seems so. You'll have to ask Bryce."

We make it to the door and I turn the key in the lock, but before I can open it, a blackbird lands on the patio a couple of feet from us. That freaks me out because Enora has power over these birds. I freeze by the door.

"It's okay," Maddie says with a chuckle. She kisses the cat again and puts him down on the floor, letting him roam freely around the house.

It's so bright inside. Too bright.

"Maybe Uncle Hanley called the electrician?" Maddie suggests, reading my mind. But no, not just some lights but *all* the lights are on inside. "It turns on sometimes by itself for a couple hours," Maddie adds with a shrug. "AC too. Even when it's impossible. The whole house is screwy, you know. Haunted."

"Well, why are *all* the lights on?" I ask.

Right?

The lovely crystal chandelier above glows, reflecting light

throughout the room. It's so bright, but pitch black upstairs. It's always creepy up there in Alondra's bedroom.

Maddie shivers and presses her hands together, blowing on them. "Fuck, it's cold. The AC must have been left on again too."

"Beatrix should have turned it off," I say, furrowing my brow. Then I yell, "Beatrix? Beatrix?"

Maddie looks around. "Hey, Beatrix. Yoo-hoo. Where are you?"

"Beatrix," I shout again. "I'll go upstairs, Maddie, and take a look."

"Well, I ain't going up there," Maddie says with a big grin.

"Check the rest of the house, then."

"Make it quick, Katesy," she says, touching my arm. "I want to catch that movie." Maddie heads down the hallway, humming. I slowly make my way up the pitch-black stairway. It's so cold that I wrap my arms around my red coat. But it smells nice. Beatrix must have been burning incense.

"Beatrix? You up there? Beatrix?"

She's doing it again. She's not responding.

When I make it to the top, I notice the bedroom door is wide open, but no light is shining inside. Not even a candle. I have to take out my cell phone and use its dim flashlight.

I'm worried. Every time I've visited her, she's been holed up in the bedroom sulking—except that one time in the guest room.

I take a deep breath and force myself to step inside. I can see the yard through the floor-to-ceiling window, its light emanating from the windows downstairs. I glance at the bathroom. Nobody's there. I have to be careful where I walk, because there are bags of food and papers all over the floor. When it's clear, I quickly head out and see Maddie beside the banister downstairs.

"Beatrix?" shouts Maddie, facing the kitchen. "Beatrix? Where the fuck are you?"

"She's not in the bedroom," I say. "I'll check the study and side room."

"Okay. But I don't get why she won't respond."

"Not in the guestroom?" I ask.

"No." Then the cat jumps into Maddie's arms. "Whiskers! Aww, boy. You're so cute. Let me take him home? Please? I mean, Crazy isn't even here."

She walks down the adjacent hallway, by the banister, petting him.

I walk into the study, still using the flashlight of my cell phone. I run the light along tons of books on the bookshelf. They're Alondra's. History books and witchcraft grimoires. We never packed them away.

Then I jump like thirty feet in the air. I *feel* a scream in my chest and then I hear it. It's Maddie's voice from downstairs. And she won't stop screaming.

"Katie! Oh my God! Come quick. Katie. Come here!"

I rush down the stairs, nearly skipping a few steps; I could have sprained my ankle. When I get to the living room, Maddie's standing by an open sliding glass door with both hands over her mouth. She spins around and her eyes are bulging. In the center of the brightly lit patio is one of our black cloaks, shifting ever so slightly as it hangs from a wooden rafter.

"Look, Katie! Look!"

I run outside. Bare feet dangle underneath the black cloak, and I get a glimpse of a girl's pale naked body. I recognize Beatrix's long golden hair inside the hood. Her head droops over a rope, her eyes are open, and her face looks ghastly white.

"Look at her hand!" Maddie screams, in tears. "Jesus, Katie! Look! Look at her hand! Look at it!"

Red fluid drips from her palm. I grab her limp arm and turn

it, thinking it's blood from a cut. But the red isn't blood. It's paint. A red pentagram has been painted on her palm. I look up, doing everything I can to avert my eyes from her face. I can't. I can't stop looking at Beatrix's lifeless blood-red eyes staring down at me.

8

———

UNCLE HANLEY

Within a few minutes, the house is packed with my friends. Alondra's house is only a short walk up a hill from campus. Maddie's still in the living room being comforted by some of my friends. She's in shock. I'm with Tammy and Frida in an adjacent hallway.

Uncle Hanley arrives. We call him "uncle" because he's Alondra's uncle. He owns the place since she passed and has been letting us use the house. He lives in Flintwood, but he told me he was in Hawthorne when I called. He walks into the hallway with his farmer suspenders, thin glasses and sparse gray hair. Usually the guy is boisterous, talkative, and in great spirits, but now he walks slowly in a morose silence. He pats me on the shoulder.

"Cadence," he says with a nod. Then he nods at Tammy and Frida beside me. He gazes hesitantly toward the living room. He knows Beatrix is hanging from a rope outside the sliding glass door there. "Wish we were meetin' under better circumstances."

"It's terrible," I say.

"None of you girls were home when it happened, I hope?"

I shake my head. "Just saw it after."

"Called the police?"

I nod.

"Still not here, huh? You do know it's a suicide, you reckon?"

That's the question that's been haunting all of us. Maddie's convinced it wasn't, and I know Beatrix was afraid of death. Sure, she threatened to slice her wrists, but I never felt like she was actually going to do it. It wouldn't surprise me if Cordelia had come back and killed her. Enora's involvement makes me feel caught between anger and feelings of sadness and fear. Beatrix was such a young girl. I feel like maybe she could have straightened herself out and lived a normal life had this not happened.

Uncle Hanley takes a deep breath and says, "Well, it's my house, I suppose. If you'd excuse me, Cadence, I'm gonna take a quick look."

He gestures above his head with a finger, as if tipping an invisible hat, and makes his way slowly into the living room. Most of my friends soon head out the front door. I think only Uncle Hanley has the guts to walk into the living room. I hear Maddie talking to him. I remain in the hallway doing nothing. I don't know whether I should get out of the house with my friends or wander into the living room and see Maddie. But I don't want to go back there. I can't.

It's still so bright. And that's weird and irritating. That night Bryce and I spent together, we would have given anything to have the lights on. Now I'd do anything to turn them off. I switched a few lights off, but they just turned themselves back on again.

"Katie?" It's Bryce behind me. I'd recognize that comforting voice anywhere. I spin around. "I came as quickly as I could."

"Oh, Bryce..." I fall into his arms. "It's horrible. I...I'm so upset."

"It's okay, babe," he says, rubbing my back.

Someone shouts and I jump. It's Uncle Hanley's voice, which is really weird because I've never even seen him scowl, much less shout. I squeeze Bryce tighter, looking down the hall.

"It's okay, Kate," Bryce says.

I nod. Then I gently push him back and gaze at my man. He's wearing a light-blue button-down with brown slacks. Handsome as always.

"How was your meeting?" I ask.

"Unfinished. That's okay. We'll meet again later. When I told him I had to go to a student suicide, he wasn't about to stop me. Anyway, it was going about as well as your interview." He puts his hand up, smiling ruefully. "Don't worry, babe. Maybe it's not that bad. But he wants to reorganize my whole project. It's crazy. I should have asked someone else. I really like Dr. Riker a lot, but I don't have time to compulsively go over every detail with him. You know how he is. And my topic is the plague. It's like he's more interested in the architecture of medieval Europe than illness. But he's the best I could get to be my advisor now."

Maddie walks into the hallway wiping her eyes. Her change in mood is incredible. She was humming and practically dancing when we entered the house, but now she looks like she can barely walk.

"Poor Mr. Hanley," Maddie says. "He got so furious. I've never heard him so mad. He started cursing up a storm at Bill Reardon. He thinks it all has something to do with him. When he came back inside, he apologized to me for the outburst but told me that seeing that palm made him crazy ... I can't believe Enora did this."

"You really think Enora did it?" I ask.

"I *know* she did it, Katie."

"You saw how desperate Beatrix was," Bryce says, shaking his head. "Her coven..." He stops for a moment and looks over his shoulder at the living room, probably worried he's too loud. "They might have driven her to do this, but it was *her* suicide."

"Then how do you explain her hand?" Maddie asks. "Why would someone paint a pentagram on their hand before killing themselves? She wanted a faster way to go to hell? And the cloak? Why would she dress up in *our* coven's cloak? She never associated herself with Hawthorne. That was a message too."

"Maybe," I say.

"It could have been a spell preparing herself for the Summerland before taking her own life," Bryce says, turning back to Maddie and me. "Katie said she dressed up in our cloak when she drew up a protective circle."

"And she decided to draw a pentagram on her hand?" Maddie asks, raising her eyebrows. "Katie also said she was terrified of being damned. So...she decides to kill herself while worshipping Satan with a red pentagram, Bryce?"

"Why are you protecting Enora, Bryce?" I say. "I think Maddie might be right."

"Come on, Kate, I'm not. I'm just saying we don't know."

"I know it was Panthera," Maddie says.

"Look, even if it was, so what? It's not our business."

"No. It's mine." I hang my head. All of a sudden, I feel horrible. "I kept visiting her all week. You heard her. She wanted to die, but she was more afraid of damnation. And ..." I take a deep breath and lean against the wall. "I think it's my fault, guys."

Shit. It is totally my fault.

"It's not your fault, Cadence," Maddie says. "Don't be ridiculous."

Beatrix came to me for protection and I failed her. Maybe Enora cast a spell that drove her to do this. Or maybe Cordelia returned and tied a noose around her neck. Who cares? It doesn't change the fact that it happened. It happened in Alondra's house, essentially my coven's house, and I'm sure I could have stopped it if I'd stayed here to protect her. How is that not my fault?

I feel a tightening in my chest. I'm thinking of Beatrix's beautiful blond hair and large eyes. She was so young and vulnerable. She could have become a normal girl. Enora ruined her life.

I start crying. Bryce takes me in his arms and comforts me. And now, so does Maddie.

That's when Uncle Hanley walks out of the living room. He approaches the three of us, shaking his head.

"I ..." His hands are shaking too. "I'll talk to the police when they get here. They're going to inspect everywhere around the house and probably block off the backyard. I'll talk to them ... poor girl. She's so young. It's so horrible. And she was into that weird devil stuff Bill used to get involved with." He looks at Bryce. "Did you see her hand?"

Bryce nods.

"Yeah," Uncle Hanley says, nodding back. "Look, I appreciate the cleaning you guys have been doing, but maybe for a little while, you kids should stay away from the house."

That's how nice Uncle Hanley is. The house is a complete mess. We hardly cleaned anything.

"I saw a pile of burned wood at the center of the backyard again," Uncle Hanley adds, scratching his head. "That's suspicious for Satan worshipping. You guys know if there's been any of Bill's stupid devil worship still going on outside?"

He looks at me. Damn, he has to ask me? I hate lying. Maddie is standing behind him, and she quickly shakes her head, worried I'm going to mess up our favorite gathering spot.

"No devil worshipping here, Mr. Hanley," I reply, wiping my tears with my arm.

He examines me, and for the first time, there's distrust in his eyes. But then he nods.

"Okay. But that doesn't mean it's not going on outside of you guys' control… that poor girl. Poor girl. Maybe I should put up security cameras? Yeah, I think I should… I'm just so happy to find you're all okay."

We hear sirens from outside.

"We shouldn't have had her stay at the house without asking you, Mr. Hanley," Bryce says. "I'm really sorry about that."

"No. No, I reckon with everything that happened, that girl needed all the love she could get. Alondra would have wanted you to help her. She would have supported that. Don't blame yourself. Just hope Jesus can forgive her tormented soul, the poor, poor girl." Then he looks down, shaking his head.

"Sorry we had to bother you, Uncle Hanley," I say with a nod.

"No bother." He forces a smile. "No bother at all."

We all walk slowly out to the front of the house to greet the police.

9

____

STROLL WITH A FRIEND

MADDIE'S HUFFING AND PUFFING BESIDE ME AS WE MAKE OUR WAY down a leafy, muddy path beside a stream. The trickling water running over stones under the foliage of leaning trees is simply gorgeous, and the outside temperature is perfect. Birds are chirping and there's a light, pleasant breeze. The leaves on the ground and above us, on the sheltering trees, have turned my absolute favorite fall colors: various shades of red, yellow, and orange. It's so beautiful that you'd think we were in the middle of a national park or something, but we're not. We're about thirty minutes from campus.

"We need to hold a Sabbath, Cadence," Maddie says between breaths.

I adjust the water bottle attached to my belt for a firmer grip, grabbing her hand to help her climb over a large tree branch.

"This is serious," she says. "You know as well as I do that Beatrix was murdered."

"I don't."

"Come on. You saw her hand."

"That was the symbol of her coven and she was suicidal."

I told Dr. Bainer that I loved the woods around our school. I do. And I love hiking. But I could never get Maddie to go with me before. Well, unlike me, Maddie is very out of shape. She doesn't exercise. But the walk was her idea for some reason. I told her this morning, on the phone, that I had to study because midterms are coming up, but the silence on the other end was enough to tell me how important it was for me to meet with her.

"We have to meet. You told me you felt ..." She doesn't complete her sentence. We reach a steep hill full of brush, which covers the dirt path, and Maddie shakes her head. I take her hand again and we maneuver around more bushes on our climb up the hillside. She's really hating me over this hike, but I keep telling her it's worth it. She takes a deep breath and finally says, "Beatrix never really wanted to kill herself. Come on, Kate, that was Enora. We need another Sabbath this week. This Friday. Stop avoiding it."

We get back on a straight path under the trees, and Maddie looks relieved. The trees are so dense above that it's a little dark, but at least it's flat. But even though it's a straightaway, Maddie stops and rests. She leans over with her hands on her knees.

"Fuck, how do you do this? You're barely even sweating... Katie, Enora planted Beatrix. Beatrix told you. It was all to fight us again. I don't know what the bitch is planning, but it's trouble. We should meet with our sisters to plan what we're going to do next. If we don't, she's gonna do something first. She planted Beatrix and then killed her. It isn't just a warning. She's in our business just like Reardon was last year."

"I've got midterms Monday. Maybe we can meet next week."

"Goddammit," Maddie snaps. She quickly turns away. "Okay. I know. I know—"

"Maddie, I screwed up my grades last fall, I'm not going to

do it again. Dr. Brainer made it very clear. If I mess it up again, I won't make it into any graduate school."

"You're the leader of our coven. It's your job, babe, to do something."

"Isn't it enough to just meet with Mira?"

"It will help. I want to know her thoughts too."

We start walking again. This part of the trail is easy. You know, it's the climbing that's the killer, but because it's a tough hike, no one's around and it's peaceful.

"This is the easier part," I reassure her.

"Better be, bitch," Maddie says, but she smiles at me. "Damn, the things I do for my bestie."

"We could meet Wednesday. I can do that. Instead of me seeing Mira, I could have the gang meet—"

"Don't talk to me like you're not a witch. It has to be Friday, if at all, and you know that. There's no magic on Wednesday. At least meet with Mira." Maddie takes my hand and holds it, which is cute. "I'm really spooked, babe. Please, just talk to her. At least do that for me. But not on the phone. Go see her and ask her about their coven. I'm really worried something else is going to happen. Mira will tell us. I don't think she'd ever mean to hurt us."

"You want to go with me?"

"I really do, but I can't. You know Aunt Jane's going into surgery."

Aunt Jane has been having stomach pain all month. I visited her at her house last week, and she couldn't stop throwing up. She has gallbladder surgery scheduled. That's another reason Maddie has been so glum.

"Maybe you can convince Mira to come down and join us for a gathering next week, Katie. We've got to hold a Sabbath. With Mira, the wait could be worth it."

"Okay, Maddie, got it. I don't want to talk about it anymore."

"Okay," she says. "But...there's something else I need to tell you, Kates."

"Yeah, what?"

But she stops in her tracks when we pass some bushes and see another steep, grassy hill above us. She puts her hands on her waist and stares. Then she looks at me. I try not to laugh. She looks really pissed. There's finally a clearing in the woods about fifty yards up. She looks down at another stream, meandering around the trees, that we have to cross.

"How much further?" she asks, shaking her head.

"Right over the top."

"You're such a bitch. Don't ever forget the..." She carefully jumps on a few rocks, trying not to fall in the water. "Things I do for you."

"It's gonna be hard with Bryce this week too. He's busy with his dissertation."

"Then go alone. But do it. At least talk to Mira. Mira will tell you what's going on. Brainwashed or not, she'll be honest. Mira's always been honest."

"For sure."

That makes the old Maddie I know come out. She smiles. "Are we almost there? I don't think my out-of-shape bones can take much more of this, babe."

"It's right over this last hill. I promise."

We finally get to the top. It's breathtaking. Maddie nods at me, still out of breath, and seems to forget her complaining. Below us are miles upon miles of yellow, red, and orange trees in the valley below. It is truly gorgeous. In the far corner, we can just make out Hawthorne Lake near campus. Then straight out, about thirty miles from the cliff, is a mountain range. But below are miles and miles of trees.

It's a long drop down there. Maddie takes a rock and throws it down. She chuckles. Then she pulls out her cell phone from her shorts pocket.

"Come here," she says, putting her arm around me. She holds the phone in front of us, with an extended arm, for a selfie. Behind us is the sheer drop and a gorgeous view. "That's a keeper."

After staring for a little longer, she sits down on the wild grass and smiles up at me. "You were right. I should have taken you up on this a long time ago. It's amazing."

"Beautiful, isn't it?"

"Incredible. Just like you said it would be. We should do this stuff more often."

"I'm just so busy."

"I know." She loses her smile and looks away. "With you and Bryce."

"I'll go see Mira, 'kay? I'll see what she says."

But Maddie keeps looking down. She picks up some of the grass and brings it to her nose. Then she tastes it. We're witches, you know. We can tell what's edible. She even offers me some.

"What's wrong?" I ask. "Why so down? I told you I'll go see her, okay?"

"We need the Sabbath this week," she says with a shrug, still staring at the grass. "But I knew you'd say no."

"Then what's the matter, Maddie? I've never seen you so blue."

She nods her head, throws her dark hair back, and focuses on me. I look into her eyes, behind her witch makeup, which looks a little smudged from sweat. I could swear her eyes are tearing up.

"You know, Katesie, honestly, I knew this would be a tough hike. I never wanted to do it. But I thought suggesting it would be enough to finally see you again."

I furrow my brow.

"I miss you so much. That's all. I miss you. And I'm so

worried about next year. I'm worried I won't see you after we graduate."

"Oh, Maddie, stop it. You will."

"Unlike Bryce, I don't have a ring to lasso you in."

"Come on," I say, plopping down on the grass and putting my arm tightly around her. I lean my head against hers. "We're best friends forever. BFFs. Remember?"

"The very best. Absolute best."

10

———

MIRA

I take Maddie up on her suggestion to meet Mira, at Piedmont Park in Atlanta, at noon on Wednesday. Bryce isn't too happy about it, but that's why I love him to death. He has so much work to do on his dissertation, but he still drops everything to take me there. He drives me, parks his car under a tree, leans his seat back, and closes his eyes. He hasn't been sleeping well, and I told him I'd rather speak with Mira alone anyway. As long as he can sleep in the parking lot, he's content enough.

Piedmont Park was actually my idea. I've loved the park since I was a kid. My dad and I used to walk on the grass and feed the ducks in the lake when I was a little girl. I still have fond memories of my brother running after the ducks in this silly sailor outfit and hat mom used to dress him in when he was little. I must have been only nine. He would have been, like, six. It was fun times back then.

I couldn't have chosen a more perfect day. The sky is clear and it's, like, a perfect seventy-two degrees again.

After Bryce drops me off, I walk alone in my saffron T-shirt, black shorts, and white tennis shoes. I realize that Mira and I didn't agree on a particular meeting place. I take out my phone but remember that she never answers her phone. But I don't worry. The park is huge, of course, being Atlanta's "Central Park," but I feel like Mira or I will *feel* our way to one another. I know, that's weird. But somehow, I just know. So I amble along the cement walkway beside the grass, constantly moving to the side so as not to be run over by bicyclists. There are a lot of families out. We started the semester early, and early October is still warm. A lot of kids are running around on the grass, playing ball or picnicking with their families. In the not-so-far distance beyond the fields, I see the Atlanta skyline.

I'm right about Mira. She isn't hard to spot. She's the only one wearing a long black dress trailing along the ground. I think she's gained weight. She's always been overweight. And I can spot the black paint on her face from a mile away—she's wearing much thicker eyeliner than I am. I try to be discreet with my goth look, but she's never cared. She never cared at all what other people think.

It seems to take forever for us to catch up to one another and get close enough to hug. "Yatu, Windstorm," she says. Then she backs up and looks at me quizzically. "How's Hawthorne?"

"How are you?"

"Fine. Maddie and Bryce? You and Bryce still sharing the same bed?" She gives me a sly smile, the bitch. Then she laughs. "Where is he? I'd have guessed he would come with you."

"He's in the car sleeping. What about Derek?"

"Split."

"Oh, that's too bad."

She just shrugs.

"Well, all Bryce cares about is rest. He's working so hard on his dissertation that he's not sleeping. Anyway, I thought you and I would talk alone first."

"Alone?" She squints and nods slowly. "Hmm. Must be very important."

"Bryce and I are doing fine. Real fine." And I put up my left hand and show her my ring. It doesn't take much for me to parade my ring around.

She just nods dismissively. "About fucking time. I see little Katie's growing up."

"It's so lovely here," I say, throwing my hair back and trying to deflect her usual sarcasm. She's already annoying me. Somehow I had forgotten her prickly ways. It's funny that distance and time can do that to people.

"I don't like it," Mira says with a deep breath, annoying me more. "I hate this park. I'm not interested in seeing large man-made buildings over lots of fake manicured grass. But I guess it's a lot like you, isn't it?"

"That's insulting."

"I've really missed riling you up." Mira laughs. "I like watching you get all flustered. Your lovely tanned skin flushes, and you get all hot and bothered. It's hilarious."

"Shall we?" I ask, gesturing to the walkway.

She nods, walking with her arms folded.

We fall silent. I've lost the nerve to raise the question I'm dying to ask her.

It doesn't take long for Mira to veer off the walkway onto the grass. I follow her across a bridge over the lake. The water reflects like glass the surrounding fall leaves on one side and skyscrapers on the other. Two dogs rush by, and Mira dips down and pets one. We both do. We love dogs. But we still don't say anything to one another. We just enjoy the view of the fake manicured grass and buildings.

"You want to know why I joined the Abaddon coven?" Mira finally says, cocking her head, with her arms folded again, as we make our way across the beautiful bridge. "Is that it?"

"You always knew how to get to the point."

"So did you," Mira says with a chuckle. "That's why we became friends."

I stop and turn. She puts her hand on a rail on the bridge. She smiles a wily grin, waiting. Then I just spit out what I've been dying to say.

"Why would you?" I ask. "I mean, I don't get it. After everything that happened? Last I heard, you were looking for a job back in Jacksonville. What happened? I asked you on the phone, and you just laughed it off. What did Enora do to you? Hypnotize you or something?"

"Enora's my friend."

"Seriously?"

"What's wrong with her?"

"She's evil. You told me that last year."

"Alondra was never good, Katie, but you joined us. Alondra taught us that there's no such thing as good and evil. You're the only one who's insisted on being good. You've limited your freedom. If you allowed Hawthorne to be free, like Enora, I probably would never have left. Why are you so worried?"

"Are you for real? Do you really have to ask me that?" I'm staring at her. Then I say more quietly, "You were there when she stabbed Professor Reardon to death."

"She had the courage to do what I'd always wanted to do." Mira looks down, serious. "What I didn't have the nerve to do. I hated Bill Reardon more than anyone. Bill lusted after me, along with most of the other girls in Hawthorne. He was a pervert and after he raped me, I wanted him to die."

"Not to be murdered."

She annoyingly shrugs again.

"What about Bryce?" I remind her.

"Katie," Mira says and takes a deep breath. She turns and gazes at the lake. She gestures to the water. "You know, this water is a little like you. Gorgeous. Pretty... but fake."

"Don't be mean," I snap. "I didn't come here to fight. I'm worried about—"

"I know," she says, smiling. "But you *are* fighting. If you're asking me if I'm okay, I am. But if you're here to convince me to leave the Abaddon coven, I won't." She looks around the park she hates again. "Bryce was the one thing that almost stopped me from joining. But Enora explained that she had to erase all the men who had humiliated her publicly from our coven. As much as she once loved Bryce, she assured me it wasn't personal. She wanted him gone because she blamed him—"

"It wasn't personal that she tried to burn him alive? I don't believe this."

But she doesn't join in my anger. She smiles. "And this is the reason you're here. Not to see me, or to check on me, but to get information?"

"I told you, I'm worried about you."

"No, you're not." Mira shakes her head. "You would have visited before. You're worried about your coven."

"Well, I care about our friends. And my fiancé." I lift my eyebrows, sounding really condescending. I can't help it. She's really pissing me off. She's acting like she's being logical, but it's all crap.

"You know, Alondra loved you more than any of us, but she and I always marveled at the conflicts in your head."

"What conflicts?"

"Your not accepting being a witch." Her dark eyes just stare at mine as if we're in a showdown. Like she's daring me to disagree. I don't.

"I accept being a witch, I just wish I weren't one."

"That's funny, Katie, because, you know, I would do anything to have your power. You were given a gift, but you don't accept it. I've pored over books about the occult. I studied and pestered Alondra, sucking out every morsel of information I could from her before she died. Now I'm learning from Panthera. But I don't have your gift. I'd give everything for it."

"You can have it."

She laughs. "You asked me why I joined. Enora accepts who

I am. She practices the occult. She doesn't care if she is "good" or "bad." Those are Western concepts. She asked for my help, and we work together in order to work magic. She sought me out because of my knowledge of spells and incantations. Of divination. Where else can I practice what I love? Not with you. Not in Hawthorne. Do you see what I mean? Why is it so hard for you to understand?"

"Your leader is a murderer."

"Katie, I would have stayed with you in a second if you had asked me. You're not thinking this through. If Enora had killed Bryce, I'd agree with you. Bryce didn't do what Reardon did. But Bryce wasn't killed, and Enora agrees that what she did to him was wrong. But Reardon? Why are you upset that that prick died?"

"She really did brainwash you," I say, staring at Mira in amazement. "You didn't trust Enora last year. Why do you now?"

"Enora explained to me everything I told you," she says with a shrug. Then she gazes into my eyes, challenging me again, and she gives me her infamous smug smile, very much like the old Mira.

"Beatrix hanged herself."

Mira loses her smile. Her eyes examine mine and she shakes her head.

"And I think your Abaddon coven was behind it," I continue. "Maddie's convinced Enora is. Isn't that enough evil for you to turn from Enora? What other crimes do you have to see from that bitch?"

But Mira loses her infuriating smugness, along with all the color in her face. Then she turns from me and leans her head in her hands over the rail of the bridge. I hear whimpering.

"Oh, God... you didn't know?" I can't believe it. "How? Your coven knows. Gilda knows. How can you—"

She shakes her head.

"Mira ..."

"I've been wandering," she explains with her head in her hands. "My first. I haven't been there... I've been away all week. I... I think I'm going to be sick..."

"Mira, I thought you knew."

"I heard Beatrix had run away to you. Cordelia said you were protecting her. Enora was furious. I know she visited you to bring her back. But...I can't believe this."

"Mira, she was hanging by a rope, with a red pentagram painted on her left palm. You know that's Enora's symbol. Your satanic coven. Beatrix told me Enora had sent her. And she wasn't wearing any clothes except—"

"I don't want to hear this!" Mira snaps, staring wide-eyed at me. She shrugs my hand off her back and walks fast, not seeming to care whether I follow her. She rushes over to the shade of a tree, puts her head in her hands again, and cries.

"Mira, I'm sorry! I'm sorry. I thought you knew."

"God," Mira says, wiping her now smeary mascara on her sleeves. "I loved her. We loved her so much. It's...it's like hearing something happened to you or Maddie."

"She was young."

"Very." Mira nods. "And she was sweet like you. She was just mentally ill."

"Mira, she said Enora sent her. She said Enora sent her to start a fight between our covens again."

"Stop worrying about Enora, Cadence!" she snaps, wiping her eyes with her long black lace sleeve. "Enora's left you alone like you demanded. I know she didn't do anything to Beatrix. That girl did it to herself. She's been attempting to kill herself for years."

Mira's never lied to me. She's irritating as hell, but she has never lied. Even Maddie and Bryce have lied to me. Not Mira. In a weird way, I trust Mira even more than my best friend and my fiancé. Obviously, she really didn't know. And she really believes that her coven had nothing to do with it.

"Mira …" I hesitate. Then I just say, "I'm sorry."

"Forget it." Mira shrugs, wiping her eyes again. "I understand. It's okay. It's…good seeing you, Cadence."

Is it? All we've done is fight. But, come to think of it, all we ever did was fight.

"We should have lunch," Mira says, trying to change the subject. "Bryce too. I'd love to see him again."

"Sure."

But I'm not done. I have to ask her more. Now. Now, when she's upset. I don't want to bring this up later and upset her again.

"Mira, Beatrix told me she was running away from a blood sacrifice. That's why she wanted to stay with me."

"We do blood sacrifices," Mira says. "You allowed Alondra to cut you at your initiation, if you remember."

"She said sex ceremonies."

Mira nods again.

"And she said Enora threatened her life."

Mira shakes her head.

"She said she was given a choice…it's disgusting." I look at Mira and I'm hoping that she gets what I'm saying so I don't have to say it. But Mira just wipes her nose and eyes. "She told me that she could either birth a fetus and drink its blood or be sacrificed and killed in a ceremony."

Mira chuckles. That's definitely not the reaction I was expecting.

"She was manipulating you. That's Beatrix. That's what she does. She needed a home. We love her, but she's very sick."

I turn and gaze at the Atlanta skyline. The *fake* concrete buildings Mira hates. Well, I think the view is pretty. I believe Mira. At least I believe this is her understanding of the situation.

"Okay, Mira. But ..." I'm remembering that Beatrix also said Mira was doing sex ceremonies with a girl in the coven. "Mira, are *you* doing sex ceremonies again? After hating Reardon for—"

"I'm not going to talk about that," Mira says quickly, shaking her head.

"Okay, sorry...and I'm sorry I had to be the first to tell you about Beatrix."

Mira nods. Then she looks down at my ring finger and forces a thin smile.

"You know, Beatrix and I were so close...because of her friend. Congratulations, Katie. I'm so happy for you and Bryce. I'm finally going out with someone I love too. Her name's Courtney. I wish you were here longer so I could introduce you. She was Beatrix's best friend. I don't know how Courtney is going to get through this."

11

BACK TO THE DORM

I'M RUSHING DOWN THE MAIN STRETCH OF CAMPUS ON MY WAY TO Maddie's place, because I can't wait to give her the 411 on Mira. I feel better. Now I think Beatrix just committed suicide. Mira was sure of it, anyway. Our lunch went so much more smoothly than our first meeting at the park. That could be because of Bryce. He gets along with everyone. And, you know, Mira and I always had a rough relationship, but we still love each other. And I'm so happy that she found someone and is happy in Atlanta.

It's late, about eight in the evening, as I make my way to "our" place. Bryce is being a bookworm, working late in the library. Since it took us all day to drive to Atlanta and back, the poor guy is exhausted. The plan was to get a hotel, but Bryce convinced me to come back tonight. He said he's got a ton of work to do in the library. I suspect he's probably not working. He's probably sleeping in a cubbyhole—he was so tired.

Anyway, I walk down memory lane and use my extra key to get through the glass door to the Yorkshire Dormitory. I feel a little guilty when I unlock the door, since it reminds me of how

Dad's paying for my room with Maddie. That's when an old neighbor of mine, Sophia, waves at me in the hallway.

"You back here, Katie?"

"No. Just visiting."

"Everyone misses you so much." She gives me a hug.

"You going to the outdoor concert next week?"

"No. I have to study." Like really study. Like, if I don't get it together, I'm gonna mess up another semester.

"It's gonna be fun. You should go."

"I'll try."

Then she smiles goodbye, and I mosey down the dimly lit hallway. I head around the bend to the other side of the hall. Here everybody's got their door open, welcoming me. I miss them. If it weren't for Bryce, I'd love staying here my last year.

Finally, I'm in front of Maddie's room. I take out my keys, but when I check the doorknob, it's unlocked. I open the door. The room is dimly lit by a single lamp, but I can see well enough.

The key falls from my hand. First, I hear what I don't want to see, then I see it. On my bottom bunk, Maddie is naked, straddling a boy and moving up and down on him. She's moaning, which is super gross because she's my best friend. And her tits are moving up and down while the boy is breathing heavily under her. That's grosser. I am so embarrassed. I'm about to throw the door closed, but as Maddie's naked body rolls off him in surprise, and she sees me and shrieks, the man she was fucking falls off the bed. Damien. My little brother.

"Oh my God!" I yell.

"It's not what you think, Kate," Maddie says.

Ewww! How is this not what I think it is?

Damie jumps over to the desk and grabs his clothes off a wooden chair. Unfortunately, my eyes see his bare ass, and I can't stop staring. In my eyes, his naked body seems childlike.

Maddie has a white sheet over her chest with her hand extended. My heart is bursting in my chest.

"Sis, it's not what you think," my brother says, pulling up his pants.

Not what I think? I think it's exactly what I think. And did he call me SIS?

"How is this not what I think!" I yell. A few people in the hallway probably hear me screaming.

"I know you're not staying in the dorm with Maddie," Damie says. "You're living with Bryce."

Is he accusing me? Seriously? Is he going to go tell Daddy after I tell him he's fucking my best friend! REALLY?

"What … huh?" I don't know what to say. I look at my best friend. Her eyes are filling with tears. So are mine. She's still stupidly clutching the bedsheets over her chest. "Why...why would you—"

"Gotta run," Damie says. And that's exactly what he does. He runs out of the room so fast that I can't stop him.

"I'm sorry, Kate, but—"

"My brother?"

"Kate…" Tears are streaming down her face. "We really like each other. I've tried to tell you, but you won't listen. You just ignore me when I mention him. Your brother is so nice. He's like the first boy I've ever been with who's got it together."

She had to say *been with*. She could have said *dating*. She could have said *going out with*. But she said *been with*. Like *fucked*!

"I hate you!" I say, wiping my tears. "How could you do this?"

"Oh, Cadence," she says, squinting.

"He's...he's just a boy."

"He's not," she says. "He's an adult. More of a man than anyone I've ever been with."

"Been with! Stop fucking saying *been with*!"

"Katie," Maddie says, putting her hand up again.

"Just don't talk to me. God, Maddie. Just...don't talk to me ever again!"

And I slam the door.

I feel horrible. There's a pit in my stomach. I can't believe this. I feel alone.

I could go to the library. See Bryce. But he's finally studying —and a little mad at me. I coerced him into leaving in the middle of the day to go to Atlanta when he's got so much work to do. I can't go to him after all I've done. So what can I do?

Maddie said she couldn't go see Mira because of her mom's surgery. *Aunt Jane*, even though no one understands why the hell Maddie tells everyone to call her mom "Aunt Jane." She's her mom, right? Does it matter if she's not biologically her mom? A mom is a mom, right? And now her mom's sick. She just had surgery. But, apparently, Maddie had some spare time to go fuck my brother instead of visiting Mira or taking care of her *aunt*. What a bitch!

I run out on the one-lane road near our dorm. I look at Krunner Hall, the tall building where Damie stays, across the street. Then I look back at our room. It's too dark to see inside. The drapes are closed and all the lights are off now. Maddie probably has her head in her hands, bawling on my mattress— you know, the one she was fucking my brother on.

Some of me, the really small, gentle part that's buried, wants to go back into Maddie's room and hug her. But most of me wants to go back and slap her across her face! I keep seeing her having sex with my little brother. It's imprinted on my mind. I don't think I'll ever forget that nasty image.

I walk into the woods.

Mira's right. Piedmont Park is fake. So is the lake and the ducks. I want to live in the woods. In nature. Away from people. Because I'm a witch. I don't love people. I don't think I like people. I love the forest. I love nature. Fuck people. They're too busy fucking themselves.

12

TEATIME AND TRYING

I don't really want to meet with my former best friend. I'm so angry with her that I'd rather just not talk to her ever again. But there's something I learned from my tall, dark, and handsome fiancé—when you're angry, sometimes it's better to communicate than to shut down. You need to talk things out.

When I get mad, I withdraw. Last year I fought with Bryce for months. Enora had showed me images of her and Bryce having sex, making me jealous as hell, and I got so angry that I refused to talk to him. Well, I'm not going to do that again.

Sort of. Okay, Bryce convinced me to meet with Maddie. I had every intention of ignoring the bitch until she graduates, but Bryce said it's been long enough. It's time to "talk things out."

I told Madison to meet me in the morning at the university coffee shop. It's our favorite hangout. Unfortunately, since we're still in midterms, it's so crowded that the four large wooden tables at the center of the place are packed with students. But I'm early enough to find one of the nicer two-person tables by the window.

I gaze at the decorative murals on the brown walls of the coffeehouse. A runner is crossing the finish line, and a soccer player is kicking a ball. Then I bury my head in my textbook on the Industrial Revolution, but it doesn't take long for me to look out the window. It's a cloudy day, and the wet main walkway on campus is packed with students carrying books, laptops, and backpacks. A few people are sitting along the grassy hill. It's not too cold, but the lawn is wet from the morning rain. That's where the two of us once loved to study—on the grass beside the library.

The Industrial Revolution is not my favorite part of history, but it fulfills one of my requirements. This chapter talks about the flying shuttle and spinning jenny. It's boring stuff, really. If I'm going to study the eighteenth or nineteenth century, I'd much rather study Gettysburg or the French Revolution.

I decide to suffer and read on.

This section is about calcium hypochlorite. Like, what does calcium have to do with history? Bleach. Calcium hypochlorite is bleach, apparently. Bleach for clothing.

Madison comes through the glass doors, carrying a forest-green backpack over her shoulder, with jeans and a matching green T-shirt. Her makeup is black, giving her a goth look, just like mine, but her expression is very un-Maddie-like. She looks depressing as hell. She's looking down or to the side, doing whatever she can to avoid my eyes.

When she arrives at our table, she plops her backpack by the chair across from me, runs her hand through her long hair, and sighs. She puts her heavy red coat—which is just like mine, we got them together—on the chair and sits down.

I gesture to the white cup in front of her. It's a no-foam vanilla soy milk double espresso latte. (Her favorite, when she's not stealing other people's drinks. She's a bit of a kleptomaniac.)

"Hi, Cadence," she says, forcing a grin.

"I want you to stop seeing Damie." There. Blunt enough? I figure it balances the peace offering. Might as well get to the point and "talk things out."

She sips her drink and looks out the window at the gloomy day, ignoring me.

"Out of everyone I know, maybe even more than Bryce, you know I don't want my brother mixed up in our stuff. You dating him means he'll get close to our coven. I can't have that. I don't want him anywhere near our witchcraft. Jesus, Maddie, you know that. I can't believe you want to be with him. Unless...you are dating him, right? You're not just—"

"Bitch," Maddie snaps with her eyes wide. "How dare you. What do you think I'm doing? I told you, I like him."

"Okay," I say, putting a hand up.

She turns to the window again. I'm a little surprised she doesn't jump up and leave, but what did she expect? I mean, the whole thing is gross. My brother. Maddie. I mean, what the hell—

"You're so selfish, Cadence. You always think everything's about you. I'm falling in love with Damien, okay? Your brother. So? Why is it so hard for you to understand? No, I can get how it's hard. But what am I supposed to do? I really like him."

"Do you? Really?"

"What else do you think I'm doing?" she asks, hitting the table.

This isn't going well. I told Bryce. I should have done it my way. Maybe this is why I'm withdrawing. I don't have much patience when I'm mad. And talking to my former friend is like dealing with Beatrix, but instead of "crazy," I'm dealing with someone who—

"What do you want me to do?" Maddie stares into my eyes. "Is this really important enough to break up our friendship? What do you want me to say to make this better?"

I put my head in my hands, running my fingers through my long hair. Then I rub my eyes and shake my head. I feel her touch my wrist.

"God, Katie, you know I love you," she says with her voice cracking. "I'm so sorry I hurt you. I love you more than anyone in the world."

I feel tears coming to my eyes. I shake my head. "You're not hurting me, Madison. You're hurting my brother. He needs to stay away from us. That includes you."

"I can't do that."

I look at the wet grassy hill. The two of us have had so many lovely afternoons out there together. I miss it. And I miss those times. What happened?

"This is your way of being with me, is that it?" I ask. "You told me on our hike how much you missed me. You figure you can just hang with my brother and screw—"

"Damn it, Cadence! Shut up! I told you I love him."

"You don't love him."

"I love him. And, yeah, I miss you. But think about what you're saying—you've got Bryce. Who do I have? Yeah, I've been lonely. But your brother is really cool. He's the sweetest guy I know. I can trust him, which is more than I can say about anyone else I've ever gone out with. I'm sorry he's your brother, but that's the way I feel about him. I really like him, babe."

"I'm also your High Priestess," I say, staring at the hillside again. "I'm ordering you to stop seeing him."

She gets up and stands over me, putting her wet coat back on and shaking her head.

"You don't understand what's happening. This is real love, Cadence. Love. It's like what's between you and Bryce. You don't know how close we are because I kept it from you. I've been seeing him since school started. I didn't tell you because I was scared that what just happened would happen. I can't do what you're asking, High Priestess or not. I remember when we started and you were outside our group. Then I didn't want you in the coven at first. But...but, if you can't open your heart to me and your brother the same way and accept this, I don't know what we're going—"

"I'm ordering you, Blackbird. You're a witch in my coven. You have to do what I ask. You have to stop seeing him."

"*No! I don't!*" she shouts, shaking her head violently, and grabs her backpack. People all over the room stare at us.

She's gone.

Our meeting went exactly the way I thought it would go. Now I suppose I can take my anger out on Bryce when I get home because it was his idea to "talk things out."

Shit.

I sip some of my favorite drink. A green tea latte. It tastes really bland.

Shit.

I lean on my hands again and think about crying. But I'm not going to cry.

How dare she. She's the one messing with my brother. She can just stop seeing him.

I look out at the field once more, and this time I wish I hadn't. Maddie is rushing by, on a cement walkway, holding her head in her hands, crying. I feel a lump in my throat.

Maybe I'm being unreasonable? Maybe I need to accept the two of them? How can I not? I love Maddie so much.

My phone rings. I really don't want to answer it.

"What!" I snap.

"Katie." It's Dad. He sounds awful. "Did you hear?"

"What? What's the matter? I'm not really in a good mood right now, Dad."

"It's Damie. He's at the hospital. I'm rushing down now."

"Oh my God!" I say, jumping up. "What happened?"

"A car accident. He's going into surgery for his leg. I talked to him right before he went in. At least he's all right now."

"I'll...I'll come right away."

"I'll meet you there, Cadence."

I look out the window again. It's pouring rain now. Out in the center of the grassy hill, using her red coat to shield her from the pouring rain, Maddie is on her cell phone. I run out to catch up to her.

13

HAWTHORNE HOSPITAL

We take my car. It's awful because we have to walk through pouring rain to the apartment I share with Bryce, where my old Honda jalopy is sitting in the parking lot. Maddie's a bit irresponsible, and she doesn't have a working car at the moment. We walk really fast, practically running through puddles, while we do our best to shield our heads from the deluge with our arms or backpacks. Throughout the long walk, neither of us says a word.

Before we know it, I'm driving into the hospital parking lot. It's still pouring and the rain clouds are so dark that it feels like nighttime. Maddie still hasn't said anything. Actually, I think she's only said one or two words since I met up with her outside the coffeehouse. It's really weird: we're both so worried but still so furious with each other. When I stop the car, she jumps out and runs without me.

Hawthorne Hospital is a really ugly small hospital, more of a clinic really. It's a two-story building with drab white concrete walls and a hideous silver overhang in front of the emergency room. That's it. The only thing making the eyesore bearable is the lovely Hawthorne Forest surrounding it.

When I catch up to Maddie, she's asking the receptionist at the front desk what room Damien's in. A gray-haired black lady smiles and hands us a visitor board to sign. She looks up something on her computer and tells us that Damien is still in the operating room.

"What's wrong with him?" Maddie asks.

The receptionist just looks at her monitor, bewildered.

"Can we meet him at the room he'll be staying in?" I ask.

She nods and tells us it's Room 174, on the first floor.

Maddie and I practically run again, which is really silly because she just told us that Damien is still in surgery, but we're just that worried. When we make it, the white room is empty. In fact, newly folded sheets are laid out on the bed. The drapes are open, showing rain splashing over a walkway and the surrounding dense thin trees of the forest. The room smells very fake and sterile, like Lysol. There are two chairs near the window, and Maddie removes her coat and takes one. She looks out the window for a moment; then she grabs her cell phone and calls somebody.

"Who are you calling?" I ask, sitting down on the bed.

"Oh, we're talking now, Cadence?"

"Actually, you're the one who ran from me."

She laughs derisively, leans on the armrest of the chair, and puts her ear closer to her cell phone. "Hey, Mom. Yeah. Fine. Look, can you come to the hospital and bring me some of my stuff from home in a suitcase? Clothes. Makeup. My travel purse. You know, my vacation stuff. I'm probably going to stay here overnight. Yeah. A car accident. I know. It's...terrible. I'm all right. No, I'm just worried about Damie. I don't know. I just don't know yet. Yeah, I really need stuff from home. Yeah. No. No, I'm okay. Great. Thanks. Love you. Bye."

She sighs and shoves the phone in her pants pocket. Then she stares out the window, acting as if I'm not in the room. She sighs again.

"I can get you your clothes from the dorm," I say.

She looks over as if saying "are you for real?" and turns back to the window.

I like the view of the forest even when it's raining. But right now, I don't like it so much. Not when we hate each other.

We sit like this, not talking, for about half an hour. I can't remember a tougher time between me and my former friend. But, like I told you, I'm used to ignoring people when I'm angry. Maddie's not. She's always bubbly. And right now, neither of us wants to be in the room together, but we're forced to wait.

I'm so worried. Why does Damie need to be in surgery after an accident?

My mind wanders as it always does. I'm fantasizing images of my little brother being a paraplegic or something. Maddie looks just as worried. She keeps going through multiple sticks of gum. The sound of her chewing is driving me crazy. First it was constant sighing, now it's chewing gum. These sounds mix with the incessant pounding of water on the ground outside and against the window. Normally, in our old world, the two of us would be comforting each other. At least she'd offer me a piece of gum. Instead, she keeps staring out at the trees, and I keep looking at the ugly plastic tile floor and whitewashed walls.

Finally, a nurse wheels Damie into the room in a wheelchair.

He looks fine. I jump up to gather my little brother in my arms, but Maddie beats me to it. They kiss on the lips, and I remember again why we're fighting.

"Hey, Maddie," Damie says. "It was compartment syndrome. Can you believe that? That's so rare. The dashboard in Dad's old Toyota fell on my leg."

"Oh God, babe, your face," Maddie says, brushing gently over it.

"Yeah, just a few scrapes. It's nothing."

"But they sewed some," she adds.

"Sutured a little," he says with a chuckle. "Nothing that will scar badly. It's mainly my forehead." Damie looks at me and smiles. "Hi, sis."

"I'm so relieved you're okay," I say. I can't believe how formal and fake I sound. I feel totally out of place, which is really weird because he's my brother.

"Yeah." Then he turns to Maddie and smiles again. She annoyingly strokes his hair. "Maddie, compartment syndrome. I can't believe it. They had to cut into the flesh to relieve the pressure. Isn't that cool? Fasciotomy. I asked if they could let me watch. Normally, they'd put a patient out, but the doctor was really awesome and let me watch the whole procedure."

"You need to rest," comments the nurse with a smile. She's staring at a plastic bag on a tray. "You want me to help you get back into bed?"

"I'd rather sit for a while."

"At least let's get you into the chair, then."

We all help him into one of the wooden chairs: the nurse, me, and my ex-friend. We also move the large tray with a tube hooked into his arm, placing it beside him.

When the nurse finally leaves, Maddie takes my place on the bed beside Damien, holding his hand. I'm now standing, uncomfortably alone, near an empty wooden table.

"Dad's coming," I say.

"I know," Damien says. "I talked to him before surgery. He was just glad I was okay. I did black out for a second, but I didn't injure my head. Nothing serious."

"What happened?" I ask. "You're a really good driver. I don't get it."

"It was raining. The roads were slick. I was just driving to the grocery store. I needed to restock some things, and Harvey had gone home for the weekend. I didn't think of the rain. And you know, Kate, the rain is like ice this time of year."

"So you slipped?"

"No. Not exactly. It was weird. I—" He hesitates and I can almost swear he shakes for a second. "I saw something in the middle of the road. I'm not sure what it was. I thought it was a deer. It flashed red before me under the pouring rain. Almost like fire. It just appeared suddenly in the middle of the road. This red object. I quickly swerved to miss it, and that's when the car slid on the black ice and hit a tree. I was still moving fast, probably like thirty miles per hour. And, of course, it's Dad's beat-up pickup truck."

"God, Damie," Maddie says, reaching down and hugging him again. "You could have been killed."

"I'm all right." He smiles, looking up. Maddie looks at the bandaging on his right leg as if noticing it for the first time. Damie follows her eyes. "The doctors said I probably would have just been casted if I hadn't lost blood flow to the whole leg. They had to operate."

I turn and stare out at the now very familiar view of the forest. It's still pouring rain outside. I rub my temples.

"Thanks for coming, sis. I know how it's been."

"Of course."

"She's still mad," says Maddie. "She's a bitch." In the old world, Maddie would have laughed or winked saying that. She's very serious right now.

"The strangest thing was after the accident," he adds. "I got out of the car. Smoke was coming from the hood. Of course half the engine was wrapped around a tree trunk, but when the ambulance came, I noticed two cops hovering around the center of the street. At first, I didn't really care. The paramedics were loading me into the ambulance. But then I looked more carefully. In the middle of the pouring rain was a round wooden statue. In the center was a figure shaped like a person made of leaves and straw. And it was tilted on this large, round wooden wheel. It was really weird."

I look at Maddie. She meets my stare as if challenging me to care. But then she leans toward Damie and touches his arm. "A wheel? Was it shaped like a symbol? Like the pentagram I showed you?"

He thinks for a moment and nods. "Yes, I think so. I thought it was somehow related to that witch stuff you guys do. The same symbol. A pentagram, but huge and painted red with a strawman on it. The strawman was on fire."

Maddie buries her head in her hands for a moment. Damie furrows his brow, looking at her funny. Then she jumps up and walks to the window.

"God, Cadence, Enora could have killed him," Maddie says.

"You don't know—"

"Don't you see?" she asks, whirling around at me. "I told you. I told you after Beatrix died we had to stop her. That we had to cast a spell against her on a Sabbath. Seeing Mira wasn't enough. Mira's brainwashed. First Beatrix and now... why haven't you done anything? You're our leader. You've done nothing."

"What are you guys talking about?" Damien asks.

"This isn't the time," I warn.

"Not the time?" Maddie asks. I've never seen her so angry. "When's the time? Would you have preferred talking about it in a fucking morgue? Your brother almost died! Are you and Mira going to tell me it's a fucking coincidence?"

"Maddie, stop. What are you trying to say?"

"It's Enora. It's obvious. Our coven needs to get rid of her. Just like we met to get rid of Reardon, we need to meet again and get rid of her. We should have done it after she sent a message with Beatrix. She knew exactly when and who to strike. Don't tell me you don't agree. Don't tell me you think someone else got in the way of his car." She turns to Damien again. "You said you swerved to avoid a wooden pentagram?

Red? And it just appeared out of nowhere? A pentagram? You're sure?"

"Yes."

"It's like how you almost killed Bryce last year," Maddie says, squinting at me with hatred. "It's all your fault. Alondra should never have made you our leader. You aren't one. Had you been, Beatrix would never have been murdered. Mira would never have been taken from us. Damien would never have gotten hurt. Your brother could have died, and that would have been your fault too. It's all because of you."

I don't say anything. I don't bother. I just rush out of the room.

14

HAWTHORNE LAKE

I'm walking around and around and around Hawthorne Lake. Moonlight and shadows of the trees reflect off the ripples of waves with the thick woods surrounding me. The rain has stopped, the air smells fresh, and the view is beautiful, but even this lovely place isn't enough to still my mind. Maddie laughed when I told her I was thinking of going to Sri Lanka to study Buddhism. Boy, could I do with some meditation right now. Or maybe Hinduism? A little action without thought, like in the *Bhagavad Gita*?

It's my fault?

That's what I keep asking myself.

So, it's my fault?

Maddie's right. She must be. Right?

This is my former best friend, who used to laugh off every problem we had. Now she's acting like she'd rather I not exist. Like any problems of hers are because of me.

Maybe she's right? Last year was nearly a disaster for Bryce. He almost died. I am a terrible leader. I'd be the first to admit that. And Maddie urged me to run a Sabbath. She wanted me to see Mira even more than I did. She would have gone with me had she not had to take care of her mom—or rendezvous to fuck my brother, which I learned later as you well know. Hmm...if screwing my brother was more important than the Abaddon coven and Enora, maybe she's to blame. Right? Fuck her!

My fault! You've gotta be kidding me!

I don't know... maybe it is. I'm so confused.

I'm walking my fifth lap, I think. I don't know. I keep walking around and around the water's edge, staring at the small waves lapping up against pebbles and mud. It's like I have a purpose, but I don't know what it is. I threw off my shoes and socks a long time ago—I have no idea where I threw them— and I occasionally dip my bare feet into the cold water. I feel the pebbles; most are soft, massage my feet in the muddy, shallow water. It's after midnight. I think I've been walking for hours.

Why did I let Beatrix die? She was my responsibility. She was so young. I failed her. She died because of me.

I see a vision of a pale body in a black cloak ever so slightly swaying over Alondra's patio.

About halfway through another lap, I stop and walk a little closer to the edge. I dip my hand into the water and touch the rocks. Most of the stones are rounded and feel smooth against my fingers. Then I gather some mud underwater and let it drip down my hand. The water's cold, but it soothes my skin. I dip my fingers through the opening of my shirt, probing under my bra and enjoying the feel over my breasts and along my nipples. It's a warm night.

Something startles me from behind, in the bushes. I jump and squint, searching the blackness through the trees. I hear it again. Then I'm breathless as an animal bursts forth from the thicket, its eyes shining an eerie white, reflecting the moonlight. It's a deer. She stops close to the shore beside me, slowing down to a trot, and gently dips her head in the water to drink. I walk closer to the water and pet its fur. It steps closer. Then I get on my knees beside the deer, soaking my pants, and run my hands in the cold water again. At first it's to wash off the mud and grime, but then I bring the water up to my mouth to taste. It's dirty, earthy, and bitter, but cool and refreshing. I get why the deer likes it. The deer nudges me a couple of times with her head. I giggle and oblige, petting her again.

I stand up and remove my red coat and throw it by the water's edge. Then I bring more water up to my bare arms, bathing my skin. It feels good. It cleanses me.

Why did I hurt my brother? I'd rather die than let that bitch lay a finger on him. She knew that. She taunted me at the Billington House. Maddie's right. There's no way it's a coincidence that he crashed because of a burning pentagram.

I should have confronted Enora. I should have fought her long ago. I'm such a coward.

The deer walks deeper into the water and turns as if waiting for me to join her, as if beckoning me. Perhaps the water can splash away my thoughts? I could walk in and swim? But...wait, that's crazy. It's the middle of the night.

When Mira was lost, I told Bryce a thousand times I should visit her. But, to be honest, it wasn't hard for him to convince me not to. I didn't want to mess up my grades. That sounds stupid, but I just wanted a normal fall semester. Every year, all I wanted was to be a normal student.

No, that's not honest. I was afraid. Very afraid. I'm scared of Enora.

I need to cleanse more. I have to clear my body of these thoughts. Usually walking helps me forget my troubles, but tonight it's not working. Earlier I considered just walking in circles until dawn. But now I feel a pain in my chest. I feel horrible. I'm so sad. It's all my fault.

I start crying.

I feel so alone.

Perhaps I should go to Bryce. Bryce. He's so nice. He kept calling but I didn't answer my phone. I'm not sure where my phone is now.

I need thoughtlessness. My thoughts are painful. I need to find a way to ignore them.

I pull up my T-shirt and unclasp my bra. I pull down my pants and underwear and pile my clothes by the side of the lake. Slowly, I wade ankle-deep, in the nude, following the deer, but it's really cold. I bring the cold water along my arms and belly. Then I splash the water on my face. The deer is beside me again. I bathe with her. I crouch down and run the cold water along my legs and up to my sides and waist. I walk in deeper, knee-deep. I throw cold water along my stomach and breasts. Then I feel the cold along my groin and butt. For a moment, I shiver. But I'm committed now. I enter deeper. I sink until the water is at the level of my belly button.

I smell and feel charred, rotting flesh and chalky talc powder. There's a flash of red and an upside-down pentagram. Then my skin is soothingly warmed as if I'm standing near the jets of a whirlpool sauna.

The deer swims beside me as if trying to grab my attention. I laugh. I think she's beckoning me to join her. That's crazy. The water's so black. And...wasn't there a reason I shouldn't be in the water?

Soon my whole body is dog-paddling. I enjoy the icy water as it touches my skin. It feels like it outlines my body. I feel it against my face, hands, belly, back, and arms, just like before, when I ran water along my body. It's as if I've summoned Vidar, the forest god, and he is touching me. Caressing my skin. I feel him along my chest, then running his hands over my pussy and ass. Being this bare in the middle of the night in the water is pleasurable and incredibly erotic. I feel as if I am giving myself to the forest god. I want to. I want to let go and have no thought or care anymore.

I'm a good swimmer. In the furthest reaches of my mind, I think that. Beyond the black water, I can see lights from campus between the trees in the forest. The deer and I swim toward the artificial lights of Hawthorne University.

Then I rest. I lie on my back and float on the lake, naked, staring up at the gorgeous bright stars. It's so serene. It's as beautiful as the empty, quiet forest. At my side, I catch my deer's eyes open wide while it treads water.

I roll and dip my head under the water. I open my eyes and can't see a thing, just a little light dancing in blurred lines under me. The bottom is blackness. For a moment, as I look down into complete darkness, not able to see under my feet, I'm afraid. There's this fear that some sea monster will come barreling up to the surface and consume me. I always have this fear when I swim in lakes. Sea monsters, alligators, and snakes. The fear's greater now because it's dark. But it's a small lake. It was safe during the day; why wouldn't it be at night? So I tell myself not to be stupid and scared.

When I get to the surface of the water, I realize I've lost my deer. I'm close to the center of the water now, about fifty yards from either side of the shore.

Feeling a little crazy, perhaps as if I have nothing to lose, I dive. I'm shocked by how long it takes to touch the ground at the bottom of the lake. I swim deep in the pitch darkness. My ears pop. It's much deeper than I could have imagined. I touch some sort of plant or branch near the bottom, and I quickly push myself back up to the surface for air. As dark as it is, I actually see moonlight on the surface as I emerge from the water. I spit out some of the water and rub my eyes. I'm treading water and, at the center of my chest, I feel elation. I feel happy. Wasn't there something wonderful happening in my life right now? Or was it tragic and sad?

There's a flash of Beatrix staring at me with her bloodshot

eyes wide open, hanging from a rope. My neck tightens. I can't breathe.

I splash the water, shake my head, brush my wet hair from my eyes, and swim toward the light at the other end of the lake.

When I'm close enough to the other shore, I wade until I feel rocks and boulders jut out. Then I slowly walk to the water's edge. The water laps up against my tits, and I feel aroused again. I enjoy the tingle of the dripping water falling from my neck down to my breasts. Then the water laps up against my butt and privates again. It's as if the lake is making love to my naked body. My water-lover touches me with drips of water as I emerge on the shore.

I turn from a noise in the bushes toward the faraway lights of campus, on the other side of the thick trees of the forest. It's dark, but my eyes have adjusted. On this side, there's a dirt path that leads right to campus. People are laughing and murmuring behind thick trees. Two people run out from the trees to the shoreline, about twenty yards from the water, where I'm standing. They stop in their tracks. Two boys—I think I recognize one of them from one of my classes—and they're staring at me with mouths wide open. Then comes a girl's voice. She appears right next to them. One of the boys points at me, and the girl gasps. Of course, I've completely forgotten that I'm stark naked until now. I don't think my mind is all here right now, to tell you the truth.

I'm mad. I have no interest in "talking" to anyone. Why am I angry? They're disturbing my peace. That's why. I love my lake. My joy comes from swimming and walking along its shore. I don't want to talk to anybody. People bother me.

"Cadence?" asks a girl, unsure. She's so far away, but I recognize her voice. She's standing over rocks by the river's edge.

I see a vivid vision of a witch falling from the rafters of Alondra's porch with a noose around her neck. I feel tightening along my neck again, but I cut the cord when I utter, "*Lux mortis. Ariadne. Hecate. Astraea. Gaia. Limnades.* Summon me, Nyx. Welcome. Not far from man's curse. Hecate, know my own. Blind me in darkness so that I feel Vidar's pleasure. Not pain. Fuck you. *Lacus. Aqua. Lacus. Aqua.* Fuck me. Fuck me now."

"Katie, is that you?" she asks again, squinting.

"*Somnus*," I say, waving a hand before the girl. She collapses on the rocks. Her two friends run down the rocks from the woods and grab her, trying to revive her.

I walk up, swaying my naked hips. When I'm beside them, I look down at the two boys. They're so worried about their fallen comrade that they didn't even hear me approach. They're pushing and tugging at the girl. I know her. Her name is Kendra. She's an Asian girl who was in my economics class last year.

I don't know the boys well. One is a nerdy-looking boy with glasses, a button-down, and slacks. The other's cute, wearing just a T-shirt and jeans. I smell alcohol. The boys reek of it. The moonlight shines on their faces. The cute one has short hair and a thick beard, which I like. He's broad-chested and really muscular. He looks up at me. I smile, remembering that I'm not wearing clothes. I have a strong urge to fall to the ground and fuck him. I want to hit the ground right now, run my hand along his short hair and all the strands of that bushy beard, yank down his pants, and have at it. And with his gaze, I think he wants it too. It wouldn't be hard. He'd have no way to stop me. Not in my current state. I could easily *make him* love me.

The other boy's staring now. In fact, both of them have stopped even caring about their fallen comrade. What a surprise if I fucked the nerdy one too. Just grabbed those glasses, licked his face and cock, and squeezed my body against his thin girlish figure—like I really fucking care about his figure at the moment—and screwed the virgin until the sun rose. Or I could fuck both boys together. Why not? It would be fun.

I kneel down and touch the fluffy beard of the buff one. He just stares like a frozen rabbit playing dead, allowing my dripping wet fingers to run along his hairy cheek. I see him stare at my tits. I smile. I look at his T-shirt. Both boys are staring at my tits. They're on their knees, looking blankly at my breasts.

"Take your clothes off," I order.

The strong guy removes his shirt first. I lick my lips, looking at the ripples of his muscular chest. His perfectly developed triceps, deltoids, and pecs. His abs. The nerd undresses too. Even his run-of-the-mill body attracts me. I rub the muscles on their arms and shoulders and then down along their chests.

"You shall be my sacrifice. *Lacus. Delactatio, delectatio, fructus.*" I gently lay the two naked men down on the dirt. "*Coitus, fructus. Fructus... coitus. Fructus.*"

They nod, obeying me, and lie still beside the passed-out girl. As I crouch beside them, running my fingers over the thin, lanky boy's hair, I use my left hand to reach down to his hard cock. As my gaze hungrily follows my hand down to his groin, I see a twinkle in the moonlight on my finger. My ring finger.

I feel a sharp pain in my head. It becomes crushing. And fear. My confidence leaves me, and I'm feeling as if something terrible is happening. I squeeze my hands and quickly shake my head. I can't breathe for a moment. Then I jump to my feet and look at the two naked boys.

My God, what am I doing?

"*Somnus! Somnus!*" I shout, almost screaming, throwing my arm out toward both of them. They both turn their heads, close their eyes, and fall asleep.

"You are alone," says an echoing voice behind me. The voice laughs. "Only in magic are you free. Let go of your power and you are nothing. Blind."

I search the trees and the lake. I don't see where the voice is coming from.

"Why not join them? Take these men as they lie here as

your sacrifice. You have that great a power. Take them. They're yours with magic. Don't you want to? You can have any man with your power. Afterward, you can even wipe away his memory. Take whomever you want, whenever you want. You are a witch. You can do whatever you want to men under the rays of Selene's blessed darkness. No longer be a part of God's deception and guilt, descendant of Escoba. Roam free, descendant of Hawthorne. Rise up in this baptism. Join me. Your friend. Once you have a taste, you will never go back. You won't want to. Join me. Be free. Within the water or upon the walls of the forest, you can be reborn and finally be happy. You can finally feel free."

"Who are you?"

"*Amica.*"

Dread deepens. My blackbird, my majestic raven, who I haven't seen in a year, stands beside the shore of the lake. I hate her. But...part of me misses her. Part of me feels free before my bird. Cleansed. And the raven nods its head, as if reading my thoughts.

I see my brother sitting in a wheelchair with his leg bandaged.

"What did you do to Beatrix!" I shout, and the bird flutters its wings. Then I jerk my head in every direction, looking around the lake. "What did you do to my brother! How dare you bewitch me! How dare you put a spell on me!"

"*Et nos unum sumus,*" says the voice, bursting into laughter. "*Et nos unum sumus.*"

Laughter echoes from a thousand trees, surrounding me.

* * *

I wake up naked in a bush beside the lake. It is still dark.

15
____

LOVE ME

IT TAKES ME ALL OF EARLY DAWN TO FIND MY CLOTHES. I CIRCLE like thirty times to find where I placed them. It doesn't help that the sun hasn't risen above the trees on the horizon, so it's still dark. But at least it's still summer, so I'm not too cold.

I run barefoot to my apartment. By the time I get to the door, the sun's rising. And the minute my key is in the lock, the door swings open.

"What the hell happened!" Bryce exclaims. "Oh my God, I've been so worried! Maddie called and told me about Damie. She's been desperately trying to reach you. She said she was mean to you. She said she thought you went crazy when you left them. You haven't answered your phone!" He's hysterical. He won't stop talking. "I've told you a million times to answer your phone. Damn it, Cadence, I've been pacing all night!" But he lets go of his rage, looking at my head and touching my hair. "Your hair's wet and dirty." His tone becomes gentler. "Why? Are you okay, baby?"

"I went walking," I say with a shrug, entering the apartment. "It was a warm night. I walked to the lake to take my mind off things."

"What?"

"It was a spell. Enora's, I think."

He closes the door and I sit down on the couch and stare across the living room for a moment. Then I start crying.

"It's all my fault," I say when he puts an arm around me. "Beatrix and now Damie. They're all being poisoned by Hawthorne. Beatrix thought I could protect her. And now Enora's after my brother. God, Bryce! You know how much I didn't want him to come here."

"Damie's fine, Katie. That's what I was trying to tell you. He's fine. Everyone is fine. And Beatrix wasn't your fault. She was going to kill herself sooner or later, with your help or not. I've told you this a million times. Hell, you even said she probably killed that cat she told you about."

"She was murdered." I shake my head violently. "It wasn't suicide. Maddie's right. And now Panthera is going after us. My brother."

"It's so late. Just stop worrying." He holds my hand. "Why don't you go shower and rest? I'm just relieved you're okay."

"Fuck you!" I toss his hand back to him. "We could have saved her! Maddie's right. We could have watched her and stayed at the house and stopped it from happening. Seeing Enora in the Billington House should have been enough to convince us to never leave that little girl alone at Alondra's house. I should have stayed with her. What sort of protection did I give her? I made it worse. It's all my fault. And Damie could have been okay if I had just told him. I should have just said to stay away from Hawthorne. I should have just told Dad about us. That would have done it. Daddy would never have let him come here. But I'm a coward. I'm such a coward. If I had told Dad that I'm a witch, he would have done everything he could to keep Damie from becoming one too."

"Calm down, Cadence. Please. That's not true. None of this is your fault."

"What do you mean!" I yell, standing up. He falls back on the couch, furrowing his brow, looking at me like I'm insane. "How the hell can you say that! Beatrix was just an innocent, confused little girl."

I'm looking down at Bryce like I hate him, but his blue eyes look up at me with this mix of confusion and sweet concern. He looks worried. About me. I don't think anyone else cares about me. Nobody in the whole world. Only he cares.

His care finally disarms me. I fall back on the couch and put my head in my hands. But I don't cry. Crying reminds me of Beatrix.

"I'm sorry. I...I'm so sorry, Bryce. I'm really confused right now."

"You're not being yourself. You were in a wandering tonight, right? A trance... was it triggered because of what happened to Damien, or do you really think it was Enora?"

"I don't know. I heard her. I saw Amica. It...was her."

I am in a witch trance. Even now. A witch's trance is set off by extreme emotion. Seeing Beatrix hanging from a rope certainly provided the first impetus. Then seeing my sweet baby brother having sex with my best friend spurred me on. His surgery probably threw me over the edge. No, my fight with Maddie did.

But I think I would have gone swimming in the middle of the night whether influenced by Enora or not. So, in a really weird way, I'm not so sure whether the trance was because of her or because of me. Maybe she came to take advantage of it?

My heart is racing. My senses are heightened. Even though Bryce's door is closed, I can hear a student throw her keys and purse in her car and start her engine outside. That's beyond the wall and around the corner in the parking lot. The scent of my body overwhelms me—it's of the ground and the fresh water of the lake. I love that smell. The earthen scent soothes my anger. It makes me long to be back in the lake again. It's funny because Bryce wants me to shower and stay home, but I would be happy right now just sleeping in mud under a tree.

"I am in a trance," I admit with a nod.

I look at Bryce. He's sitting beside me, running a hand through my hair. He's probably been worried about me all night. I run my hand along his forehead, touching his feathery hair. Then I lean over and kiss him on the lips. I love him so much.

"I'm sorry I worried you," I say. "I lost track of the time."

"It doesn't sound like you had a choice," he says with a nod.

He's breathing more heavily. I think he is. Or maybe I'm noticing his breathing? I'm not sure. I know I'm breathing more heavily.

I reach closer and press my lips to his, harder, entering with my tongue. And we make out. It's nice. I run my hand over the curves of his biceps and along the muscles of his neck and back. Bryce doesn't wear a shirt to bed until we're deeper into winter. It's too hot. With my other hand, I make my way down his pecs and along the ripples of his abs to his boxer shorts. I sneak a hand in and start rubbing his cock.

"Cadence, stop," he says, pulling my hand out of his pants. "What are you doing? We were just talking about Beatrix and your brother. Let's not do this again. You're in a trance."

I laugh.

"Go shower, baby," he repeats. But his words seem almost sultry to my ears, like a whisper.

"Why, do I smell?"

He chuckles despite himself. That brings my lips back on his.

Ooh, I want him so badly. I don't think I've ever wanted anything so badly before. Trances do increase sexual drive but...so? I really love this man.

"I probably do smell," I say between kisses. "I swam in the lake."

"What! You swam in the lake!" he exclaims with eyes wide, pushing me back again.

"Aha."

"Jesus, Cadence."

The apartment doesn't feel like my home. I can't explain it. It feels like Bryce's. Sure, I've been living here. My stuff is here, and I've slept here for many months, but it doesn't feel like home. The forest is my home.

He takes my hand and pulls me to my feet. He helps me take off my red coat. Next is my shirt. I just stand there and stare at his naked chest. He undresses me. He's taking care of me. It reminds me he's the only one in the world who cares about me. Why? Why should he? I hurt everyone I love.

He removes my bra. I feel the circulating cool air brush over my nipples, and that arouses me more. They feel hard. The air conditioner is like the lake. Like when Vidar caressed me in the water. Now the air touches me. I want Bryce to do that now. I feel every stroke of his fingers as they graze the curves of my breasts and belly and massage my soft skin. I feel it in slow motion. He is probably moving quickly, but it all seems slow. It feels so good. This is part of a spell too. My spell. I look at his wide eyes, and they're staring at my body. I think I'm confusing his mind. He thinks he needs to undress me to help me, but really he's undressing me to touch me. I feel his fingers as they slowly pull my pants and underwear down from my hips. Then he strokes my skin, brushing lightly along my legs and ass while breathing more heavily. He touches my inner thighs and the hair between my legs. Purposefully? I don't know. I catch his eyes and he quickly averts them. I'm naked.

"Where's your phone, Kate?" he asks.

"Huh?"

"Your phone?"

"What?"

"Where's your phone?" he asks sternly.

Oops. I laugh. He doesn't.

"That explains why you didn't answer our calls," he says with a sigh, shaking his head.

"Aha." I'm staring at him, thinking of his stern tone of voice. "Did you want to punish me?"

The question makes him really nervous, and he blinks his eyes and turns from me.

He takes my hand to lead me to the bathroom, but I don't move. That's one thing I'm not going to let him do. I'm not going anywhere. I'm staying put right here by the couch. I told you, it doesn't feel like my apartment. It feels like his. I love that. It's like I'm visiting his place. His things. His body. I can smell him. His scent permeates the whole place. His smell. Not just his cologne. His body scent. It's irresistible.

"What's the matter?" he asks, looking at my dirty feet. "You need to go shower."

"I want to fuck you."

"Katie," he says, closing his eyes and shaking his head. He looks angry. "You're in a trance. Let's not do this now. And... you're bewitching me. Stop it. Go shower."

"I want to fuck you, Bryce," I repeat, and I run my hand along his short hair. He freezes. It reminds me of the students. He is under my spell. Really, I could do whatever I want with him. I could make him fuck me. Enora was right about that. With Bryce, it...wouldn't be so wrong. Would it?

I look at my ring. I don't want him to fuck me. I want him to love me.

He's wearing his pajama pants. I remember having sex with him one night last year, practically attacking him and yanking them down. That was after a trance too. I don't want to do that tonight. I won't do that. I want to make love *with* him. I know the trance is spurring us on, but is that so wrong? When we love each other? I slowly run my hands along his chest, over all the ripples of his muscles. He's so cut. I make my way with my hands down to his boxers once more. Then inside. His penis is large. He may be telling me to stop, but his body isn't.

"I'm sorry I worried you," I say almost in a whisper, stroking his cock.

"Cadence," he says, closing his eyes. "I said you were in a trance. We should stop."

"You don't want to?" I ask, pouting like a child. He regains his smile.

"I do ... of course, I do. But I'm worried. It's Enora? You're sure?"

"I think so. She was trying to hurt us. Separate us. But I stopped her." I'm still rubbing his cock.

I look into his gorgeous blues. God, I almost had sex with those boys by the lake! That's almost enough to break my arousal with Bryce. To think that I could have done that. It would have destroyed me. I would have been lost forever. Was that Enora's plan? It must have been.

"How? How...did you stop her?" he stammers. He closes his eyes in pleasure.

"You. You stopped me."

"What do you mean?"

I shrug. Then I drop to my knees and pull down his pants and shorts. I hold his large cock in my hands and bring my mouth next to it, but he pushes me away. I move close again and take it inside.

"Cadence! You're in a trance."

"So?" I ask, looking up at him.

I drop to my knees again. That drives him mad. I never have oral sex with him. It just feels too dirty. Nothing's too dirty at the moment. I still smell the grime from the lake on me. And dirty is something I yearn for right now. In fact, it makes me even more wet. I take him inside again.

"Stand up," he says. But he doesn't push my face away. "Please...Cadence...just stand up and go shower."

"Okay," I say, obeying him with a laugh. I'm guessing he's disappointed. "I'll go shower."

But I'm not done. Not even close.

I stand up and touch his beard, staring into his eyes again. Then I press my lips hard against his, tasting him. I kiss him passionately, entering his mouth slowly, rolling my tongue along his.

"God, Cadence, what are you doing to me?" he asks, breathless.

"Loving you. Would you prefer I stop?"

"No. I mean, yes, if it's a spell."

"This isn't a spell, husband."

That word does it. *Husband.* It drives me wild. The word *husband* drives me absolutely over the edge. It's like throwing open a jammed door between our true love and our passion, now mixed with my witchery. I have never felt such strong attraction before.

Somehow, we land on the carpet. We roll from the couch to the center of the room.

"What are you going to do to your wife?" I ask, with a sly smile, in his embrace.

"Make you shower."

I giggle. "Can I tell you a secret?" I whisper in his ear.

He nods.

"After," I whisper.

I roll him on his back and straddle him on the carpet. Our lips touch again. Then, slowly, I gyrate my pelvis up and down along his shaft while running my fingers through his hair. Already, I'm feeling what I've wanted in my pussy since jumping into the lake. I suppose if I didn't have Bryce, I would have the lake. And the trees. But I do have Bryce. And that makes me forget all my troubles.

He runs his hands along my breasts, tracing around my curves and touching my erect nipples. I run my hand along his beard again and his short, feathery hair. I grind around him, teasing him, only making him crazier. I want him. I want him inside me so bad.

"I love you, Cadence," he says. He enters me. "You're... you're unbelievable, Cadence. You're—"

"Love me."

He's so slow and gentle, moving up and down inside me, just holding me by the hips. Then he runs his hand along my back, and his other hand squeezes my boobs. He brings his fingers up and traces my areolas and erect nipples. Then he brings me really close, his hands rubbing lower, down over the crack in my ass. My face is an inch away from his. I smile and suck his lips hard. My heart is racing. I feel his race too. But he doesn't smile. He's determined.

It's quiet otherwise. The door's locked. The lights are dim, only coming from the kitchen. There's nothing to disturb us. No distractions. Nothing. I don't hear anything outside our apartment anymore, because I don't want to. There's just us.

He jerks faster, moaning. I bounce on him harder, and I can hear the sound of me riding up and down on him. It feels so good. All the while, I'm sucking and kissing his lips hard. I even bite him. That stops him for a second. He answers by lifting himself deep into me, even harder, lifting my entire body as if punishing me.

"Oh, Bryce," I say quietly in his ear. "Yes. Fuck me. Fuck me hard. Fuck me. Do it. Do it to me now. Fuck..."

"Is this...a spell?"

"No. Not a witch's spell. It's me. Love. I love you so much. Don't...stop. Please. Please just don't stop."

I feel him climax inside me. That puts me over the edge and I come with him, falling into his arms. It's only then that I realize I'm still covered with muck and grime from the lake. *Gross!* I realize that he wasn't asking me to shower just to stop himself from making love to me. I'm filthy. I get off of him.

"Come here," he says, laughing, gesturing for me to fall back into his arms. Hesitantly, I do. I lie back down on the carpet with him and close my eyes in his embrace.

We lie quietly for a little while. Then—

"Bryce."

"Yeah?"

"The thing that stopped me from losing it, you know, from giving up everything, from being lost, was your ring. Your love. Otherwise, I think I would have been lost forever. I love you so much, Bryce. Do you love me?"

"Oh, Katie," he says, squeezing me tighter, kissing my cheek. "I love you. What am I going to do with you?"

"Love me."

16

FAMILY DINNER

AUNT JANE'S HOUSE IS ALWAYS A COMPLETE MESS, AND IT'S amusing how she's hidden all her junk behind unhung paintings and rugs. I know better. I've stayed over at her house many times and attempted to clean it. She usually just leaves stuff all over the carpet, but tonight, in order to entertain us, she's cleared out the whole dining room. She's also set fancy silverware along the long light-oak table with elegant white tablecloths and candles. The room is dimly lit with lamps.

Jane's also not a great cook. There's turkey, mashed potatoes, and cranberries on the table, but I know that she microwaved it or took it out of cans. But that's okay. Who cares? Because, like Maddie, Jane's one of the most fun, smiley women I've ever met.

Well, Maddie used to be. I haven't talked to her since the hospital. She's still blaming me for Damie's car accident, so we're back to ignoring each other. In fact, she's even been intervening with my other witch friends. I actually listened to her and finally scheduled a rendezvous with the coven to talk about Enora, but we didn't meet because only a couple of girls showed up. Frida told me Maddie had convinced the rest of the gang not to go. That's how crazy she is. Maddie was the one who originally told them we needed to gather. Now she's sabotaging our Sabbaths. It doesn't make sense, right? I'm telling you, she's gone cuckoo.

Anyway, Aunt Jane is wearing a bunch of fake gold necklaces, these large red-jeweled gold earrings, and a long trailing multicolored dress. No makeup. And she has her hair short and gray. I really like her. I think she's the coolest mom in the world. I never can understand why Maddie fights with her (but again, she's crazy). My dad is sitting beside Aunt Jane, and the two look like polar opposites. It's funny. Dad's wearing a formal button-down and slacks. His hair's getting grayer, and the wrinkles are deeper around his gentle gray eyes. He's smiling and laughing a lot. And my fiancé and brother are dressed really sharp too.

My brother is sitting across from Bryce and me, with his cane leaning on the wall behind him. I'm sort of talking to him. I mean, if he talks to me, I talk back, but we're not really communicating with each other anymore.

"Bryce," Damie says after another minute of silence, "can you pass the mashed potatoes?" Bryce pushes the bowl over.

"Your leg's feeling better, man?" asks Bryce.

"Yeah. I can't run, but I'm doing physical therapy. I should be able to be back to exercising in a few weeks. I'm working my arms with rowing now. I want to join the rowing team."

"That's a fun sport," Bryce says with a nod. "And a good team."

"You guys were discouraging me so much from fraternities that I thought I'd give it a try. You know we have a great lake. And the upper-body work is fantastic."

"If I were to join a team, I'd join rowing." Bryce smiles at him and I love that. He always gets along well with my brother, even when we're fighting. But I mess up that niceness by turning to my brother and saying, "Where is she, Damie? When did she say she'd be here?"

"Now," he says with a shrug. "I don't know what's keeping her."

"Maybe we should just start eating," I say to Bryce.

My brother's already eating, but that's Damie. He doesn't really care if he's rude. Somehow, he can get away with it. He's always gotten away with stuff like that in my family, and Dad and I just expect it. Aunt Jane watches him eat with a big smile. I don't think she minds either. I don't know how he does it. Honestly, Damie seems so happy about rudely eating that I don't really care either.

I hear a key jostle in the front door. Then my former friend Madison walks into the room. She's wearing a long black dress and dark makeup. It's ridiculously goth and witchy for a family dinner. I'm in a similar black dress but "normal" makeup, including red lipstick.

"Sorry I'm late," she blurts out.

Yeah, sure.

"We've been waiting for you," Aunt Jane says, losing her smile for the first time.

"Sorry."

She walks over to the chair beside Damie, leans down, and kisses his lips. My dad watches the kiss and doesn't seem to mind. I mind.

"Hi, Maddie," Bryce says.

"Bryce."

"Maddie," I say. The bitch doesn't even look at me.

"Hi, Madison," says my dad.

"Hi, Mr. Hawthorne."

"Well, now we can eat," Aunt Jane says.

"Wait," says my dad. "We should give thanks." Damie finally looks guilty, puts his fork down, and pushes his plate away. We all look at my dad, and he looks at each of us and smiles. "It's times like these"—he turns to my brother and Maddie—"with family, that all of us, together, can be thankful for what we have. I am always so grateful for what I have. To be with you two."

"Now we can eat?" asks Damie.

Dad smiles again, but before he nods, he says, "Things are happening so fast. I see my two favorite people in the world with partners now. People who really care about them. Who love them. It makes me so happy." He stops for a moment and looks at the table thoughtfully. He suddenly looks sad. "It's so special to find someone...someone who loves you." He's probably thinking of my mom. "This is what family is about."

"That's so sweet, Rick," says Aunt Jane, touching his arm.

Dad turns to Damie with a grin. "Now we can eat."

"Rick" talks to Aunt Jane for the next few minutes. The two hit it off. They always have. Aunt Jane is constantly laughing. She's in great spirits.

Bryce holds my hand while we eat and, for a moment, I feel good. I forget all my worries. Maybe everything is all right now? I wasn't so hot about meeting with Maddie for dinner, but perhaps it will all work out okay.

But then Maddie kisses Damien again in front of all of us. And I could swear—no, I know—that she's making sure I see it.

"How are classes, Maddie?" Bryce asks.

"All right," Maddie says with a shrug. "European and African history. It's really interesting but I'm burning out. I just want to graduate."

"Then what?" Bryce asks.

"I don't know. I've thought of helping out in the history department at Hawthorne. Maybe I'll end up helping you if you're a professor next year."

"How's that dissertation coming along, Bryce?" asks my dad.

"Nearly finished, Mr. Hawthorne."

"It would be great if you teach here," Dad says. "You want to teach at Hawthorne, right?"

"Of course. I love Hawthorne."

"Why wouldn't he want to stay here?" asks Jane with a smile. "It's so lovely. The woods and the hills. I wouldn't want to live anywhere else."

"Maybe you and Katie can work here together if Katie gets in," Dad says.

Bryce looks at me. I know what he's thinking. That's not going to happen. But then I feel his hand pressing the finger wearing my engagement ring. I get it. He's so cute.

"Where else have you applied, Katie?" asks Aunt Jane.

I try to swallow some cranberries and sip some white wine. The wine is really good. Jane may not know how to cook, but she knows wine. I lie, "All the big ones."

"Like where?" my dad persists.

You want to know the truth? None. I haven't applied to a single school except Hawthorne. I know, that's super dumb. But Jane's right—where else would I want to go? And I'm sure Bryce is going to work here. But if I tell my dad the truth, it's going to ruin the rest of dinner. So I lie a little more.

"You know, Harvard and Yale."

"Wow, sis, nice schools," says Damie. He smiles a little too wide, probably suspecting that I'm full of cranberries.

"This is why I didn't apply," says Maddie to my dad. "It's so stressful. I'd rather just complete my time at Hawthorne and figure that stuff out later."

"Well, you lovebirds will have to decide soon," says Aunt Jane.

At first Maddie and my brother irritatingly look at each other, thinking she's referring to them. She's not. She's looking at Bryce and me. That gives me a wicked sense of justice. Maddie doesn't have a ring from my brother keeping them together. *Haw!* Nor does the bitch deserve one. *So there!*

"Have you decided where and when the wedding will be?" Jane asks. "I'm so thrilled for you two."

Leave it to her to talk about something pleasant. I laugh and raise Bryce's hand over the table and kiss it. "We don't know yet, Ms. Taylor."

"How about Alondra's house?" Bryce asks me. It makes my heart jump, because he looks into my eyes so seriously. I never even thought about that.

"Yeah, maybe."

"Damie and I will probably get an apartment together off campus next year," Maddie says. "I just need a break from everything, but Mom's right. I don't want to leave here."

I laugh and that's super mean. Living together before marriage is forbidden by my dad. It's one of his biggest rules. Bryce and I still haven't even told Dad.

Damie coughs and says, "Well, I'll probably do the dorms again with Harvey next year. But I'm hoping Maddie doesn't go anywhere."

Maddie puts a hand over her mouth, realizing how stupid she's being.

"I don't think two people should live together until they're married," my dad says.

"Really?" asks Aunt Jane, amused. "That's kind of old-fashioned, don't you think, Rick?" She's not trying to be mean. She's being Aunt Jane. She really looks sincerely surprised.

My dad tries to manage a smile. I know he likes her. "Two people who love each other should have their love recognized under God. That's my belief. I think cohabitation is a sin. Marriage under God is special."

I force some turkey down my throat.

"I didn't know you were so religious, Rick," says Aunt Jane. "I didn't know." She puts a hand up. "I don't mean any offense."

"Can you pass the gravy?" Maddie asks Bryce. She doesn't dare ask me, even though I'm closer to the dish.

"I'm not that religious," my dad says. "But I believe that things are just too relaxed these days. You lose how special love is between a man and a woman if you don't sanctify it under God."

"Interesting," Jane replies.

Now Damien laughs, and it's really bad timing because it looks like he's making fun of Dad. In a weird way, I suppose he is. And even though he can get away with eating before we do, making fun of my father during dinner goes too far.

"What's so funny, Damie?" asks Dad.

I glare at my brother, ready to jump over the table if he fesses up to what he's thinking.

"Nothing, Dad. I'm sorry. You're just...a bit quaint in your beliefs sometimes."

"We're Catholic," he responds. Then he turns to Aunt Jane and she just nods and smiles.

"I think times have changed a lot, Mr. Hawthorne," Maddie says. "You know, nowadays people are getting together younger and marriage is an important thing for commitment, but look at how many people divorce. Love is what's important, not marriage. Just like you said, giving thanks. It's not about God, it's about love."

"I don't agree with that," my dad says.

I really don't like Madison right now. Who gives a shit what she thinks? It's as if she's getting upset with my dad. My dad is the sweetest man I know, next to my Bryce. Just because she hates me, that doesn't mean she should hate him. But, luckily, Jane talks before I do.

"Everyone's entitled to their own opinion, Maddie," says her mom. "I agree, but we must respect his beliefs."

"I do. But some opinions hurt people."

"What?" I snap. "How do my dad's opinions hurt people?"

"Are you serious?" Maddie says, laughing. "This coming from you?"

Bryce squeezes my hand, telling me to shut it. I look at him and see the unspoken warning on his face.

"What do you think about the subject, Bryce?" Maddie asks with a wry grin.

I squeeze Bryce's hand tighter. I feel blood rush to my face. How is it that my very best friend is my archenemy now? What happened? I really hate her.

"Alondra taught us to respect each other's beliefs, Maddie," Bryce says. "Even if they're different. You know that."

"Sure. But what do *you* think? Do you think two people in love should live with one another before marriage?" And then she leans on her hands with a really nasty grin, anticipating his response.

What are you doing?

She looks at me but quickly turns back to Bryce. She's playing us. Is she purposefully trying to get me in trouble? She must be.

"I ..." He looks at my dad, unsure. "I think if two people really love each other, truly, then it's okay for them to live with each other before marriage. True love's bond doesn't break even before the ceremony. But...I totally get Katie's dad's point too."

Dad shakes his head and goes back to eating turkey. He doesn't look up. He eats some more, pours some gravy, and takes more bites without looking at anyone.

Everyone eats in silence. Even Aunt Jane just picks up a roll and munches on it, staring at the wall. Any semblance of a pleasant dinner seems over. All because of my fucking bitch former friend Maddie.

"Do you know why Katie and I like to wear black makeup, Mr. Hawthorne?" Maddie asks.

I drop my utensils on my plate and stare at her. Then I shake my head, warning her. Everyone stops eating.

"What are you doing?" Damie asks her. "Stop it." But she's

looking at my dad with this evil smile. I feel like Maddie left the house and bitch Enora's taken her place. Like my former friend is possessed or something. What's gotten into her? My dad furrows his brow.

"You can hate me, but you don't have a right to go after my dad," I say.

"Who says I'm going after your dad? I like your dad."

"Why did you even invite me?"

"I didn't invite you, Cadence. My mother did."

"I invited your friends, Madison," says Jane, furrowing her brow. "So be nice to our guests."

"Cadence isn't my friend."

"You're being a baby," I say.

"Am I? And you're being a liar. And it's because of your lies that Damie got hurt. Mom, do you know why we wear dark makeup? Being truthful was once very important to Katie."

Jane looks at Madison and loses her famous smile. "Yes, I do, Madison."

She does?

"No, you don't. We're not a part of the latest vampire fashion craze. Ours is a tradition passed on—"

"Just shut up!" I snap, pounding my fists on the table. "What are you trying to do?"

"This is why Damie got into a car accident. Because of your family's lies." *My lies?* "You need to be out in the open about what's going on. And I need to be open with my mom. People shouldn't be kept in the dark. If something's bad, it should be brought into the light, right out into the open."

"What's going on here?" asks my dad.

"Well, you see, Mr. Hawthorne," Maddie says, "your daughter is a witch. So is her boyfriend, Bryce. Except in our coven, we call Bryce a *High Wizard*."

The lights flicker in the dining room. Everyone looks around the room in surprise. Bryce squeezes my hand so tightly that it hurts. Maddie's rage dissolves for a moment, along with the color in her face, but then she regains her bitchiness and frowns.

"Damie's been suffering for weeks, ya know, Windstorm. You'd think if you can mess with the lights, you could have used magic to help him with his broken leg."

"He didn't want me to come over. He told me to stay away."

"We could have held a gathering to stop Enora. Could have—"

"Shut up, Maddie!"

I stare at my dad. He doesn't understand what's going on. Jane's looking at the wall.

"Why not be open? Why not—"

"You're such a bitch. If you really wanted to do something about my brother, you guys wouldn't have been so evasive. You would have let me through the door—"

"Of *our* dorm room?" Maddie asks with a nasty grin.

"You guys, we shouldn't be talking about all this right now," warns Bryce.

"Instead of sleeping with your fiancé, Cadence," Maddie continues, "you could have met with the coven and planned your revenge."

"You didn't let us meet!" I jump up from the table and slam my fists down. Bryce jumps up to pull me back. "You didn't let me anywhere near you!"

"You never answered your phone."

"Why are you even here? With my family? On Thanksgiving? Haven't you had enough of me? You thought being with my brother would bring me back after I left you? I don't want to be anywhere near you. I never want to see you again. Ever! I hate you!"

Maddie jumps up and scowls at me. No one else dares say a word. Then she looks at my dad, pointing. "She's a witch, Mr. Hawthorne. Your Christian daughter is a witch. So is your future son-in-law. Not only that, but they've been living together for months. Two witches cohabitating before marriage. How does that fit in with your moral Catholic beliefs?"

"*Get out!*" I scream.

The lights shut off for a second, and I hear banging against the window and the pounding of a rush of wind.

"Where?" Madison says, looking all over the room, when the lights turn on again. "Where do you want me to go? You want me to leave my own *fucking house!* Why don't you go?"

"Maddie!" Aunt Jane stands up too. "These are our guests."

"So? Isn't that what I am to you? Aren't I just your guest too, *Aunt* Jane?"

"You're my daughter."

"Well, you're not my mother."

Jane looks stunned. She puts her hand to her mouth.

It's clear to Bryce and me, and probably to my brother, that Madison has completely flipped her lid. She's beyond nuts and she's hurting everyone in the room. If there weren't a shred of love from our past, I think I would blow open one of the windows and have her sucked out of it.

"I don't want to ever see you again, Cadence!" Madison yells in tears. "I hate you too!" Madison rushes out of the room. My brother hobbles after her with his cane. We hear the front door fly open and slam shut.

They're gone. Everything falls silent. We just stare at the ceiling or look away from one another, but nobody picks up a fork or says a word. Then Aunt Jane runs into the kitchen with her head in her hands.

"We'll talk about this later, Cadence." My dad throws his utensils on the table and joins Aunt Jane.

I sit down in shock. Bryce and I are alone in the dining room. I lean my head on Bryce's chest, but I don't cry. I just sink into his arms. "God, Bryce. I told you we shouldn't have come. She's flipped."

He doesn't reply, but he holds me. Maybe he thinks I have too?

In the other room, Aunt Jane is crying. "I'm so sorry, Rick," she says. "She's so difficult. She's never accepted me. Now it's the accident. The car accident with your son made her even crazier. She keeps telling me it's Cadence's fault. I adore your daughter. I told her that's just crazy. I can't control Maddie anymore. I guess I never could… that accident must remind her of the death of her parents. Your son said something about the occult. He saw a pentagram. There was witchcraft involved in Maddie's parents' car crash too. I think I should never have told her about that. This town has been into witchcraft ever since I was in grade school… I'm sorry, Rick. I'm so sorry. I'm so sorry we spoiled your Thanksgiving."

"It's all right. You didn't spoil it."

No, she didn't. Maddie did. I hope I never see her again.

17

FORGIVE ME

It's dark. Not because it's dark outside—it's not, it's morning and cold—but all the lights have been turned off and the drapes are closed in a white-walled hall with a vaulted ceiling. A heavyset pastor is up on stage in an umber suit. His words echo throughout the room as he covers a candle with a golden snuffer. He has lovely dark golden skin, short dark hair, a mustache, and black eyes. Every time he discusses a sin, he douses the flame of one of the candles. There are seven candles. Right now, he's about to snuff out the last candle: pride.

Frida's sitting beside me on a wooden bench near the central aisle. I look over and she's all smiles. She loves it. We're both wearing formal black dresses, but our makeup is light and not too witchy. A lot of people are dressed up. It's church, you know. She's so happy I came. This is the last day her brother, Liam, will be here from New York. It's Liam who's preaching. I think the service is almost over.

"Take a look at Proverbs 11:2," the priest says, dousing the candle. "Pride is our greatest sin." He has a thick Brazilian accent like Frida. He smiles like her too. "Get rid of pride, reach out your hand to the Lord and savior, and allow the light of Christ to fill your heart." It's really dark as the last candle goes out. "Pride leads to anger. If you care so much for yourself that you darken your soul towards others, you live in darkness like the devil."

I bite my lip. I think I have a lot of pride. And you know I have an anger problem.

Liam turns to a young boy sitting on a piano bench by the side of the stage. "Open the front drapes, please, and let in some light." The boy jumps up to help. As he opens the drapes, light shines forth over the large cross behind the altar. "Now let us light the seven heavenly virtues. Humility. I will light a candle for each virtue to represent God's grace." He smiles. Again, his smile reminds me of Frida's. I look over and Frida gives me the same look.

But then I see someone I didn't notice before, sitting behind her. My brother. I haven't spoken to Damie in weeks. I'm not speaking to Dad either. Well, Maddie did that. My dad isn't very happy I'm a witch. Nor is he very happy I'm living with Bryce. He really loved Bryce, but not anymore. Maddie was right in thinking that unveiling our coven to him would hurt me. She knows me too well. She knew exactly where to strike.

Frida turns because I'm staring at my brother and she sees him too. It's the first time she's lost her smile.

"She's loco, Katie," Frida whispers in my ear. "You know, crazy. She started screaming and crying one night on the phone. Then she told me how we need to protect each other from *you*. Maddie blames you for everything. Like you're worse than Enora or something."

I nod. I'm not arguing about Maddie flipping her lid. I don't need to hear it; I saw enough on Thanksgiving. But Damie doesn't look happy. Something else is wrong. Damie's like Frida, always smiling. This morning he seems disturbed.

"How can God lead us to the light?" asks Liam.

The church is now bright, with all the drapes open. I look at a window and see reflections off the snow outside. It's warm in the church but really cold outside. Winter is not my favorite time of the year, but this week is winter break. That's nice. And I actually did exceptionally well with my grades for the first fall semester since my freshman year. All As. This year I—

"Loco, Katie," Frida whispers again. "She blames you for Damie's accident, as if Enora's better. As if you're hurting her and our circle. But you know, I reminded her what Enora did to us."

"Give your heart to Jesus Christ and allow his light to fill your soul," says Liam, moving his hands over the seven lit candles. "Now, please stand."

"She went totally loco and I had to hang up on her," whispers Frida quietly, getting up. "I took your side and told her she's totally crazy, Katie."

I nod while looking at Liam. Liam looks down, closes his eyes, and clasps his hands in prayer.

"Let us pray. Lord, thank you for this church, which allows us to gather together under your grace. I ask for your blessings. To the Father, Jesus Christ, and the Holy Ghost, thank you for this congregation this morning. Amen."

"Amen."

"This concludes our service," says Liam with a smile. "Blessed be our Lord, Jesus Christ, our savior. Remember that through God's forgiveness, you can all see the light. Thank you for coming."

Everyone gets their things and prepares to leave. The church is pretty full. Frida takes my hand and, after we wait for a line of people to move down the aisle, she rushes me to the front of the church to meet her brother. She's so excited about it, and I love that.

Liam's shy. That's surprising to me after watching him lead the congregation, but when Frida brings me up to the altar, he seems to avoid my gaze. But he smiles the family's famous smile as he gathers his Bible under his arm and the candles in his hands.

"Hi," I say with a wave.

"You must be Cadence. My sister has talked a lot about you."

"Frida says you're heading back to New York. We should get together today for lunch or something."

"I wish I could, but my plane leaves from Atlanta this afternoon."

"Shit, I should have come to watch you sooner." Then I cover my mouth. "Pardon my French. Damn. I mean, too bad. I've just been so busy with studying, you know."

"Katie's a bit of a bookworm," Frida says with a chuckle.

"Nothing wrong with studying a book," Liam says with a wink, lifting his arm to show us his Bible.

"So ..." I put my finger to my lips in thought. "You just became a priest, or something?"

"Yes. Just ordained."

Frida laughs. "Cadence isn't Christian, Liam. You don't know what it took to get her to come to church this morning. I told her it was your last sermon in Hawthorne."

"Honored to introduce you to the Lord's teachings, Cadence. To *my* favorite book."

"Yeah," I say. "Uh...about that. Can I ask you a question?"

He looks at me with his kind eyes. So does Frida. With those same sweet brown eyes. "You said forgiveness helps fight pride. Do you...do you think some things are unforgivable?"

He furrows his brow. "What sort of things?"

"Sins and stuff. Damnation."

"The Lord, our God, was crucified for our sins. Sin is a part of our existence ever since the fall in the garden. You can't live without sinning. But you can ask for forgiveness."

"From *all* sins?"

"You like books, huh?"

I nod.

"Take a look at Isaiah 55:7, Cadence. In the Bible, you'll find your God forgives you if you accept his love. Where I think people err is when they give up trying. Let God light your heart, and do not fear darkness. Your trespasses through the seven deadly sins can be forgiven if you accept Jesus. If you accept him in your heart, your soul, you will find the seven heavenly virtues feel natural. Goodness is the natural way of things that leads us to the light. That was the point of my sermon this morning."

Interesting. Christianity is so much more based on a book than Buddhism. I like this forgiveness stuff. It reminds me of my teacher, Alondra. At the time of her death, I told her I'd never forgive her. I've felt so guilty about that. I feel like, in my heart, I can't forgive her, and I feel like she can't forgive me for not forgiving her. Does that make sense? Do you see what I'm saying?

Am I damned? Beatrix said I was. Is there hope for me through Liam and Frida's God?

"I don't know if I can believe in God's light, Liam," I say. "I've seen evil in light sometimes too." Like Beatrix hanging from a rope in the brightest light. I wake up seeing her like that in nightmares almost every night.

"Find a quiet place, then, Cadence. In darkness or light. It doesn't matter. I am talking about lighting your heart, not physical light. The physical light is only symbolic. Sometimes, God reveals himself in darkness when you're alone. Pray. Accept the love of God. But you have to find God within your soul. The Holy Spirit. I can only preach. Only within can you find your true faith. But when you do, I promise you will find great joy. We all have the potential to find the Holy Spirit within. I have, and I've never been happier."

He touches my chest with a finger and smiles gently.

Frida laughs. "You'll never convert her, Liam. You can try, but she's the stubbornest girl in the world."

I nod.

That's when I feel someone else's finger tap me. I turn and it's my brother.

"Cadence, can we talk?" Damie asks.

I turn back to the pastor and reach out my hand, but his hands are holding candles. Frida helps him, and with a free hand he shakes mine. "It was a lovely service, Liam. And so nice to meet you."

"Thanks for coming. I will have to take you up on lunch next time, Cadence."

And we shake hands again. He's definitely Frida's brother. He's so nice. Frida helps him move the candles from the altar.

"What is it, Damie?" I follow him down the aisle. The church has emptied out. "Are we talking now?" But he doesn't say anything until we're about halfway to the exit, then he turns. He looks so nervous.

"Maddie and I had a fight." He shakes his head and puts a hand up. "That's not what I want to talk about... after the fight, she left for Atlanta. I know because I got in contact with one of her friends. She told me she never wants to speak to me again." He pauses and shakes his head. "That's also not what I'm trying to tell you. Katie, Maddie didn't leave for Atlanta during winter break. She left before finals. She didn't complete her classes. Not only that, I got a few calls from Aunt Jane. Her mom's so upset that she called the police to look for her. Unlike you, her mom has been in touch with her—until she went to Atlanta. Now Maddie's nowhere to be found. And her friend doesn't even know where she is. You said you're not talking to her. But do you know where she is?"

"No, I don't."

He takes a deep breath and runs his hand through the long side of his hair.

"Why didn't you tell me before?" I ask.

"You haven't been answering my calls."

Oops. I'm doing that anger thing again. You know, the thing where I don't speak to the person I don't like for weeks. I block calls too.

"Jane never called me," I lie. But I think I might have blocked calls from her too.

"It's only been a couple of days that her mom's been worried," he says. "It's been a week for me."

"Who's the friend you were talking to?"

"Gilda. Gilda said something about how Maddie was going to go see this girl named Mira. There's some weird witch thing going on in downtown Atlanta, but Maddie didn't tell me what it is. She never told me anything about your witch stuff. She said that was the only thing she agreed with you about.

"But Maddie's been acting so strange since last time you saw her. She never sleeps. She spends the whole night lighting candles around her. She curls up in a ball and just cries all night. She shuts down and stops talking. She doesn't talk to anyone. When I couldn't take any more, we fought and I stopped seeing her. But the last night before she left the dorm, I came back for one more attempt to make up with her. The door was unlocked, and she was curled up in a weird dark cloak in her dorm room. She had spray-painted a red pentagram on the carpet and placed candles all around it. And she was whispering this weird chant. I tried to rouse her, but she wouldn't lift her head. All she did was flash her left hand up at me. She had a red pentagram painted on her palm. It really creeped me out. So I gave up. I stopped visiting. I wish I hadn't. It was after that night that she went missing."

He wipes his eyes.

Now I'm the one freaking out. I have this sudden mix of fear and anger building in my chest. I'm having flashbacks of Beatrix sitting in the center of the guest room just like that. And to think Maddie's doing that now? And she painted a pentagram on her hand? I'm scared. All my anger at Maddie has left me. Now I'm only scared for her.

I look toward the altar and blurt out, "Frida! Frida, come here! Come over here. Quick!"

She touches Liam's shoulder and rushes over.

"What is it, Katie?"

"It's Maddie. Damie's saying she's been taken. She's in Atlanta. Panthera took her."

"Oh my God!" Frida says.

"What's happening?" asks my brother. "What do you mean? Who's Panthera?"

I jump into Damie's arms. He's so surprised. I start crying and hugging him so tight.

"I'm so sorry, Damie. Forgive me. I've been so mean. I should have accepted you two. Now I'm scared for Maddie. I'm so worried something's going to happen to her. I just hope I'm not too late to help her. I love you both so much."

"I love you too, sis," he says, sounding confused. "It's...okay. But what's happening?"

"It's a spell," I say, shaking my head. "Maddie's under a witch's spell. She must be. That might even be why she did what she did on Thanksgiving. That wasn't the Maddie I knew."

Liam runs over. He looks concerned.

"And, God..." I feel so heavy. I feel like the ceiling and walls of the church are falling on me. "It's my fault. Again. Maddie was right. I've done nothing with our coven, and this is my punishment. And now...I did this to Maddie. My friend."

"It's not your fault, Katie," Frida says. "Don't say that."

I search around the church. Then I look into Liam's caring eyes. And I think, *Can your God really forgive all sins?*

18

___

RED

I'm descending narrow, muddy concrete steps, and I'm smelling red. It's a burning smell of cinnamon mixed with sandalwood and rotting meat. Red smoke rises from below. Cold concrete walls enclose me as I crouch down to avoid hitting the ceiling. After a few steps, I stop and look back. There's bright yellow light along the sides of a metal door above me. I'm guessing it's sunny outside. There's a slow drumbeat. And voices—whispering, repeating themselves over and over, as I slowly descend.

At the bottom, the thick red smoke surrounds me, but it clears enough for me to see a large room with a central bonfire, similar to what I've seen in our witch gatherings. The flames rise to about the height of a person. This must be a conjuring, for I doubt a fire like this could be coming from the concrete floor. In front of the fire is a circle of witches in crimson cloaks. Dancing around the women, jumping up and down like a bucking bronco, is a naked man, the man I saw with Enora at the party. Gus, the creepy, freakishly tall guy with fangs. He's nude with a tail and long beard, reminding me of a Greek satyr.

Like Pan. He's even playing a flute. And in the center, near the pyre, a nude couple is fucking on a red pentagram painted on the dirty concrete floor. The woman has short hair with antlers and very thick black makeup. She is sitting on a man, riding him up and down with her tits bobbing. The witches around the couple are bowing. Each bow, each thrust, follows the beat of a drum. So does the satyr, who is synchronously jumping up and down. A circle of white candles illuminates the walls of the room. And along the walls I see red painted pentagrams and upside-down crosses in the flickering light.

"Blessed be thy servants," says one of the cloaked witches, the central one. "O holy Baphomet, we unite under the number six hundred and sixty-six, your servants under your power. Let our offering hang by your feet so that you may feast on the virgin under the stars. Hail Astraeus. Hail Selene. Hail Satanas. *Lucifer. Lucifer. Lucifer.*"

Everyone falls prostrate before the copulating couple. They all freeze, repeating the word *Lucifer* in whispers.

"Fire from the pit of hell!" the central cloaked witch yells. I finally recognize her voice: it's Enora. "Enlighten us so that you may reveal secrets to your beloved servant!"

"Did you kill Beatrix?" I ask. It takes all my energy to form the words. I'm so sleepy. I don't even know how I'm here. Is this a trance? A dream? How did I get here? I feel so disoriented.

The witches turn and start shouting at me. Then I see a face I recognize under one of the hoods—Maddie. She looks back at me, emotionless and curious, as if she's as confused as I am. Enora turns and faces me with creepy white eyes and an evil grin.

"Maddie," I say to my friend, "come back with me. Please. Please come with me. I'm so sorry."

"She's here, Cadence," says Enora. "Come here and get her if you care."

But Maddie turns back to the couple having sex.

Then everything freezes. All the prostrate women, even the couple having sex, freeze as if being paused in a movie. Only the third witch in a cloak turns. It's Mira. She has bright white eyes, like pearls, just like Enora. Mira stands and points at me.

"*Serpentus*," Mira says.

Enora laughs. Mira rushes to me with those creepy eyes. Then she wags her finger by my face.

"*Serpentus. Serpentus. Serpentus.*"

All the witches cackle in derisive laughter.

"*Muta! Serpentus! Serpentus! Serpentus! Muta! Muta!*"

I fall to the ground, shaking. Then I watch Mira and Enora grow as I fall closer to the cold concrete. My arms and legs merge with my body. I feel frigid. I shiver. I'm so cold.

I twist and slither, desperately trying to escape up the stairway. But the steps are too steep. They laugh harder behind me, but I can't get up the stairs. I can't run. I'm trapped. And they will come and get me. They will tread on me. They will finish me.

* * *

I awake with a start. I'm in bed and it's dark aside from the light from a streetlamp in the parking lot shining through a crack in Bryce's curtains. He stirs.

"You okay, babe?" he asks sleepily.

"No."

I sit up in bed, throw my long hair back, and hold my head in my hands. I'm breathing so heavily and I'm covered in sweat. My heart is pounding. The white sheets fall from my breasts, making me realize I'm not dressed.

"What's wrong?" asks Bryce.

"I'm naked."

"You fell asleep after we made love."

"Bryce …"

He lies on his side and just looks at me. I can barely make out his eyes in the shadows. He nods. "It's just a dream, babe."

I take a deep breath. Then I touch his hand, and he plays with my fingers. I'm so grateful to have hands. I know that sounds weird but, you know, I really was turned into a snake last year. Yeah, that's what Bryce meant, in his letter to the dean, when he said I was "sick." I was an actual snake. I'm not kidding. For two weeks, I was a slithering serpent. And you'd never guess who made me a person again. Enora. But she wasn't being nice. She needed my coven so she could use me and my magic.

I touch Bryce's face, but I'm not doing it to be loving, I'm doing it to make sure he actually has one. I make sure he's not another figment of my demented imagination.

"Tell me this isn't a dream. Oh God, please, Bryce."

He loses his smile, takes a deep breath, and shakes his head. "Not a dream. I heard you talking in your sleep. But you're awake now."

"I was underground. With Enora. I think she wanted me there to witness one of her Sabbaths. To show me that Mira and Maddie have become a part of her coven now."

The white covers fall from my naked body as I push myself to the edge of the bed. He rubs my back. I throw my hair back and turn with a smile.

"I'm scared, Bryce. She knows how to upset me. She knows we're going to try to get Maddie back. And I think she wants me to come. It was like she was taunting me."

"She used to haunt my sleep at night after our breakup. She did it for weeks. But they're just dreams. She has no power to do anything to you in them."

"She could drive me crazy. Make me keep having nightmares during the day. Or turn me insane like Maddie."

"She'll try, but you know they're just dreams."

"What does she want? At the lake, I thought it was to join her. Then I realized she wanted me to cheat on you. To hurt you. To hurt us."

I stand up with my back to him. The moonlight casts my shadow on the wall. I have arms and legs, a human form, thank God.

"Maddie was right, I did do nothing. We had enough of a warning with Mira. Then Beatrix. My brother. I've endangered all of us. I don't think she's going to stop. And now that wicked witch has Maddie. Who's to say she won't take us all away?"

I hear the sheets shift, and he stands up and touches me from behind again. I cradle my head in his arms.

"Everything's okay," he says, kissing my shoulder. "They're just dreams."

"We need to face her," I say with a nod. "To get back our friends."

"We're going to. I already spoke with the others. We're meeting this Sabbath."

I turn. The dim light is so dreamy that I almost fear for a moment that Bryce will change into a monster or something. He doesn't. He just shows me his lovely, warm smile.

"Oh, Bryce. I'm so scared. We can't wait till Friday. We need to do it now. Today. It can't wait. I need our coven to meet tonight."

"School starts today," he says, sitting back on the bed.

"I don't care. We have to meet tonight."

"All right," he says. "We'll meet tonight, then."

I walk over and turn the lights on.

"What are you doing?" he asks, squinting.

"Not sleeping. Not after my dream. I'm getting dressed." I walk over to the dresser. I smile, catching him staring at me. I turn to him. "And no funny business. I am sooo creeped out, babe."

"I'll try to resist."

I crack a slight grin. But then I turn serious again. "She's taking everyone from me," I say, grabbing clothes from the second drawer. I get dressed. "If I don't do anything, there'll be no one left. She'll even take you."

"I'm never leaving you, Cadence."

19

THE MEETING

My friends and I sit around our fire, holding hands. We are all on white chairs in the center of Alondra's backyard. White chalk has been poured in a circle around us. I'm shaking a little because it's really cold, but thankfully it's not snowing or raining. The flames are the height of a person, but not warm enough on this winter night. We're all wearing sweaters or jackets under our black cloaks. Bryce is sitting closest to me, and I feel like if it weren't for the ceremony, he'd have his arm around me. Tammy and Frida, the other witches closest to me, are on my other side; they're shivering a little too.

"We should get started," Bryce says to me.

"Let us begin," I say with a nod. Then I turn to the circle. All my friends, with hoods over their shoulders, look over. "*Lux alba.*"

"*Lux alba,*" they all repeat.

"Blessed be the day that our circle is brought together once more. Blessed be the coven under the gods Gaia, Selene, *et* Astraeus."

"Atman," says Bryce.

"Atman." We all nod.

My good friends Tammy, Helen, Frida, and Bryce are all smiles. Mandy, Natasha, and Hannah aren't. They're across from me, behind the flames, and I think they chose to sit there on purpose to avoid my gaze. Maddie had convinced them, for the past few weeks, not to come to our Sabbath. It was only when Maddie went missing that they agreed to come. The new recruits, Josie and Debra, are wearing black cloaks and sitting to my left, near Frida. They look really nervous. To my right, sitting beside Bryce, is Damie. Yeah, my brother is here. I know, that's really weird, but at this point there is no reason to lie to my brother, pretending that we're not witches. And he's more concerned than anyone else that Madison is missing. He doesn't have his leg bandaged anymore, but he still walks with a limp. The weirdest thing is seeing him wearing a black cloak.

"You all know why we're here," I say earnestly. I might as well get to the point. "Maddie has been taken by the Abaddon coven."

"Was she taken or did she go 'cause she wanted to?" asks Mandy.

"We're here to find out," Bryce replies.

"It sounds like she's been in a trance," I reply. "I can't help but think it's a spell cast by Enora. She's also been messing with my dreams."

"Mine too, Katie," says Frida.

"Me too," says Hope. And a few others nod.

"Damie, tell the group the changes you saw in Maddie."

My brother tells them what he told me in church. He talks about how she stopped leaving her dorm room and sat on the floor, catatonic, staring at the wall and murmuring incantations. She stopped going to class. She didn't take her final exams. She withdrew and disappeared.

"Like Beatrix," says Tammy.

"Maybe Beatrix wasn't crazy, Katie," says Frida. "Maybe she was under a spell too."

"I've felt like Enora has been up to something since she threw me into a spell a couple of months ago," I say. "I had a wandering at Hawthorne Lake...no, I felt it even before that. You guys know. Beatrix. Maddie said Beatrix was killed and she didn't commit suicide. I believe that now. So if Maddie truly believed that Beatrix had been killed by Enora, why would she go join her coven and blame me? It all just doesn't make sense. She's not herself."

"Why wouldn't she blame you?" asks Mandy, acting like a total bitch. "We're in this mess because of your fight over your brother. It doesn't sound like you were very welcoming to her. I've spoken with Gilda. Mira's fine in Atlanta. She said Maddie ran to Mira. She probably accepted Enora after that."

"Enora's been conjuring nightmares, Mandy," I remind her.

"Katie's right," objects Tammy. "I spoke to Maddie too. She's totally nuts. Not our lovable Maddie, but transformed into a person I don't even recognize anymore."

"She's not herself," says Frida. "That's for sure." Mandy's scowl fades a little.

"I'm not sure you're right about this either, Cadence," Natasha says.

"Guys, we have to stick together," Bryce says. "This is what Enora wants. She wants us to be divided."

"Because Cadence never should have been our leader," snaps Mandy. "She never even wanted to be."

"I didn't," I snap back, opening my eyes wide. "But I do want my friend back." Then I look at all my witches under the flickering firelight. "We all do. This isn't just about dreams. This is about Maddie." I put a hand up because Mandy's about to say something, and I can already predict her nastiness. "When Mira left, it was assumed she left because she wanted to. Now I doubt that too. But Maddie kept asking us to meet. *To stop* Panthera. Why would she join her? Come on, guys. It doesn't make sense."

Everyone pensively stares at the flames. Mandy just turns from me in disgust.

"Last year we gathered to get rid of Reardon," I say. "I thought I could trust Enora because she helped me. But you know what happened. And then she threatened Bryce. I feel like she's been finding a way to get back at us since Lammas. Beatrix told me she was sent to disturb the peace. The bitch is scheming. And now she has two of our sisters."

"Maddie hasn't even spoken to her mom," interrupts my brother. "I'm so worried."

"It's okay, Damie," says Frida.

"I think we should—"

"Are we going to hurt Enora?" Helen asks. Helen rarely says anything in our coven. She's a shy, bald, dark-skinned girl who joined our coven when Tammy, Maddie, and I joined. "What are we planning, guys?"

Then Tammy and Bryce make suggestions again. And then there's more arguing.

I stop paying attention. This isn't a Sabbath. We might all be wearing witch cloaks, but it's really just a meeting. In some ways, that's better, because it means I'm avoiding magic. But in another, it means that we're wasting time.

I look up at the moon and stars. There are a few wisps of white clouds, but it's really clear and beautiful. Alondra's backyard really is peaceful. Everything is peaceful here, even though my mind isn't. And though we've still neglected caring for her place, the backyard was, and remains, wild and the best reflection of Mother Nature—a witch's paradise.

I hear howling in the distance. And a full moon. And there are sounds of scurrying animals among the bushes and trees. But it doesn't bother me. I'm a witch. Wolves, full moons, and creepy-crawly things in bushes are my thing.

I hold Bryce's hand. I feel like it's a beautiful night, if only it weren't so cold.

It's our first week back, but I didn't go to class today. I'm too worried about Maddie.

In the background, witches are still arguing. One subject that finally perks my attention involves an ancient summoning that Bryce, now the oldest member of our group, remembers Reardon conjuring once as High Wizard. The idea is to enter a trance by the fire and summon spirits who can provide us protection from the netherworld. We can cast a shield spell. But the last time we tried this against Enora, I was transformed into a snake. And even if we protect ourselves from Enora, how is that going to bring back my best friend?

"No," I interrupt, shaking my head. "No way, Bryce. I'm not going through that again."

"Then what can we do, Kate?" Tammy asks. "What do you propose? You're the only one not saying anything."

"We should go to Atlanta and demand that they give Maddie back."

"That's her territory," Tammy reminds me, shaking her head. "Her hallowed ground. You might be a powerful witch, but we'd be on her turf."

"Why not?" suggests my brother. "I'll go tonight. What are we waiting for?"

"Bryce and I are going," I say. "I met with you all to try to convince you to go with us. The only way to confront this evil is to face it. I've been avoiding it, hoping Enora would stop, but she's slowly destroying our circle. She'll take all of you, and there'll be nothing left of our coven if I don't do something."

"It's just not safe, Katie," says Frida, shaking her head. "We're not sure what we're getting into there."

"I'll join Bryce in a conjuring," Mandy says, frustrated and in a huff. "Or I'll go with you to Atlanta...but we need to do something. Seems Katie's already made up her mind."

But before I can say another word, cries of "*Yatu!*" erupt. The interruption is jarring. I turn. The sound's coming from

Alondra's house. Two witches with hoods over their heads are wearing cloaks similar to our own, only crimson. The tallest is carrying a fiery torch. The other one is much shorter. When they're close enough, I recognize their faces: Cordelia and... Mira.

"Yatu, witches," Cordelia repeats, bringing up her left palm to show her red painted pentagram. Mira lifts her left hand, flashing the same symbol.

"Mira!" A few witches are happy to see her. Mira looks over but doesn't smile.

"Celebrating Thoth and Diana, Cadence?" asks Cordelia. "On a Monday? What a strange coven. You don't gather on the Sabbath, you choose Monday. No doubt Selene holds power, but this is very unorthodox. I can see why Raven and Blackbird left you."

"We come on behalf of the Abaddon coven," Mira says. She's deadpan. Morose. I squint at her. Typically, she's infamously smug and derisive, but tonight she looks depressing as hell. I'd rather she made fun of me. She doesn't seem like herself.

"This is our business!" snaps Tammy to Cordelia. "Your circle is evil."

Mira looks at me. "You invited me, Cadence."

"Yeah, I did. But I didn't expect you to come after you hung up the phone. Nor did I expect you to bring her."

"Sorry," Mira says. And for a second, I do see her old sly smile. "I brought a friend."

Adder is your friend?

There's an uncomfortable silence.

Do they really think we're just going to let down our guard and let them sit with us? Let them hear us discuss our plans to take back my best friend after they kidnapped her? So no one says a thing. They just stand over us staring as we stare back.

When they finally walk to our bonfire and add the flames of

their torches to the fire, I say to Mira, "I need to talk to you alone."

"Fine." Mira nods.

The two of us leave the circle and walk across the backyard. From the corner of my eye, I watch a very uncomfortable coven squaring off against Cordelia.

Mira and I walk away from the house toward the forest. Alondra's backyard is large, and when we're beyond earshot and I'm about to say something, she beats me to it.

"Why are you threatening Enora?" She stops by a tree trunk and turns. It's dark but the full moon is bright enough for me to see her face. With her red hood and thick, dark goth makeup, she looks evil. But her expression is pained, as if I hurt her, which is ridiculous being that I fully believe Enora is attacking me. "I belong to Panthera now, Katie. You know that."

"Yeah. I know. Mira, Enora's messing with my dreams again. A month ago, she cast a spell on me and made me nearly cheat on Bryce. She hurt my brother, then she possessed my friend. Our friend. I want Maddie back. And I'll do anything to get her."

"It just isn't true, Kate," Mira says, shaking her head. "It's not true."

"Bring Maddie back to me."

"Maddie came to us," Mira says. "She's having a hard time. She said she had a fight with you. Then her boyfriend and her mom." Mira cracks a smile for the first time. "I heard about her and your brother." She gestures toward my friends. "Cadence, you're playing with fire. It's very dangerous to provoke her. I'm a powerful enough witch now to know you were considering a conjuring. You best be careful. Enora has a bad temper."

"No. We were talking about coming to see you. And it's Enora who's been provoking me."

"You took Beatrix into your home. You refused to give her

back. Then you rejected your best friend. Enora gave her a home. What's the problem here?"

"Mira," I snap, quickly shaking my head. "I've had enough of this. Why do you think everything's all right? You hated Enora more than anyone last year. And Maddie was convinced that Enora killed Beatrix. Either you two are brainwashed, or something's up with your memory. Be straight with me. Deny to my face that Enora has been entering my dreams and casting spells."

"I can't deny it. I don't know. But you're not listening. I came to warn you. She views you as a threat because you're minding her business. My master's coven is her coven. Yours is yours. You're all meeting here to hurt us. Now deny *that*."

"You're calling her *master* now?" I ask in disbelief.

"So?"

"*Master?* Alondra never had us call her master. Certainly never me. We wouldn't have allowed it."

"This is what you do," Mira says with a sigh. "You judge people. You should just leave her alone. Maddie told me how you stopped speaking to her over your brother. Do you think that you're guiltless over everything—"

"He's my brother!" That makes me furious. "Fuck! Mira, your bitch 'master' knows exactly how to get under my skin. The fact that you don't see what's going on is incredible. You're either bullshitting me or you're under her spell. I'm sure Maddie is." I see Damie turn in the distance. I wasn't being discreet. All the witches are staring at us now. "Did she tell you about the car accident?"

She shakes her head. "Lies. These are lies. You have no proof that Enora did that. Of course Maddie told me, but there's more witchery in Georgia than just our two covens, Katie. I explained to Maddie that there are many satanic covens. Maddie doesn't blame Enora anymore. Why would you guys blame Enora for that? You have no proof. Cadence, if you knew my master better, you'd know that if it was her, she would have killed your brother, not hurt him."

I shake my head. "She's playing games. Why are you protecting her?"

"You're paranoid. You're as delusional as Beatrix."

Clouds develop over us, covering the clear sky. That's my anger. Mira looks up but she doesn't become afraid, she gets angrier.

"You violated our peace!" Mira closes her eyes and shakes her head. "I warn you. If you attack Enora, I'm on her side now. You're attacking me. We all know your powers, but with my help and my knowledge of spellcasting, I can make her equally strong. Be warned. If Enora entered your dreams, that was a warning too. Stay away. Stay away, or I can't tell you the harm that'll come of it."

Her eyes are ablaze in rage. I search them. I don't get it. What's she doing? Has she been hypnotized?

Then I think about that girl Mira talked about. When I told Mira about Beatrix's suicide, she seemed so concerned about her friend's welfare.

"It's the girl, isn't it?"

"What?"

"It's Beatrix's friend. That's why you're doing this. Beatrix told me Enora's dangling a carrot. Your new girlfriend. That's why you've betrayed us."

"I haven't betrayed you!" she says, shaking her head. Her rage leaves her, and she looks terribly depressed again. "I loved you," she says in a broken voice. "I would have stayed with you had you practiced real magic. Now it seems like the only way for your gang to assemble is to hurt us over fantasy."

"Fantasy?" I snap. "What do you mean, fantasy? She took you. Then she took Maddie. She'll destroy everything. She hates Bryce and she hates me. If you don't help us, she'll kill us."

"I just said I'm on her side. I'm a part of the Abaddon coven now. I'm not one of your sisters anymore."

"Then go! Get the fuck out! If you're not a part of my circle, Alondra wouldn't want you in her yard. Go love your girlfriend in ceremonies under your new master, the master who hanged your other friend by a rope."

I point and when I turn back, Mira looks like she's about ready to deck me. But she doesn't. Instead she quickly turns her back on me and rushes back to the fire.

There's a crack of thunder in the skies. It starts to rain. "*I want my friend!*" I shout. "Damn you, Mira! You hear me? I don't care about you! I want Maddie! Bring her back and I won't do anything to Enora. Just bring back my friend!"

"She's with us now."

Oh, no, she isn't! "Your master can have you! I don't care about you. But she can't have Maddie! Tell her that, Mira. She can't have Maddie. And stay away from this house! Don't ever come back! Alondra wouldn't want someone like you here anymore."

"We're leaving." Mira nods with her back still turned to me, but her voice cracks again.

My friends rush over to me.

"*You're not my friend anymore!*" I'm still screaming like crazy in the pouring rain.

Cordelia grabs their torches and runs to Mira. She puts an arm around Mira as if comforting her. That makes me even angrier. She's acting like I'm hurting her. As if Mira hasn't hurt me.

My friends catch up to me, turning to watch the two red-cloaked bitches quickly leave Alondra's side yard. They don't look back. The whole time, my friends stand behind me in silence. They just stare with me under the pouring rain.

"I'm going to Atlanta," I say to my witches. "With or without you."

Meeting adjourned.

20

ABADDON

I'm standing in the dark on a sidewalk, staring at the plain, boring white house, across a one-lane street, at the address that Gilda gave me. This is supposed to be Enora's new home in Atlanta. It's not what I expected. In my imagination, her house was a gothic fifteenth-century tower, all in black and white, sitting by its lonesome at the summit of a hill. Instead, her two-story house is wholly unremarkable, no different from any other house on the street. She's not far from downtown. I can see the windows of the skyscrapers a few miles away. There's a train of cars beside the road with windows open and heads hanging out, staring at the boring house too. These are my friends from my coven. Bryce is standing beside me. We're wearing heavy coats because it's really cold.

I look back and see my brother sitting in Bryce's BMW, waiting impatiently. He keeps asking in a hushed voice what we're doing.

I'm tired. It's early in the morning, around one o'clock. The drive from Hawthorne to downtown Atlanta takes two to three hours.

"Let's just knock," Bryce says. I finally turn and Bryce is smiling, with his hands in his pockets.

"Maybe I should have driven here alone. I'm putting you all in danger."

I hear a car door and see Gilda jumping out of her white SUV. She met us here from Savannah. She's worried about Mira and Maddie too.

"What the fuck's the matter?" Gilda asks, rushing to us. "Why are you guys just standing here?"

"Katie's getting cold feet," says Bryce.

"I'm not." *Okay, maybe I am.* I feel uneasy and a little queasy.

Gilda shakes her head and runs across the street, up a concrete path, and to the door. Bryce and I follow her. Then I hear another car door. It's my brother, standing impatiently on the sidewalk, eagerly watching us. Bryce signals for him to stay back.

Gilda knocks on the door.

The door swings open with laughter. A young girl with long blond hair and dark makeup, goth like ours, opens it. She's wearing a tight violet lace cami and gray sweatpants. She's attractive. She squints at us and laughs again. "What? Huh?"

"We're looking for Maddie," I say. "Is she here?"

"Who are you guys? It's really late."

"I'm Gilda. Is Madison here? We came a long way to see her."

The young girl just shrugs.

"What about Mira?" asks Gilda.

"Mira went someplace down to nowhereland," the girl says. "Some really boring college town in the woods or something."

But she should be back. We left a couple of hours after they did. For all I know, we were traveling together on the freeway.

"Is she here?" I ask, raising my eyebrows.

The teenager just shrugs annoyingly again.

"What about Maddie?" Bryce asks impatiently.

The girl turns and calls out Maddie's name. I look over her shoulder, hoping to see her. Directly behind her is the kitchen, lit by a dim yellow light. A girl with a protruding belly is standing by the kitchen entryway, wearing dark goth makeup and a black nightgown. She's smoking a cigarette and staring at us.

The room smells like incense mixed with perfume attempting to cover sweat, rotting food, and weed. Plastic chip bags, banana peels, and magazines are strewn all over the floor. A couple lying in each other's arms are asleep on a beat-up couch close to the door. The woman has only a thin T-shirt and underwear rising up her butt crack. The boy is in his underwear.

"Who are you?" I ask the girl who greeted us at the door.

"Courtney," says the girl. "How you guys know Blackbird and Raven? You close or something?"

"Friends from school," I say. "Can we come in?"

"Oh." Courtney puts her hand to her mouth and chuckles again. "Oops. Sorry. You guys must be from that place from nowhere."

Gus appears beside Courtney at the door. You know, the really tall, thin, deathly pale monster with long blond hair and a rippling shirtless chest, wearing only jeans. What a creep. I think he came from an adjoining room. He looks at Gilda and then Bryce. When he sees Bryce, I could almost swear Bryce stands on his tippy-toes.

"What's up, Courtney?" asks Gus. "These guys bugging you?"

"Nothing I can't handle," she says, running her fingers along his naked chest. She stumbles a little and Gus quickly hunches over to catch her.

"What do you want?" Gus snaps, looking at us.

"We want to—"

"They want to see Blackbird and Raven," Courtney says with a laugh, rubbing her hands along Gus's hard pecs again.

It finally dawns on me who this girl is. She must be Mira's lover, Courtney. The one I yelled at Mira about but couldn't recall her name. Mira said her lover's name was Courtney. Beatrix told me Courtney was her close friend. She looks young enough. So why is this girl, who's supposedly Mira's girlfriend, fondling Gus's chest?

"Do you have any idea what time it is?" asks Gus.

"It's important," I say. "We drove really far. If you can't show us Maddie, at least let me talk to Enora, the owner of this house."

"Enora's not the fucking owner of my house," Gus says with a laugh. He slaps his chest. "I am. And I'm not letting in people in the wee hours of the morning. Goddammit..." He looks at the couple sleeping on the couch. "Are you crazy? People are sleeping 'round here." Then Gus looks out at the five cars across the street. Some of my friends have their heads stuck out the windows again. "Hey, what the fuck's going on?" And he walks right up to Bryce.

"We told you," Bryce says, looking up to meet his gaze. "We're just here to see our friend Madison."

"Get the hell out of here," he says, sticking his finger in Bryce's chest. Bryce slaps his hand away. Then Gus raises his fist, ready to strike him.

"Stop it!" I snap. "We'll go, but not until—"

"I'm here, Cadence," says Mira. She is walking down a very dark stairway to our right. She looks solemn, like she did at Alondra's—no, even more depressed. She's wearing a thick turquoise robe and her hair's wet. All her makeup is off. It looks like she just showered.

By now the couple on the couch have woken up, and another three girls have rushed over from another room, standing near the girl smoking by the kitchen, staring at us.

"Get away from them, Gus," Mira says. Gus steps back. "Why did you come here? You guys crazy? You demanded Cordelia and I leave. I think, Cadence, you yelled that you never wanted to see me again. Now you're here? That was only a few hours ago, wasn't it? And now you're on Enora's hallowed ground. Are you nuts? After I came to warn you. And you think Maddie's crazy? Get out of here."

"Where is Maddie?"

"Get out of here, guys," Mira repeats. Then she sees the cars outside. She slowly shakes her head. "What the hell are you doing? Get out now."

"I'm not here for you. I'm here for Maddie."

"You made that plain enough." Mira looks at me and shakes her head again. "You have to be the most infuriating witch in the world, Cadence."

"Is she here?"

Mira rolls her eyes. "Yes."

"Can we see her?"

"Will you leave? If we prove she's safe, will you go?"

I nod.

Mira rolls her eyes again and walks over to Courtney, hugging her and kissing her passionately on the lips. Gus narrows his eyes. I have a feeling there's some sort of love triangle going on between the "vampire" and these two witches.

"This is Courtney, Cadence," Mira says with a big grin, still holding her in her arms. "On better terms, I would have loved to introduce you guys. But you hate me now, right? And anyway, Courtney's totally fucked up and baked."

"I'm not baked, Meer!" Courtney snaps.

"You are," she says with her old grin. "You're also drunk." Mira turns to Gus. "High Wizard, meet Cadence, the leader of the Hawthorne coven."

"We've met."

"She wants to see Maddie. Show her. I think Blackbird is in ceremony. Do you know if she's with Panthera underground?"

"She should be."

"But not you, Gus?"

"Not yet. I was told to wait until after the witching hour."

"Why don't you go take the three of them downstairs. Show them Maddie's safe. Then they'll leave."

"Okay, Raven," he says.

"She won't want to go back with you," Mira adds with a shrug. Then she pecks Courtney on the cheek one more time. She turns from us and heads sleepily back up the stairs.

As Mira walks upstairs, she cocks her head back. "Oh, and by the way, Cadence, fuck off. I don't care about you either."

"Goodbye, Mira," says Gilda. Gilda looks confused. I think she thought it was really weird Mira didn't even say hello.

"Bye." But Mira doesn't look back.

"Shall we?" Gus asks, showing his filed teeth and fangs. He gestures to the door.

Gus walks out into the night shirtless. Of course, Gilda, Bryce, and I are still wearing coats. I think Gus goes out without a shirt to be tough. He even scowls at the other members of my coven in their cars. Damie jumps out of the car again, and Bryce and I shout and gesture once more for him to stay back.

We walk around the house to a side metal gate. This dark iron gate creaks open into the backyard beside a wall separating the yard from the neighbors'.

The backyard is just a small dirt lot. Tall trees surround the cement walls of the house. By the far end of the yard is a small wooden shedlike structure. It's wide but very short, looking too shallow for anyone to stand in. On the shed, in the dim moonlight, there's a painted red lion. And surrounding the caricature of the lion, in the same red paint, are small backward pentagrams and crosses.

Gus lifts a heavy metal door. Warm air rushes from inside. Steep concrete steps are lit by red smoke at the bottom. That makes me lurch back. Bryce tugs on my hand, but I don't want to go down there. This is exactly what I saw in my dream.

"One of the perks when I bought this house was this old nuclear fallout shelter," says Gus with a chuckle. "Wait till you see the space. It's huge. It's ready for Armageddon. You know, when the nations of this world finally lob bombs, this will be the safest place in Atlanta. I think it's the only shelter for miles. It's really cool, but the steps are muddy as hell, so watch your step. Guests have been known to slip and get hurt. Wouldn't want that. Watch your step. And head."

I smell incense trying to cover the smell of sulfur and burning meat. The same smells from in my nightmare. But it's brighter than it was in my dream. The red is almost blinding. And there are no drumbeats or whispering chants. I feel unsettled. Usually with this much stress, I'd feel magic. I don't. I just feel fear.

When we make it to the bottom, another metal door opens into a very large chamber. It's warmer, almost hot, here. Once again, like in my dream, there is a thick red fog, but this time no central bonfire. But the walls and ceilings of the chamber are the same gray concrete with backward pentagrams and crosses scrawled in red paint. The room is very large. It could fit three rooms of a house, I think. But there's a drab, dirty carpet and sparse raggedy furniture lying around. At the farthest end of the room is a circle of witches wearing the crimson cloaks of the Abaddon coven. They're kneeling with their hoods over their heads, and in the middle of the circle is a couple. The couple is naked, a man on top of a woman, on what appears to be a very large brown cowhide rug. The woman has small antlers tied to her head. Unlike in my dream, the witches surrounding the couple are calm. They're just observing instead of bowing and worshipping. It's almost as if they're studying the act. Other than the couple, the room is quiet.

"We buy the men," explains Gus, talking softly to Gilda. "We advertise it as a modeling job. Of course the witches in our coven like handsome ones. So when I'm not fucking the girls, like tonight, we hire models. They take mandrake and become disoriented. If they have moral problems when they wake, Enora threatens to kill them. Of course few of the models have ever dared challenge us." Then he shines his fangs at Bryce and me. "Those that do become a different sort of sacrifice, if you know what I mean? It's one of the advantages of living near downtown. You guys use models in your coven?" Gus is not asking for a response; he's trying to intimidate us. He's a real asshole.

"You're disgusting," I say.

That makes him smile, showing his carved animal teeth. My disgust satisfies him.

A few witches hear us talking and turn. One rises. As she walks over, I can just make out the infernal face under the red hood. I'd recognize those pretty features anywhere. Enora.

"Welcome," Enora whispers. "It's been a long time, Red Fox. Welcome. And Bryce."

"Mira asked me to bring them," Gus says quietly. "They want to see one of their friends, Blackbird."

"Well, you saw Mira, didn't you, Windstorm? Wasn't Mira once one of your friends?"

Oooh, I hate her!

Enora walks over to Gus and kisses him passionately on the lips in front of us. She makes out with him while rubbing his chest. Gus runs his hands inside her cloak and fondles her breasts. Enora's completely naked underneath her cloak. He runs his hand slowly down, opening the cloak more, so we can see her silhouette, caressing her chest and down over her butt.

"Well done," Enora says, releasing her lips. "Well done.

Return to the house. Guard it from the rest of them. Make sure none of the others step out of their cars. If they do, put them back in, would you?"

"I don't like them," Gus says, shaking his head. "I don't like the way they look."

She takes his hand and pats it. "Just don't touch them unless they leave their cars. 'Kay?"

He nods.

"Prepare my room for later," she says, reaching up and kissing him again.

"Tonight?" he asks, suddenly opening his eyes wide. He breathes more heavily in rapture. "Oh, tonight, my love?"

"Your reward, my dear," Enora says, patting his hand again. "Your reward."

The beast leaves. Enora turns to me and loses her smile.

"I need not ask what you think of us. I can already see it in your eyes."

"You're disgusting."

Enora laughs. A couple of witches turn toward us. Others continue to watch the sex show.

"Perhaps you three would like to partake in our sacrifice?" Enora asks with a laugh. "There's vital energy when it comes to lovemaking, especially with confused men. This one's quite handsome, don't you think, Cadence? Did you see his penis?"

"Where's Maddie?" I ask.

Enora looks at me, confused, and turns to Bryce. "I would be willing to consider you two as replacements." She runs her hand along Bryce's arm. "But not you. No, not you. You know, Gus may be well endowed and a good caretaker, but he's not smart. Oh, how I missed jousting with your mind, Bryce. And you were bright enough to keep up with me, weren't you? No, I'm not going to let you into our fucking ceremony. I would much rather hurt you."

"Where's Maddie!" I snap. "We came for her. We'll take her and leave."

The witches who were watching the couple suddenly whirl around and hiss like snakes at my outburst. The couple having sex seem disturbed too. They stop moving.

"Shh, Cadence," Enora says, putting a finger to her lips. "Your tantrum is messing up my ceremony."

"Where is she?" I repeat. "Where's my friend?"

"Blackbird," Enora says, turning to the witches in the circle. "Sister Madison Taylor. Please exit the circle and come here."

One of the witches in red cloaks slowly gets up and walks over. When she takes her hood down, I nearly fall apart, fighting back tears.

"Maddie," I say, "come back with us."

"Please, Maddie," Bryce says.

Maddie says nothing. Then she looks at Enora. At first, I don't know why, but then I surmise it's to ask permission to speak. Apparently, this is how much control the bitch holds over them. Enora nods.

"Why are you here?" Maddie asks me. Tears form in her eyes, and she violently shakes her head. "Go. Get out of here, Cadence. Hurry. Leave. It's not safe. This is Enora's coven."

"Maddie, come back to us," says Gilda. "We're so worried about you."

"*Come back to us,*" a few red-cloaked witches repeat quietly. "*We're so worried about you.*" And as they mock us, many of the witches in red cloaks rise and stand behind Enora. The man who was having sex falls on his knees with his head in his hands. He seems sick. The nude woman with antlers gets up and walks over to a bunch of red cloaks hanging on the wall, nonchalantly throwing one over her naked body. Then she joins the other Abaddon witches surrounding us.

"Master, you told me you'd leave them alone," Maddie says

to Enora. She shakes her head as if trying to shake off Enora. "You promised. You lied to me. I was right about you. I shouldn't have trusted you. Now Katie's here? What are you planning to do to her?"

"Well," Enora says, walking right up to Maddie. "I wasn't expecting this tonight. She's early. See, Friday you were going to give yourself to Gus. If little Katie had seen you then, that might have been enough to make her lose her senses."

"Let's go, Maddie," I say. "She's crazy."

"You swore!" Maddie cries to Enora. "You swore you'd leave them alone if I joined!"

Enora nods to Gus, who's standing behind Maddie. The man lifts Maddie from behind and pins her arms behind her.

"Let her go!" I shout.

"*Sopor*," Enora says, displaying the painted pentagram on her left palm to me. "*Sopor*." It makes me so drowsy. Enora signals to some of her witches, and they walk over and grab me, pinning my arms behind my back. For some reason, I can't fight. I'm so weak.

"Madison, I didn't lie to you," Enora says, turning back to her. "You're still a Hawthorne witch. You can't join us. I didn't lie because you can't live up to your end of the bargain."

"What are you doing?" I ask. It's strange, but it takes all my effort to just ask the question. I feel as if I'm in a dream again. I barely have enough energy to open my eyes.

"I don't need her, Windstorm," Enora replies, cocking her head back. "I have you. Now I have my true sacrifice." Enora addresses the witches who are now standing around us. "Take Bryce and chain him to the wall. He won't give up his seed, so instead I will hurt him."

My eyes open wide. I cry out with all my energy, "*Ad infernum! Exite! Ad infernum! Exite! Exite!*" From my chest to my head, I focus my energy and imagine Enora being thrown back.

But nothing happens. There's silence. Enora and her witches stare at me. Then... Enora chuckles nervously.

"No incantation can hurt me here," Enora says. "You're too weak."

Three witches who I don't recognize grab Bryce. Bryce struggles, but he seems too weak. They drag him over to the wall, where there are handcuffs on chains.

"Bryce!" I cry out.

"*Bryce*," repeat some of the witches. "*Bryce.*"

"What's going on!" Gilda asks. She seems to be the only one able to move now. "What are you doing? We just came to take Maddie home."

"Oh, you're free to go, Red Fox," Enora says, waving a hand dismissively. "You're not a part of the Hawthorne coven anymore."

"Let them go," Gilda mutters desperately. Gilda looks at me and Bryce and shakes her head.

When Gilda doesn't move, Enora's eyes open wide. "Go! Get the fuck out of here. Go before I change my mind. *Run!*"

Gilda runs. I hear her rush up the cement steps.

Enora walks right up to Bryce as they chain him to the wall. I try with all my might to fight her, but I can't even move my legs. I'm standing, but completely immobile. Then my heart pounds as I watch her run her fingers along Bryce's beard, over his face, his chest and down to his legs. But he's as immobile as I am.

"Bryce, you're as gullible as little Katie. Why didn't you stay away from here? You knew it wasn't safe. You've changed. You were always so responsible...except that night." She licks his ear and says, "Oh, for that night, I loathe you. I shall never forgive you."

"Don't touch him!" I yell.

"Pity you didn't get to marry him, Cadence," Enora says, looking back at me. Then she walks up to me and raises her left palm, showing the pentagram again. "*Sopor. Sopor.* Sleep. Shh. Sleep, Windstorm. Sleep. Don't fight it." I'm standing, but I can't move. I can barely open my eyes. "You're not dumb. You just do dumb things. It took me a year to plan this. You thought you could just walk in?"

I can't open my mouth.

"I thought that it'd be enough to take Mira." She taps her black nail on the center of my chest. "I thought she'd send you running over, but I was wrong. Your friendship with her was weak. In your snobbish mind, she wasn't good enough. Well, no matter, I used that too. I gave her Courtney so I could get her to work magic against you." She looks down for a moment, and when her eyes look back at me, they're solid pearly-white. She wags her stupid finger at my nose. "You see, Mira likes you, only she likes Courtney more."

Behind her, her witches slowly surround me whispering: "*Sacrificium consecratum. Sacrificium consecratum. Sacrificium consecratum.*"

"I can't get myself to forgive Bryce," Enora says, shaking her head. "Sorry, I never will. I wanted to kill him in Hawthorne, but Alondra's ghost stopped me. Or...you stopped me. But now that he's here, he's mine."

I can't respond.

"I will bleed you," she says with a nod, staring at me with solid pearly-white eyes. "If I can't destroy your book, I will destroy Windstorm. Not you, but the High Priestess. Every day until Friday, I will bleed you, undoing the magic given to you in your initiation. With the magic of the Abaddon coven, Windstorm will be no more. Then, though you'll feel sicker than now, I'll enjoy watching your expression as I slice Bryce's throat."

"Don't...touch...him!" I blurt, my tongue slurring each word.

"What are you gonna do?" she asks with a sly smile.

My eyes fall on Maddie. With all the strength I can muster, I stammer, "I'm soorry...I...loovve you." Tears run down her face and she nods.

"Oh, stop," Enora says, closing her eyes and shaking her head. "Just stop. Don't feign kindness. You're an evil witch. The only reason it took so long for me to trap you is because of your selfishness. I don't think you care about anyone. You certainly don't care about Mira.

"The last days will be unpleasant. I will bleed you. Slowly. Other covens will hear. They'll judge me, but I think they'll be on my side when they hear how you stole one of my witches and she killed herself. I will bleed you. Your blood, the blood of Escoba and Maverick, will be the most powerful of sacrifices. With it, I will finally destroy Hawthorne."

She comes up to me and runs her disgusting fingers along my cheek. Her eyes are still solid white. I feel no control of my head. I can't even turn away from her.

"You will suffer. But don't worry. After all is done and you're just a normal little girl again, I'll let you go back and study."

She smiles, but then she narrows her eyes.

"*Sacrificium consecratum!*" All her other witches join her, echoing her words. "*Let the first drop fall now, Windstorm!*" She pulls out a curved dagger from her robe and slices my arm. Bryce cries out from the wall.

I'm dizzy. There's so much pain. I fall backward and witches behind me grab me. Everything blurs. The pain is unbearable. Enora laughs and licks my blood from the end of her blade. My arm stings. When I open my eyes and look down, some of her red-cloaked witches are on their knees, feasting on the blood dripping from my fingers. When I try to say something, only a grunting sound comes forth.

"Our real Sabbath is in four days, blasphemer. Four days. This will be the end of the Hawthorne High Priestess. Perhaps that will teach you the importance of a witch's traditions.

Friday. Sabbath. Never have a gathering on another day, unless it is one of our holidays. And never come to a witch's coven uninvited." Then Enora looks at the witches surrounding my feet. "Take her into the supply room. Let her and her best friend spend their last days together, since little Katie wants to talk to her friend so badly. That is why you came, right?"

21

———

THE SUPPLY ROOM

"Katie, wake up. Come on. Wake up, Cadence! Wake up."

I blink my eyes. I'm lying on my side. I'm so weak. My hand, pressing against the floor, feels like ice. The air is cold too. Maddie's standing over me, shaking me.

"What... what's happening?"

I look up at the gray concrete ceiling. There are three recessed lights and a fire alarm above me. I wince. There's an unbearable sharp pain along my arm.

"Cadence, you collapsed when they threw us in the room. Then I blacked out too. It must be Enora's spell."

I can't move. Maddie carries me and props me against the wall. The wall is concrete and as cold as the floor. It smells. It smells of feces and urine. And a metallic putrid smell. Blood. Behind all the unpleasant smells is a background scent of food. I see the source—there are wooden shelves along one wall filled with stored food: canned foods, cereal, bags of rice, soda, and water. We can survive here for a long time, even if they keep us locked up. I don't see any candles. If they turn off the ceiling lights, it will be pitch black.

I see a flash of Enora's pearl-white eyes in my mind. That

reminds me of why Maddie and I are alone in the concrete room.

"How... how long have we been here?"

"I don't know." Maddie shakes her head, looking around the room.

Her black makeup is smeared on her face, and she's still naked under her red witch cloak. I'm not. I'm still wearing my red coat and blue jeans.

I think of Bryce chained to the wall. That's enough for me to stumble to my knees. I tip over and Maddie catches me. I see blood dripping on the gray floor from a large gash in my left arm.

"You have it worse than me," Maddie says. "That bitch cut you. She cut you real bad."

I look up into her eyes. She looks pained. So sad. She forces a smile.

"I'm sorry, Maddie. God, I'm so sorry. Can you forgive me?"

She nods. "I know." She tears up and looks around the room. "I know. I am too, babe. And now it's my fault that we're in this mess. I'm always getting us into trouble."

"I thought you were blaming me?" I ask, actually managing a faint grin.

She shakes her head hard. "I know you came for me. I love you more than anything in the world, Katie. Even with our fight, I never stopped loving you."

"Did you know Enora was going to attack?"

"Of course not." Maddie shakes her head. "I saw bad things happening here, but she was always nice on the surface. She used me. I should have seen through it. But I've been in a trance. I've been so upset that it flipped me into a trance, like you. At first, I was proud of myself, thinking I was finally feeling my power as a witch. My wandering, you know, from the initiation was never very—"

* * *

"You went out again," Maddie says.

I feel myself being propped up against a wall. I touch the wall. It's cold.

"The supply room?" She looks at me with an empty expression. "We have to get out of here and help Bryce."

I struggle to rise, but then I feel so dizzy. She helps me lean back against the wall. "Outside are the rest of our friends. They're waiting by the street. God knows what that creepy Gus is doing to them."

"He's a vampire."

"What?"

"He lives off blood," Maddie says with a nod. "I've seen it. At first, we just saw the fangs, but he really does everything he can to live like a vampire. He never eats real food. He gets most of the blood from the hospital. And Enora uses magic to strengthen him. He's like her dog, but he's inhumanly strong. He's the strongest man I've ever seen, Kate. But he's part of the sick stuff I've seen here too. I've watched him beat up strangers on the streets. He does it just to make them bleed. Then he drinks their blood."

"Gross."

Maddie nods.

"Well, this *vampire* is outside with my brother. Our Damie."

"*Our* Damie, Cadence?" Maddie smiles faintly.

I roll my eyes. "We'll figure that out later."

The metal door swings open. Maddie gasps when Mira, still wearing her blue night robe, is thrown into the room by two witches wearing red cloaks. The door is slammed behind her.

"You fuckers!" cries Mira, jumping up and spinning back toward the door. "For everything I did! All my sacrifice! Damn you all!" She slowly turns to us as if noticing us for the first time. She throws her dark hair back, takes a deep breath, and straightens her blue night robe. Then she gives us a big wave. "Hi, guys."

"You bitch!" I run to tackle her, but I don't have the strength. I fall on the ground right in front of her. She actually reaches down to help me up. "We're in this mess because of you!"

"Sorry," Mira says, looking down at me. "I warned you at Alondra's. I warned you to stay away."

"Why did you trust her?"

"Katie," Maddie says, grabbing me and helping me up. "We can't fight now."

"I should be fighting with you too," I snap, snatching my arm back. But I feel woozy again, ready to faint. I put my head in my hand. The room spins. I say more quietly, "God, what happened to you two? If you wanted to be stupid, leave Bryce and me out of it. She's gonna kill him."

"She's gonna kill all of us," Mira says. She seems surprisingly contemplative.

We stop talking. We just sit in the center of the room, feeling hopeless. I wait for my nausea to pass. Then Mira starts crying.

The room smells disgusting. That's not helping my nausea. I glance at the pile of towels at the corner of the room and finally realize that's the source. It's a "bathroom." No doubt there's human excrement on those towels. Where else do prisoners go to the bathroom?

"What can we do?" I ask, looking at Maddie. She doesn't look at me. She just shakes her head. I stand up slowly. I'm grateful for enough energy to do that. Mira's still bawling on the floor.

I dawdle over to the shelves and start looking for things that can be used to open the door. A crowbar would be nice. I'd even settle for a hammer and chisel. But I'm so weak that I'm leaning against the cabinet in order to stand.

"Mira, shut up and help me find a way out."

Mira just shakes her head and cries.

"Have others been thrown in here?" I ask.

"Yes, prisoners," Mira says.

"Why would you join this coven knowing they kept prisoners!" I say.

"They were criminals. And she let them go free after our ceremonies. That's what she told me, anyway."

"You hated Reardon for sex ceremonies. So did Enora. Why would you guys do them again?"

"I don't want to talk about it."

"Yeah," I say, putting my hands on my hips and glaring at her. "Well, you have to. Start talking. You got us in this mess. You've been here longer than anyone. Get up and help me find a way out so I can help Bryce."

But Mira keeps shaking her head, staring at the ground.

"You're still bleeding, Katie." Maddie touches my arm. It's dripping with blood. "You're not only dizzy from a spell, you're losing blood. The first thing we should do is find a bandage or something to stop the bleeding."

"No. Don't worry about me."

"You need to be strong," Maddie says, shaking her head.

I turn my back to her and start searching the shelves. I throw cracker and cereal boxes on the ground, desperately searching for something to use to get out of this pantry from hell.

Mira cries again. That takes me over the edge.

"Why did you join her!"

"For the magic!" Mira snaps between tears. "Okay! I told you."

"No, you did it for Courtney. For sex with her. You'd been hitting on me since we met. You did it to have sex with her." Then I turn to Maddie. "And as for you, I don't understand you either."

"I told you I fell into a trance," Maddie says, putting up a hand. "But we can't fight now, Cadence."

"I helped Enora put a spell on her," Mira explains miserably between tears. "Enora lied to me and told me it was to bring Maddie to us. I...I was fooled into thinking Maddie wanted to come here. I thought I was just helping Enora communicate with her."

"Just shut up," I say, shaking my head. "I don't want to hear any more."

Mira doesn't object. She just cries. But Mira's not a crybaby, crying all the time, like Beatrix. It's just that once she starts, she can't stop. During Alondra's funeral, she bawled through the whole service.

Maddie finds bandages. She takes two out of a box, rolls up the sleeves of my red coat and shirt, and sticks them on my gaping wound. It doesn't stop the bleeding. I ignore my arm and keep searching the cabinets. I don't care about me. But I do have to pause a few times and close my eyes to fight off the spinning sensation.

"They won't open the door until Friday," Maddie says. "It's no use. They figure we can survive until then. Then they'll gather us and ceremonially sacrifice us. Probably kill us."

"There must be something we can do?" I look up at the ceiling. There's the small fire alarm near the recessed lights. Hmm... "What about the fire alarm? Can we set it off?"

"Even if you could start a fire, what are you going to do?" asks Maddie. "We'll die of asphyxiation or smoke. They won't open the door."

"I think they will. They won't let their shelter burn. If they hear the alarm coming from the room, they'll open the door and we can fight our way out."

"They'll let us burn to death," interjects Mira miserably. She's sitting on the ground, leaning on her hands now. At least she stopped crying.

"Mira, Enora needs us Friday," Maddie says. "Why? Why on the Sabbath?"

"If Enora bleeds Cadence in ceremony," Mira says, wiping her nose with the sleeve of her robe, "she'll get rid of her power. Just as Cadence got her power from blood, Enora can take it away by bleeding her in a ceremony with her coven. Once she does that, it's like burning her book. She can destroy the coven. She hates Hawthorne. Alondra. Bill. And Bryce." Mira rises slowly. Then she throws her long hair back and straightens her robe. "She hates me, I suppose. I see that now. She lured you here for the right time to strike. It was all to get you here."

"But why?"

"She'll never forgive Hawthorne. She told me she felt publicly humiliated. She only let Bryce go because you stopped her on Hilltop Bluff, but she intends to kill him. She's told me otherwise, but I can see through her lies now. She's been scheming since. When she recruited me, I thought it was just plain jealousy over Katie's power. That's what she told me. She said she needed me to make the Abaddon coven greater than Hawthorne's. But now I see she just wants to destroy the coven."

"If she's so upset about rape, why would you guys hold sex ceremonies again?" I ask. Mira doesn't like that. For a second, she clams up.

"Our ceremonies are different," Mira says, staring at the ground. "Here, it's men who are drugged, not women. Strangers. Criminals. For the women, it's voluntary. Not so for the men. Except...for rare punishment."

"And that makes it better?"

"For Enora, yes. You know a sex sacrifice is powerful magic. In a way, for Enora, using men is part of her revenge. But I, I don't want to talk about it anymore, Cadence."

"Because you're guilty with Courtney."

"Guys, stop!" cries Maddie. "Please. We have to work together."

"Why?" Mira asks. "I don't give a fuck what Katie says. We're as good as dead anyway."

Well, I don't want to talk to her. I've had enough of her.

I return to looking frantically along the shelves. Maddie watches over my shoulder, but I can't find a single lighter or match in all the boxes on the shelves.

"It won't work, Katie," Maddie says. "I've seen terrible things here. They'll let us die if you set the alarm off. They're animals."

"What else can we do?"

I have some hope when I find cleaning materials. One section of the cabinet is storage for household bleach and toilet bowl cleaner. Beside them are combustible things like paper towels and plates, but nothing to light them on fire. That's when Mira surprises me by walking up from behind and handing me a piece of steel wool. I look at her like she's nuts.

"Here," Mira says, "if you want to start a fire and kill us, this will do. Maybe I deserve it."

"What's this?"

"There's some batteries stored on the second shelf over there." Mira points. "Take a nine-volt and rub it against the wool. It will cause sparks and start a fire. All we have to do is place it near the alarm."

"How do you know that?"

"Mom and Dad loved camping," Mira says with a shrug. "It was the first time I started to like the outdoors. They were the only vacations my sister and I ever had as kids."

"You have a sister?"

"I told you that a long time ago," Mira says condescendingly.

"This will work?" I ask again, holding the silvery piece of metal in front of her. "You're sure?"

"With a battery, yeah. It'll start a fire that will burn us alive in the supply room, Cadence, if that's what you want. I suppose you're my High Priestess again. Upon your command, we can die together."

"I want to see Bryce," I say, holding the piece of metal as if it's a lifeline. "I want to make sure he's okay. And my brother. And the rest of our gang."

"You're still bleeding," Mira says, looking at my arm.

"So?"

"No," Mira says. Then she points to the line of blood following me from the center of the room. "You need to be strong. Maddie's right." She takes my arm. I look at her funny and snatch my arm back.

"Not now."

"Stop being stubborn, Cadence. Give me your arm."

I hand it back. Mira closes her eyes. "*Claude,*" she says. Then she repeats it again and again, hovering her palm over my bloody arm. *Claude. Claude. Claude.*

Before my eyes, the gash running down my forearm closes and the blood stops dripping. Mira looks down and smiles at her work.

"How'd you do that?"

"Magic," Mira says. Then she touches my chest and closes her eyes. At first, I'm not sure what she's doing. Then I feel energy. Some of the weakness I've felt since seeing Enora is lifted from my chest. "I'm getting better," Mira says to me, opening her eyes. "I told you I had my first wandering a couple months ago. You might not agree with left-sided magic, but it's made me very powerful."

"Mira, how can you have magic when Katie doesn't?" asks Maddie.

"I'm an Abaddon witch," she says with a shrug. "I renounced your circle. This is my hallowed ground."

"Then Katie can," says Maddie excitedly.

"No. I was initiated into Enora's coven. My magic still works here, hers doesn't."

"Then get us the fuck out!" I cry. I can't believe this. I mean —*really?* If she can do this, why are we yapping? Why doesn't she just open the goddamn door!

"I don't have your power, Cadence. I can't break open the door. And I can't start a fire out of thin air like you can."

"What can you do?"

"Simple things. Healing spells, like that one. I can kindle a fire, I suppose. But I'm not..." And she really annoys me with this smug grin. "Not a Firestarter like you."

I turn from her stupid grin because I'm about to slug her. I stare at the metal wire and battery again. "So how does this work with the battery?"

"You just rub it. If we do it under the fire alarm, it should go off. But it could also light up the cabinets. And if they don't open the door, the smoke could kill us."

"Show me, Mira. Start the fire."

We look up at the fire alarm. The problem is the cell has a high ceiling. Mira tries to climb the cabinet, but she's nowhere near the fire alarm at the center of the ceiling.

"We could just light it down here."

"No," I say. "I'll carry you up."

"I'm too heavy. And you and Maddie are too weak. We can light it and carry it up there. I'll rub the battery along the coils. But ..." She grabs a broomstick near the cleaning items. "I'll attach it to this with some paper towels."

"What do we do when they run in?" asks Maddie. "We don't have any magic."

"We just fight," I say.

"I have a little magic left in me," Mira says while tying the metal coils to the broom. "I can conjure up an illusion of smoke. I can make the fire appear much worse than it is. Hopefully, you two won't have to fight at all. They'll run."

I nod. So does Maddie.

"Okay," Mira says, "but even if we get out of here, how are we going to stop them? We're outnumbered. And if Gus is there, forget it. I've seen that man pin down five people."

"We have to," I say. "God knows what he's doing to Bryce."

Mira gets to work on her homemade broomstick torch. Then, after she inspects it, she says, "Okay. I can light it when you're ready."

"The fire alarm is our diversion," I say to both of them. "They'll be in a panic. Do what you can to make them think the cell is burning completely, Mira. Build up the smoke with your spell. Can you do that?"

"Of course. Not sure I can unlock the chains on your boyfriend's wrists though. But usually in ceremonies, we leave keys along the altar."

"Well, if the cell really does catch fire and Bryce is trapped, he'll die. Then I'll die with him. I'm not going to leave him down here. If he goes, I go."

"Wish Courtney loved me that much," Mira says with a shrug.

"When, Katie?" asks Maddie.

"Now. But, Mira, what if they're not outside the door? How will they hear the alarm?"

"Gus rigged the alarms to sound in the house. You might be right about this, Cadence. I think he cares more about his chamber than the house. So does Enora."

"If all works well," I say with a nod, "we'll race up the stairs, free Bryce, and make a run for it."

Mira nods. But she looks worried. I'm really worried too.

"It could work," Mira says.

"Best friends forever?" Maddie asks with a wry grin.

I hug her tightly. "Forever." Then I reach for Mira. She looks surprised and slowly joins our embrace.

"I love you guys," I say. "When we get out of here, *forever and ever*. Okay?"

Maddie smiles. Mira just nods.

22

MIRA'S CAMPFIRE

IT SURPRISES ME HOW FAST THE FIRE ALARM SOUNDS. IT SEEMS like all Mira had to do was wave her burning broomstick on the ground to set it off. The shrill sound irritates my ears. Then Mira makes it worse. She places her hands together, as if in prayer, and dips her head down while standing in concentration. Gray smoke starts covering the whole cell. And it's weird because I expect to cough, but I don't. The smoke is an illusion. It's her conjuring.

I hear noise from outside the door. There's banging and people are shouting. We all stand to the right side of the door, waiting for it to open.

The door swings open. A woman with black tattoos on her face rushes in: Cordelia. But the minute she enters, she's covered in smoke. She starts screaming. All three of us duck around her. More witches circle the exit—most are wearing red cloaks—and we have to shove our way out.

Bryce is still chained to the wall, staring at the growing cloud of smoke.

"Katie," he says with a big grin.

I yank at his wrists, but they're chained. I pull as hard as I can, but they won't budge. Of course they won't; they're chained to the wall.

"By the altar," Mira reminds me, running there.

I look at the altar and see what I don't want to see. Enora. She's walking over to us with her head down and those creepy white eyes raised. The smoke is surrounding her, but she doesn't care. I feel weak as she approaches. She's casting a spell again. Bryce says something to me in a panic, but I can barely hear his words. I collapse. By my side, Enora stands over me. She crouches down to touch me, but then someone comes behind her and tackles her. I see a turquoise robe. It's Mira. Mira throws me the keys then rolls with Enora on the ground.

"*Vade retro!*" cries Mira. "Black witch! *Vade retro! Vade retro!*"

"Traitor!" cries Enora. "Me? Black witch? What the fuck do you think you are!"

With all the energy I have left, I pull myself up. For Bryce. The room is rocking as if I'm on a boat. I am so sick.

I see a red cloak. I jerk away, thinking it's a witch from the Abaddon coven, but then I see her face. It's Maddie. Maddie grabs the keys from my hand and jumps up to unlock Bryce's restraints. Enora and Mira continue to wrestle on the ground. The rest of the witches are running to the stairs, away from the smoke, as we planned, thinking the chamber is on fire.

Everything blurs.

* * *

There are glimpses of houses and a road as I blink. Streetlights. Cars. I recognize Bryce's dark gray BMW. It's cold. It feels so cold. I'm outside on the street. Bryce's bright blue eyes are looking down at me with sweet concern, and for a moment, I feel peace. I can't remember how I got here, but I don't really care.

I sit up with his help. Then I try to focus. I see Enora's house. That's when I remember. My sickness returns.

An orange hue forms above the houses. The sun is rising.

"Take it easy, Cadence," says Bryce, holding me.

Others crouch down and touch me. My friends. My coven. All of them are hovering over me. They never left. Maddie's recovering too. I see her under a streetlamp near Bryce's car, still wearing a red cloak, being held by Damie.

"Where's Mira?" I ask Bryce. Bryce loses his smile. That's enough to prompt me to sit up.

"Katie," Bryce says, "take it easy." But I don't want to take it easy.

I stand up facing the Abaddon witch house. My friends look at me really oddly, probably because I was struggling to open my eyes a second ago. Now I'm standing up straight, full of energy. In fact, I feel really strong. I understand. I'm slipping into a trance again. *My* magic is growing now that I'm away from that devilish house.

"We need to get Mira," I say to Bryce. "She saved us."

"We can't," Bryce says, shaking his head. "We have to go."

"We have to go," Tammy echoes, touching my shoulder. "Every time we go anywhere near there, we're thrown back. Sometimes it's an illusion, other times it's Gus. There's no way in. We already tried to get you guys out."

I look at Frida, who nods sadly.

"We have to try," I insist.

I walk over to Maddie and Damie. Maddie appears to be asleep in his arms. I reach down and touch her shoulder. She looks up at me and smiles sweetly.

"Better?" I ask.

"Yeah," she says sleepily.

Then Maddie furrows her brow, looking at me. She opens her eyes wide, staring at my arm. "Look, Cadence." I follow her eyes to my arm. There's no cut. Not even a healed cut. Even the sleeve of my red coat, which had been sliced open, is whole again.

"You're better," she says. I am better.

But then I hear my friends gasp. Maddie's eyes bulge out of their sockets over something across the street behind my shoulder. I hear an odd growl. I turn.

Gus, still shirtless and baring his fangs, charges berserko at us like a bull. He leaps over the hood of a car across the street, growls, and runs toward Maddie and me. Bryce jumps in front of the car to protect us. I yell to my friends, "Get behind me." They obey, but it's too late for Bryce. The vampire leaps on my boyfriend and slams him against the car. The impact is so violent that it dents the side of his BMW and cracks the back passenger-side window. They struggle on the car, and in horror, I catch the beast trying to bite my boyfriend's neck.

"Cadas!"

Gus falls like a stone before Bryce. I stand over Gus, wanting to hurt him more, but then I hear my name being called from the house. Enora is in the front yard with all her witches in red cloaks. Then I see Mira. Still in a blue-green robe, she's being led by two of them with her hands tied behind her back.

"Nuh, uh, uh, Cadence," Enora yells. "Play nice or your friend gets it."

"Let Mira go!" I cry.

"Come get her. You never cared about her before."

"Let her go!" I grab Gus by the arm and drag the huge beast across the street. "I have him. I'll hurt him."

"Keep him," she says. "I've had enough of him. I'd much rather punish Raven. If you'd like, Katie, you can stay and watch."

"Let Mira go, Enora," cries Bryce. He's wincing and holding his right arm. It looks like Gus might have dislocated his shoulder.

"I get Mira and you keep Gus," I say, still dragging the huge man. "And then we call it even. Okay?"

All the red witches walk to the edge of the lawn and stop by the sidewalk. I drag Gus all the way up to the line of red-cloaked women and toss him at them. They help him up onto the grass.

"There," I say, standing on the sidewalk facing Enora. "Now give me Mira."

"No," Enora says, walking right up to me. Her mouth is bleeding. Good. It appears Mira hit her before she was subdued. "You took Beatrix. I get Mira."

"You killed Beatrix!"

It's weird. She's about a foot from the sidewalk, but she doesn't dare cross. Even with those beastly empty white eyes. Neither do her witches. And, as much confidence as I have while I'm in a trance, I'm remembering my sickness in her house. I'm afraid to cross her property line too. Just the thought of walking over there makes me sick.

"What a cruel accusation," Enora says. "Manthis was my sister. Don't worry, this isn't over. You might have stopped the Sabbath, but there'll be others."

Then she wags a finger, about to say something else, but the minute her digit crosses the line of the sidewalk, her hand bursts into flame. My anger is so strong that just the thought of burning her is enough to start a fire. Enora steps back, wailing. She covers the fire with her other hand, but her finger keeps burning.

She can't douse the flame. She falls to the ground, trying to put out the fire in the grass. Cordelia runs over to help, hissing at me.

"*Bitch!*" Enora screams, looking at me. "*You bitch!*"

"I'll leave!" I shout. "But the minute you step out, I'll be waiting for you. For what you did to Beatrix! And for anything you dare do to Mira!"

One of the witches runs to Enora with a cup and tosses the liquid over her hand, but the fire won't burn out. Enora starts screaming. She can't put the fire out. The rest of my coven is beside me, staring.

"Mira!" I yell. "Come here. Come home with us."

"I can't, Cadence," Mira says with teary eyes. "I'm sorry. I can't leave."

"*Prohibe!*" Enora screams, staring at her burning hand. "*Prohibe! Prohibe! Prohibe!*"

The flame finally stops. Enora screams some more, staring at her smoking, blackened hand. She spins around and yells something unintelligible at me.

"Mira, please," I yell. "Come with us."

"It's too late for me, Cadence. This is my home. This is my family now."

Enora scowls at me, holding her smoking hand. Then, with a mischievous smile, she whirls around to Mira and screams, "*Lux!*" Mira's hair lights on fire.

"*Mira!*"

"I'm not the only witch who can burn!" Enora exclaims.

I run to help Mira. Some of the witches who were circling Enora run to the sidewalk to stop me, but something grabs me from behind before I cross into the front yard. I turn and Bryce has his arm around me. I could easily shrug him off, but he's shaking his head desperately. "Stay back, Katie! Stay away from them! Please! Don't cross the line!"

One of the witches in red grabs Mira and throws her to the ground, trying to douse the flames.

"*Prohibe!*" cries the Abaddon witch over Mira. "*Prohibe! Prohibe!*"

The hood falls from the witch's cloak as the two roll on the grass, revealing blond hair. I recognize this witch. She's the drugged, inebriated girl who greeted us at the door. Courtney. She's desperately trying to douse the flames on her lover.

Thank God, her incantation works. But then Enora approaches them.

"*Stay away from her!*" I shout. "*Leave her alone!*"

Bryce is still holding me back. His hands are so weak I could easily throw him off, but I know he's right. If I walk onto the grass, I'm as good as dead. I feel weak just leaning toward it.

"Are you a traitor too!" screams Enora at Courtney. "You? How dare you help her! You actually care about her? I don't believe it."

"Leave her alone!" cries Courtney, in tears, holding Mira on the ground.

The fire's stopped, but I can tell Mira's hurt. I'm sure some of the flames burned her scalp. Enora looks down at her hand. She waves her smoking hand back and forth to ease her pain. Then she turns back to me.

"Come over!" Enora cries. "Come on. Fight me! Come here, you coward! Try to stop me from killing Mira, Cadence! I will. I'm going to hurt her. Believe me. If I can't hurt you, I'll hurt her. I swear it!"

Damie grabs me, and I'm between him and Bryce. Then Maddie grabs my shoulder. All three are holding me back, begging me to leave.

"Did you kill her!" I cry.

"She's okay," Courtney shouts at me, still crouching beside Mira. "She's okay, Windstorm. Go. Please go. Take your coven and leave before more people get hurt."

Mira looks over. She's not okay. She looks like she's in so much pain. But Mira says weakly, "Cadence...please go. Leave."

* * *

The way back home is the most unpleasant drive I've ever had. I sit in the passenger seat, staring at the illuminated windows of the skyscrapers of Atlanta. There's something about early morning that always feels like a waking dream to me. Though I'm not a morning person, I have fond memories of this feeling, like waking up during a family trip. Not today. This morning I'm filled with dread. I got Maddie back, but I left Mira again. I can't imagine Enora's doing anything less than killing her.

Soon we pass the high rises and enter the suburbs. All the while, Maddie is in the back seat, crouched against my brother, crying. Their closeness is exactly what started all this horror in the first place. I know I apologized to her, but between you and me, I'm still a little mad.

Bryce touches my hand. I hold his as he drives, but I don't look at him. I just stare out at the fields and the yellow-orange sun rising over the horizon as we make our way back to Hawthorne.

The trees get denser. I tear my eyes from the scenery, dig in my pants pocket, and check the time. Six thirty. But we're still not over the hills into Hawthorne Forest. At least Maddie stops crying. Now the two of them are sleeping.

"Nothing's changed," I say to Bryce. They're the first words I've said since Enora's house.

"What?" I think he thought I was sleeping.

"It was all for nothing."

"That's not true, Katie."

"Why?"

"You got your best friend and brother back."

I squeeze his hand tighter. He's right. He's always right.

I take a deep breath. Then I finally take my hand from his and curl up against the door. I close my eyes, but I know it's for nothing. There's no way I'm going to sleep.

"Will Mira be okay, Bryce?" I ask almost in a whisper.

"She hasn't been since she left for Atlanta. But it was her choice. Maddie's wasn't."

"We shouldn't have left her."

"There was nothing else we could do."

My trance is over. I'm so drowsy. So tired. My eyes close. I feel Bryce's hand run along my hair. I know he's trying to be nice, but that bothers me because it reminds me of Mira's hair. Mira's not feeling any pleasure on her head right now. She must be in so much pain. She probably can't even see a doctor under that wicked witch. And that might not be all Enora's done to hurt her.

"Katie," I hear quietly from behind me. My brother's snoring.

"Yeah, Maddie?"

"Thank you for coming back for me, babe."

23

THE BURNING

I'M SITTING DISCREETLY IN THE MIDDLE OF CONNOR SILL HALL, with a notepad and pen, listening to my new teacher, Dr. Stoferson. Connor Sill Hall is one of the smallest lecture halls in Hawthorne University, with rows of ugly orange swivel chairs along cream-colored walls, all dipping down an incline over a large black stage and podium. Dr. Stoferson is probably the oldest professor in school. He is way beyond retirement age, but he still teaches because he loves it so much. He even walks with a shuffle across the stage, hunching over as he talks. He's got a short beard and he's always wearing a sharp navy-blue suit. Most around campus know him from orientation. He's a smiley man who loves attending every orientation and graduation and meeting everyone. I was lucky to get him for American history.

Anyway, he's discussing the impeachment of Andrew Johnson, which is not that thrilling, but his enthusiasm gets me into it.

"Could Abraham Lincoln have been impeached had he not been assassinated?" asks Doctor Stoferson, shifting his legs slowly and staring at the ground. "Couldn't he have gone through the same process as President Johnson?"

Just as Dr. Stoferson looks up at us, my phone vibrates. I don't dare look at it, as my professor's staring right at me. There are only around thirty of us scattered throughout the auditorium. That's because it's the beginning of the second semester and the lecture is at night. As good as Dr. Stoferson is, few people attend evening lectures.

I'm really lucky to have Tammy sitting beside me. She got into his prized class too. And, as you know, unlike shy me, Tammy's boisterous and fun. So Tammy hollers out, "There's no way Abe would have done that, Professor. Lincoln could have gotten away with anything."

"True, Tammy," the professor says. (I marvel that he knows her name). "Lincoln was a wily politician. But it was troubled times. Certainly, he'd have faced tremendous challenges just as he had during the Civil War. Of course, Andrew Johnson was no Lincoln. In March of 1865, during Lincoln's second inauguration, Johnson was drunk. He was inaugurated as president a month later. Some believe he was thrown out of the Petersens' house by Mrs. Lincoln for drinking again when Lincoln was on his deathbed. But it wasn't only whiskey...he was strongly disliked by his own political party for his disregard of the South's discrimination against black Americans."

Dr. Stoferson is so into his subject that he looks up pensively for a moment as if he were talking about the most important subject in the world. I just love that. But it's hard for me to pay attention.

I'm so worried. After I missed my morning Crusades lecture and got up after noon, Bryce had to stop me, in our apartment parking lot, from running to my beat-up old Honda and heading back to Atlanta, alone, to try to spring Mira. I'm so upset. I feel like it's my responsibility as High Priestess. It's my fault. All over again. The gang's probably going to meet again on Friday, but that's too late. I shudder to think what that wicked witch will have done to Mira by then.

"And in this turbulent time in America," continues Dr. Stoferson, "the challenge of rebuilding a decimated South, our South, whose economy was based on agriculture, did not really end on April 9, 1865. I think, had Lincoln lived, this healing could have been done so much better. The Civil War was a big turning point for our country. Know all the dates. But most importantly, go beyond what you've been told in school. The Civil War was a war representing a struggle of old against new in addition to being about slavery. Industrialization versus agriculture. It was industrialization's time to win. Technology had evolved, bringing our race into a new era. So the question I pose to all of you tonight is, what do you all think will happen with the next change in humanity's evolution? I don't know. But whatever it is, sadly, I don't think it will end racial prejudice."

I can't care. I mean, of course I care, but I can't stop thinking about Mira. I keep seeing Mira's hair burning in my mind. Bryce shouldn't have stopped me. But he didn't stop me, you know. I stopped me. I don't want to go anywhere near that house ever again.

I feel a vibration from my cell phone again. Then Tammy's phone rings. Following that, the lecture hall goes crazy with phones ringing all over the place. Everybody digs into their pockets or purses to see what's going on. The noise from all the phones disturbs Dr. Stoferson. Then his own phone buzzes.

A boy bursts through a side door in the auditorium. "The Billington House is on fire! It's on fire! Fire!"

Tammy's eyes open wide. We jump from our seats.

"The Billington House," says another. "It's on fire!"

Dr. Stoferson's squinting at his phone. "Oh my," he says.

Tammy and I run outside. It's dark. We're at the edge of campus and not far from the Billington House, perched up on the forest hillside. When I follow everyone's gaze, I don't like what I see. There are clouds of gray smoke and a bright yellow-red glow on the hill.

"My God, Katie!" cries Tammy.

My phone buzzes again. It's Bryce.

"Katie, are you all right?" he asks.

"I'm fine, Bryce. Did you hear?"

"Of course I heard. I'm here, remember? Remember the reunion with Mason?"

"Oh my God, Bryce, you were inside! I totally forgot. Are you okay?"

"I'm fine. But are you, Kate? I'm checking on you."

"I'm fine."

"Bryce was in the house?" asks Tammy in a panic.

"He's fine," I say, turning to her.

"Thank God you're okay," Bryce says. "We were on the first floor. Those on the second and third...aren't doing so well."

"I can be up there in a minute."

"It's all ablaze, Cadence. The fire trucks are here, but I'm not sure there's much that they can do. I don't think there's going to be much left for you to see. First it was smoke, but in a few minutes, it exploded into flames. I heard screams. It was terrible."

"I'll be right there."

"We can drive up there, Katie," Tammy says. "My car's outside the lecture hall."

"Okay."

"Bye, Bryce. I'm coming up now."

I hang up the phone, and we run to the parking lot and jump into Tammy's SUV.

When we get on the road, we regret it. We're not the only ones who are curious. There's traffic. Can you believe that? Traffic in Hawthorne. That's something I never see. There's a line of cars heading up the hill, and we're not moving.

"Tams, I'm gonna jump out and run. Okay?"

"Yeah," Tammy says, still staring at the car in front of her. "Just go."

I sprint over to the walkway, dodging more bodies, on my way through the woods and up to the Billington House.

The smoke gets heavier, and white ash falls between branches and leaves. Many students are talking on their phones as they're rushing up the hill. Others are smiling or laughing, thinking the whole thing is funny. I don't think it's funny. I want to slap them in the face. How can this be funny? I mean, I'm a history major. The Billington House is the oldest house in Georgia. It has so much history. And it's burning. Then I think about how Bryce was in there when it caught on fire.

My phone rings again. It's Maddie.

"Did you hear?" asks Maddie.

"Of course I heard."

"Bryce told me he was trying to reach you. You were in class with Tammy, right?" I hear my brother. Maddie says in a hushed voice, "Yeah, she's fine. She's fine." Then Maddie's voice is loud again. "You coming? You gotta see this, Katie. It's so sad. The whole place is burning down."

"I'll be there in a minute. Tammy's stuck with her car still on the road."

"Well, the police blocked it off." Maddie coughs. "And they're starting to push everyone back. I think the whole school is up here. And...my God, Katie, it's horrible. I saw a few students limping out of the building. One was being carried. I think it was Nathan. I'm not sure. And one...his face was covered with blood. Then there was...I don't even know how to say it. I don't even know how to say it."

"What?"

"There were bodies wrapped in white cloths. People died."

I hang up the phone. I don't want to hear anymore. I also don't need to. I can see the house up the hill now through smoke and tree branches. I wrap my arms around myself tightly. Even though I'm wearing my red coat, it's frigid.

At the top of the hill, the smoke is thick. People are coughing and it's raining white ash. There are sirens, and red and blue are reflected off the smoke. I can't walk fast anymore because too many students are in line, heading up the path. Maddie's right, everyone from campus is here. I see many trees and grass around the house on fire too. The brick building is covered in more smoke than flame. A black-and-red cloud billows through the shattered glass of Abigail's famous haunted window. The only actual flames burn in the upstairs windows and on top of the roof. There are gaps in the structure where the wall or roof has caved in, and bricks and cement are strewn along the ground. Maddie's right, I don't think there's any hope of salvaging anything from the rubble. Firefighters are spraying hoses, but it doesn't look like it's going to save the house. I'm thinking they're trying to keep the fire from spreading into Hawthorne Forest.

I stand about fifty yards from the front door, staring, with a hundred other students. Someone touches my shoulder and I whirl around. It's Bryce. I jump in his arms.

"It's terrible."

"I don't think Nancy and Nick made it," Bryce says with a nod. "They were upstairs. And there's...so many injured. If you happened to be on the first floor with me, you were safe. God, I'm so glad you were in class. Can you imagine if you had decided to join me? One girl jumped from a window on the top floor and broke her leg. I saw another tumble down the stairs running from all the smoke. It was horrific, Cadence."

"I'm just glad you're okay," I say, clutching him tightly.

"You too."

Maddie and Damie run up to us. Maddie's face is streaming with tears. I brush my eyes and am surprised my eyes are wet too. Everything is so crazy I didn't even know I was crying. Or is it a reaction to the smoke?

We're all coughing and I'm beginning to wheeze, and the fire and smoke from the Billington House actually warms me. The police start signaling for us to back up. I think the entire police department from Hawthorne is here.

"You okay, man?" Damie asks Bryce, touching his shoulder. Bryce nods.

"That's over two hundred years burning," I say, shaking my head at my brother.

The police are signaling for us to move back. We walk backward toward the path and trees down the hill.

"Do you know what happened, Bryce?" asks Maddie.

"I thought it was the kitchen. Mason and I ran in there, but nothing was on fire. It was coming from one of the side bedrooms on the second floor, we think. It smoked the entire house. Mason told me Jill heard a window smash before the smoke started. Mason thinks someone started the fire from outside."

"Where's Mason?" I ask.

"He went in an ambulance with Jared. Jared broke a leg climbing down from a window upstairs. He's burned too, but I think he's all right."

"It was a reunion, Bryce?" asks Maddie.

"Katie was invited," he replies. "Mason was visiting from out of town. God, I'm so glad for her class. Seems being a bookworm saved her life this time."

"Guys!" We turn. It's Tammy. She's pushing through people to get to us. I'm surprised she made it through the crowds and traffic. Maddie hugs her. We all do.

"I can't believe it," Tammy says, staring at the fire. "It's so sad. The Billington House."

"Bryce," I say, "you said your friend Mason told you the fire was started from outside? Was he sure?"

His open-mouthed look of shock changes to anger. His eyes narrow and he slowly nods. He knows my implication.

"She did it, Katie?" asks Maddie.

"I think she did." Bryce nods.

"You guys don't know," says my brother.

My brother's objection bothers me. I still don't even like that he's here. Or that he even knows what we're talking about. Damie saw that "vampire" at the house. And then he saw my magic. I still can't get used to him being a part of all this craziness.

"She's the only one with a motive." Bryce looks back at the house, frowning. "She knew I'd be in there. Maybe she thought you'd be there too, Cadence."

"She burned the house down just to get Bryce?" asks Tammy.

"No," I say. "I think she burned it to burn the town. Just like my book. She wants Hawthorne destroyed. The fact that Bryce was there was an extra bonus."

"Fire for fire, Katie," Maddie says, nodding. "For what you did to her. She's gone on the offensive."

"Alondra's house!" Bryce turns toward the opposite side of town. "Shit, guys! We've got to go to Alondra's! If she did this to the Billington House, Alondra's is next."

"Tell everybody to meet there," Bryce says, turning to Maddie and Tammy. "That house is as much a part of Hawthorne as the Billington House. More so. It's our coven's home."

"Guys, are you all right!" We hear a Brazilian accent rushing through the crowd. It's Frida.

"We've got to get over to Alondra's, Frida," Bryce repeats. But I hug her first. Poor Frida's crying.

The police sirens start blaring again. Then I hear a megaphone:

"Everyone move back. Move back down the hill. For safety, we need all of you to..."

24

THE OWL

When we finally arrive at Alondra's house, it's super creepy. It's chilling that all the lights are on again in the house. *All of them*. Lights illuminate the driveway, surround the lone red carriage and weed garden, and shine through all the windows of the first floor of the house. I can still smell the fire from the opposite side of town, but here the stars are out on a clear night.

"I don't like this, Katie," Frida says. "All the lights were on when you saw Beatrix, right?"

Ah ... yeah.

We check the house. There are no ghosts or witches hanging out. But there's still the outside to investigate.

We enter the backyard by the side yard, because there's no way I'm going to go through the living room to the patio after what happened to Beatrix. In the side yard, Natasha, Mandy, Hope, Josie, and Debra meet up with us after piling out of Natasha's pink VW Bug. Our whole coven is here tonight, summoned by Bryce, and we all walk together onto the wild grass of Alondra's backyard.

The backyard's spooky too. All the lights coming from the house glow on the grass and cast shadows of the leafless branches and bushes in the forest. When I get closer to the middle of the field, I finally muster the courage to look back at the house. The patio's bright, but there's no hanging witch, thank God. But then Maddie gasps. She points at two red figures, running behind the trees, holding fiery torches and laughing.

"Our arsonists?" suggests Tammy.

"Doesn't look like they finished their job," says Damie.

"Should we go after them, Katie?" asks Frida.

I don't know. I stare at their torches, hidden behind the leaves and branches, wondering about the two witches' intentions. Bryce, Mandy, and Frida sprint after them.

"Wait!" I yell. "Let them go!"

It's like they want us to follow them. It feels like a trap. Thankfully, Bryce and the girls listen to me. Frida runs back to me in a panic but sweetly asks, "Why not go after them?"

I don't know. It doesn't feel right.

Alondra would know what to do. She was our true leader. It's times like these I wish Alondra were here.

"Why don't you want us to chase after them?" Bryce repeats.

"What are you gonna do if you catch them?"

"They're Abaddon witches," snaps Mandy. "It must be them. We have to stop them."

"And do what?" I shake my head. "They were taunting us to follow them. It felt like a trap. Stay here. Let's talk first."

"*Talk?*" snaps Mandy. "*Talk? Talk about what?*"

"We came here to protect the house, not chase after witches."

They don't agree. I can see it on their faces. They want to run after them. Even Bryce. Even my brother. But they follow my orders, not because they believe in me, but because I'm their High Priestess. I watch the torches and hear the laughter of the retreating witches moving deeper and deeper into the woods until they disappear.

"Is this your order?" quips Mandy. "You want us to just let them go and *talk*?"

"What if they burn down the school, Windstorm!" demands Natasha. "You're just gonna let them do that?"

That really pisses me off. No, I was planning on sitting down as a group and talking things over with my coven in order to plan our next step, but everyone's so crazy and in such a panic that I doubt I can even get a word in. I don't answer.

Instead, I turn my back on all of them and walk toward our pile of wood alone. And then...I feel peace. And that's super weird because all my friends are still shouting at my back. The trees feel like arms hugging me, comforting me, while the gentle breeze brushes against my hair. I just wish they'd stop yelling.

I stand before the burned logs. Then I sit down facing the house and creepy patio. I think of Alondra again. In my teacher's last days, before she passed, she chose to leave our friends for the woods. She decided to spend her last days alone. Now I understand. People can be so agitating.

I look down at the floor and feel energy flow from my belly to my neck. I become oblivious to my friends' words. Then I completely stop hearing their chatter.

It's cold. So I will the bonfire to light by itself behind me. I feel the pleasure of its heat warming my back. The breeze against my cheek is cold, but comfortable with my newly lit fire behind me. I hear animals. Then, from the corner of my eye, I see them. A red fox walks behind the bushes to my right, and a large black snake curls along in the leaves beside a tree trunk to my left. But my attention focuses beyond. Something's drawing me to look down the hill through the trees. Far in the distance, miles from the yard, an owl perched high up on a leafless black tree branch has its head dug deep in its chest. I stop noticing everything else and stare at this owl.

A few of my friends are now standing over me with their eyes bulging, their nostrils flaring, and their mouths soundlessly yapping. They're so crazy. I laugh and turn back to the owl perched on the branch.

At first, I'm not sure why this owl fascinates me so much, but then I realize that the bird looks exactly like a witch in a meditative pose. Just like when I saw Alondra and Beatrix crouched in black cloaks.

The only sounds I hear are the breeze rustling through the trees and deer and coyotes walking over leaves in the forest. And as I look down, I see that I'm wearing a black cloak and holding my book, *Broomstick*. I don't recall changing into a cloak. Nor do I know how I came into possession of the book. Did I grab it when searching the house?

Bryce appears over me, pushing my shoulder and saying something, but I can't hear his words. He looks concerned. I laugh, grab his hand, and kiss the back of it. He keeps talking frantically. All my friends stand over me now, looking at me weirdly, but I don't hear what they're saying. I don't care. I laugh again. They look funny.

I position my Book of Shadows, *Broomstick*, in front of me. Then—I've never done this before, but it seems like the right thing to do now—I crouch, just like the owl, dipping my head down into my chest and leaning my body toward the ground. I whisper, though my words seem to echo throughout the yard:

Ut videam. Ut videam. Ut videam. Lux alba. Lux Nyx.

Everything blurs.

* * *

My eyes open in a dark room with a vaulted ceiling. I'm sitting on a wooden bench in a church. There's a large cross above the altar, and standing on the stage is Frida's brother, Liam, lighting candles. He doesn't look at me. It's almost as if he doesn't see me. It's dark and all the drapes are closed. This is Hawthorne Church.

When I turn toward the windows to my left, I jump. There's a witch sitting next to me. With a black cloak, this figure appears sinister, like the grim reaper or something. But I'm wearing a black cloak too. The hood is drawn over the stranger's head, so I can't make out her face.

"Who are you?"

"You know who I am."

I recognize her voice. "Alondra?"

The figure nods but doesn't turn.

"Oh, Alondra, Hawthorne's in trouble. The Billington House was destroyed. The town's in danger. What can I do? I felt like I had to do something, so I thought of magic. I felt like I had to speak to you. Then I saw an owl bury its head on a tree, and it reminded me of you and what you did at the time of your death."

I'm distracted by singing from a choir. I turn and face the stage, but there's no one except Liam, straightening white cloths on a table under the candles.

"I am here, Windstorm," Alondra says, "calm yourself."

"Why are we in a church?"

"This is the Summerland. You summoned me here because your father is Christian and you feel at peace with the cross."

I do feel at peace. But I don't think it's because we're in a church. If anything, being in black cloaks here feels almost sinful. But I feel at peace sitting beside my teacher again. I miss her. And, come to think of it, I was wishing that I'd see her as I crouched in meditation. Maybe I did summon her?

"Alondra, Enora's destroying the town. What can I do?" I ask again. My voice sounds desperate.

"Do you accept that you are the leader of the Hawthorne coven?"

"Yes. Of course."

Her hand pats the book on my lap. I look down and am surprised. In this house of God, I had thought I was holding a Bible. It's my Book of Shadows, *Broomstick*.

"You gave it to me after it burned in the fire?" I ask.

"No, you did. Have you accepted that you are the leader of the Hawthorne coven?"

"I said yes, but what does that have to do with anything? Alondra, you have to help me stop Enora."

"If Enora chooses to fight, your fate will depend on whether you have accepted your rightful place as leader of our coven."

Liam opens the drapes and it becomes very bright. I can't see outside. All I see is a bright white light through the windows. It makes me uneasy. It reminds me of the bright light in Alondra's house when Beatrix died.

"Who turns the lights on in your house?" I ask Alondra. "There's no electricity. Is it you? Your ghost?"

"No. It's you."

I finally see a glimpse of her profile under the hood. I can just barely see Alondra's face, but I recognize her features and her infamous smile, and that makes me feel more at peace. I was scared that this was some other witch tricking me. But this is Alondra.

"You're a powerful witch," Alondra adds. "You brought me back from the other side during Yule, just like you are doing now. And when Beatrix died, you brought me back as a warning to Adder. Just as you lit up your house now, as a warning, after the Billington House was burned."

"You know about the Billington House?"

She nods.

"It's terrible."

There's the sound of footsteps. I look, but I don't see anyone walking up the aisle.

"Well, it's not my house, Alondra. It's yours."

"Maverick built the house when he built the town," she says, shaking her head. "I moved in with my first husband, but Maverick built it. That house is more a part of Hawthorne than Josiah's. The house is Hawthorne. And Hawthorne is our covenstead. Do you understand?"

I nod.

"I don't think you do. When I first brought Enora into my coven, I thought she would take my place as our leader. Like you, she was powerful. But she cannot feel the peace you feel. She cannot..." She touches my hand. At first I jerk, ready to move away, thinking that her hand will be ice-cold. It isn't. Her hand is warm. "She can't feel this, Katie. Do you understand? This is Enora's evil. When I realized this, I expelled her from the coven. In Hawthorne, she is an outsider now. Do you know what that means?"

"Alondra, you're never straight with me." I shake my head.

"I'm being very straight with you," Alondra insists with a laugh. "I'm answering your question. You asked how you can stop Enora. Now you answer me. Do you accept your position as the leader of our coven?"

I hesitate. Then she turns and faces me. I physically draw back. She doesn't look scary; her facial features are vivid and real. Indeed, Alondra is sitting in front of me. It's her. I don't know how to explain it to you, but she is not a vision and she is not a ghost. Alondra Johansen is sitting right here beside me. And she is smiling, trying to comfort me.

"Yes," I reply.

"Take what is yours." She nods and turns back to the altar. "Do it now. Don't delay. If this outsider is so blinded by her rage that she foolishly fights you on your hallowed grounds, she will not only fight Hawthorne, she will fight the Hawthorne Witch. When she realizes they are one and the same, it will put you in great danger. She will find that the only way to fulfill her revenge and destroy our coven will be to destroy you. But when *you* finally realize who you are, it will make you very powerful. The struggle is no different than it was over the fate of your book, *Broomstick*. Let the book burn to ash, and you will burn. Fail to burn you, and neither the book nor the town will burn. Cast the outsider out, Cadence Hawthorne. And do it now."

I don't understand everything she's saying, but I feel it. I feel it in the pit of my chest, and I feel determined now. I mean, I was determined before, but now I feel confident. And my newfound conviction is all because of Alondra.

But I also feel sad. As the two of us sit in the quiet church alone, I really feel like I'm sitting by my old teacher. Maybe my stress made this magic happen. Or maybe Alondra did. I don't know. Whatever the case, I feel like I won't ever see her again.

"I miss you, Alondra. And I do forgive you."

I touch her hand again. I hold it. Its warmth is pleasant. It reminds me of holding her in my arms in the woods at the time of her death. I even see an image of darkness in the center of this bright church. I'm wearing a black cloak, and my teacher is wearing the same. And I'm holding her, desperately trying to tell her those words after she died in my arms.

"I forgive you."

Alondra shakes her head. She points to the cross at the front of the church. "I'm not damned, Cadence. Whatever you believe, have faith that there is a mercy and love far greater than anything anyone can imagine."

Everything fades.

* * *

I wake up crying. I feel an arm around me and lift my head. Bryce is looking at me with concern.

"What happened, babe?" asks Bryce. "We sat and watched you after you seemed to drift off to sleep."

"I just love her so much, Bryce," I say in tears.

I'm back in Alondra's yard. My friends are all sitting around me and staring at me. They look sad for me, but I don't think they understand why I'm crying. I'm not sad. I'm crying tears of joy over being able to see Alondra again. No, not see her, *be* with her one final time.

"Who was it, Cadence?" asks Bryce.

I shake my head. Then I pick up the book in front of me and get up before my friends.

"What did you see?" asks Hope.

"Yeah, Katie?" asks Frida. "Who?"

"Who?" they all ask. "What?"

I feel this weird sense of longing. The peace I felt with Alondra, in that gateway between life and death, was so much more comforting than this moment. My friends are so worried, and I feel stress again due to all their fears.

My phone rings. I dig through my jeans pocket. The phone reads *Mira*.

"Cadence." Mira's voice is expressionless. "She wants to speak to you."

"Mira, where are you?"

"Hello?" asks another voice. "Hello?" It's Enora's voice. "Cadence, is that you?" The hand not holding the phone clenches into a tight fist. Then my friends jump up from the grass and back away from me. "Am I speaking with—"

"What!"

"You'll be happy to know I haven't killed Mira yet." She laughs. "*Yet.*"

"You better not—"

"Shh. Quiet your piehole, I warn you...don't say a word. I

have her. I offer a trade. I'll hand Mira back to your friends in exchange for you. You'll turn yourself in and go back with me to Atlanta, where I'll complete our Sabbath and dissolve your coven. And your magic. This Friday, I'll finally dissolve the Hawthorne coven by sacrificing you..." She takes a deep breath and screams, "*For my charred finger, you motherfucker!*"

I look at my friends, staring up at me, and the fire behind me. They're staring wide-eyed, as if afraid.

"Just don't touch her."

"Shut up! Shh. Quiet. Shh, Cadence. Quiet yourself. If you upset me, your friend might just die while you're on the phone. If you want her to live, you'll allow us to take you back. I tried to trap you, now I see I just have to take you. If you don't give yourself up, I'll destroy the rest of your stupid school. First the library, then the halls, then Alondra's house. Mira will be killed, of course. Either way, I will have the dissolution of the Hawthorne coven. But don't worry, I'm willing to spare your life. You can choose to survive under my circle just like Maddie and Mira did. Letting you live and watching you kneel before us is worth more than your life. It's the least you can do..." Then she screams in my ear, "*For my finger, you fucking cunt-sucking motherfucking bitch!*"

"Where are you? If you want—"

"*Shut up!*" she screams. "*Just be quiet!*" She takes a deep breath and then says unnaturally calmly, "Shh, shut...just shut the fuck up. Do we have a deal? Huh? Huh?"

"Fine. Where's Mira?"

"Why, we're where Maddie told me you two used to steal coffee. There's nobody else here at the moment, since I've got the whole school watching their stupid frat house burn down. Come share a cup of joe by the library with Amica. Hurry before the next building falls. And Raven." And she hangs up the phone.

I look behind me and the bonfire is like an inferno, rising

higher than ever before. I figure that's why my friends are all staring wide-eyed at me.

"Katie," Bryce says. "Katie."

"Yeah, what?" I snap.

"Look."

He points at my feet. I realize he's under me. They're all under me. My black boots are hovering about twelve feet above the ground.

25

MY RIGHT

I'm scared. I mean really, really scared. I try not to show it when I run with my friends, but my bowels are turning and my heart's racing. And yet, since I saw Alondra, I also feel confident. I didn't feel that when I was in Atlanta—at least not until I was out of Enora's house. Maybe it was my teacher's words. Or maybe I'm entering a trance.

Did Alondra mean that I could beat Enora with magic tonight? Or did she just mean that I had to confront her here? I don't know.

We make it to the base of the grassy hill under the library. The Abaddon coven looks super weird in their crimson cloaks, standing in the center of the field amidst the shadows. There's mist on the ground. I think it's smoke from the fire. In fact, behind the clan, I see smoke and flames over the horizon, at the Billington House.

The field is well lit. This is one of the brightest areas on campus at night. The library's open late, so most of the light comes from the summit to my left. A little yellow light also shines from path lights along the main drag, to my right.

Enora's coven have their hoods over their heads, but there's enough light to make out Enora's nasty face.

Mira's the only one with her hood back. Her hands are tied behind her back. She looks gloomy as hell, but she doesn't seem to have been hurt, though there are a few bare patches on her head. The only other one not wearing a hood is the beast, Gus. As usual, he's bare-chested, baring his stupid fangs.

We stop about twenty yards from them, coven to coven. It's a full-fledged witch showdown, only they're wearing their red cloaks and we're in regular clothes.

"I'm here," I say to Enora. "Let Mira go."

"That simple, huh?" asks Enora, shaking her head. "Nuh-uh. I doubt that, Cadence."

"Take me and let Mira go. You have my word. I'll go with you. Just let her go."

Bryce grabs my arm. "No, Katie. I told you, I won't let you go with them."

"It's okay," I reply, still glaring at Enora.

On the periphery, a few students with backpacks over their shoulders stop on the surrounding pathways to watch us. A boy even kicks up his skateboard and stares. Two couples by the library are looking down from the top of the hill.

"Katie," Bryce says, gently turning me. He lifts my chin. "You can't go back there."

I know. Does he think I want to? But what am I to do? I trusted Alondra's words, but now I feel doubt. I don't know what to do to make things right. She said, "Cast the outsider out." And she said, "Do it now."

"It's okay," I say.

"No, it isn't." Bryce opens his eyes wide and shakes his head. He looks so stern. So worried. I run my hand along his gorgeous thin beard and force a smile. Then I reach up and kiss him on his lips.

"I love you," I whisper.

He closes his eyes and shakes his head, clenching his teeth. He embraces me tightly. We kiss some more.

"Come on!" Enora snarls. "Fuck! Do we have to watch this? Are you done? Gus, go get her. Bind her so that she can't cast any tricks."

Gus nods and comes over carrying a thick rope. But when he yanks me around to bind my hands, Bryce grabs his wrist to stop him. Gus easily pushes him to the ground. My friends and all the witches of the Abaddon coven shout at each other, threatening to charge.

"Katie, let us help you!" cries Tammy desperately.

"Please, Katie," says Frida.

I shake my head and let the beast tie my hands behind my back. Then Gus leads me up to Enora, who smiles her stupid wicked grin. Enora removes her glove from her right hand. She shows me her palm. Her right hand doesn't have a red painted pentagram. It's charred and blackened. With a fake smile, she lifts the hand and strikes me hard in the face. My friends scream. I fall to the ground. I hear stupid Gus laugh.

"Katie!" yells Bryce.

"Give us Mira now," I say on the ground.

"Sit up first," Enora is still smiling and looking down at me. "Come on. Sit." She loves that I'm under her feet on the ground, I think. As I try to get up by leaning on my knees, she kicks me really hard in the stomach. I fall again, losing my breath, gasping for air. She drives her charred hand practically up my nose. "Do you see this? Huh? Do you see my hand! You bitch! You call yourself a witch? You don't know spells. You barely know our traditions. You were initiated by a hypocrite who was bullied by a pervert. That is your coven. That is your magic. It must be taken. I am the true witch. I will remove you."

"Fine...just...give me Mira," I say, trying to take in air. I'm watching her boot for another strike. "I don't care. Give me back my friend."

"Sure." Enora walks where I can't see her. "You know, I'd rather have you." And she wraps her arm around my neck and hoists me to my knees in front of my friends. My friends are ready to charge. But then—

"Stand back!" Enora brandishes a curved knife from her inside her cloak. I feel the cold metal slide along my neck. "Everyone get back or I'll cut the little bitch's neck! I swear, I'll cut little Katie's fucking throat."

"Okay," Bryce says, putting a hand out. "Just don't hurt her."

"You're really willing to sacrifice yourself for Mira?" Enora asks, lowering her head to stare at me with her flickering white eyes. "Really? I don't believe it. You have another trick up your sleeve? Is Alondra going to walk up behind me and grab me?" She chuckles and pulls me real close to the metal blade. "Huh?" I gasp. "How 'bout I kill her now?" she asks my friends. "I can just slice her throat, and that will be the end of the coven. Why bother with the Sabbath? She sure doesn't honor it." Then she lowers her face to mine again. "I am the only witch in Atlanta. I rejected Alondra and your coven because Alondra didn't have the courage to fight a man. A man who hurt us. So I gladly killed him. But you didn't let me finish."

"You never left our coven," I say. "Alondra expelled you."

She furrows her brow above those creepy white eyes, seeming surprised that I'd say anything with a knife to my throat. But, I...I don't care if she cuts me. I can't. I hate her so much.

I feel magic. There is a trance coming on, and I look up and see clouds swirling above us. A wind picks up.

"Let her go," pleads Bryce. "Please." Gus throws him on the ground again.

It starts to rain. Then there is a strike of lightning and thunder.

"More tricks?" Enora says in my ear, looking up toward the

clouds. "Careful, one slice of your neck and the windstorm's over."

"Enora, please," Bryce says. Gus is now sitting over him, pinning him with one knee. "Let her go. She said she'll go with you."

"You'll really go back with me, Cadence?" asks Enora, holding the blade closer to my throat. I feel the sharpness cut. "You'll really let us bleed you for Mira?"

"Yes."

Enora squints. Then she lifts the blade from my neck. I hear Bryce's sigh of relief.

"Bullshit." Enora lets go of my neck and throws me down on the grass. "Anyway, for what you did to my hand, there should be punishment. You can come join us Friday, if you want, but someone still needs to pay tonight. So, I tell you what, Katie. How 'bout I let you decide?"

Enora nods to Gus, and Gus chokeholds Bryce. Then Enora walks behind Mira and grabs her from behind, just like she did to me. But unlike me, Mira's so lifeless, as if she doesn't care. It's like she's given up. Enora presses the knife to Mira's neck. "After all, I think my hand was more Mira's fault than yours."

"Stop!" I cry. "Just stop it!"

Enora jerks Mira's neck closer to the knife and Mira winces, but Mira doesn't speak.

"What will it be, Katie?" asks Enora. "I've got my arm around Raven, and Gus has his around your lover. Which one dies tonight for my hand?"

"Please. Just let them go. I'll go with you."

"No, you won't go willingly. I know you won't. I'll have to take you, so stop the bullshit and choose tonight's sacrifice before I haul you back to Atlanta."

"Allow me to teach you witchcraft, *witch*," she says. "Both Bryce and Gus are High Wizards. But there can only be one *real* coven in Atlanta. Only one High Priestess and one High

Wizard. I think I'll throw the knife to Gus. Bryce should go tonight. Sorry."

"Let them go, you bitch!" screams Maddie. "Katie's offering to go with you! What more do you want!" Then a bunch of others in my circle cry out with Maddie.

"Yeah?" Enora asks them.

"Just let her go," I say. I'm desperate because I know Enora is crazy enough to kill them. "Please, Enora. You have me. Take me on the Sabbath. We have a deal."

"It's okay, Cadence," Mira finally says, looking down at me. She looks awful. "Choose me and save Bryce. I follow my master's will."

"Why not choose the Wizard?" suggests another red-cloaked witch. It's Courtney. "Won't his death weaken the Hawthorne coven the most, master?"

"Shut up, Courtney," says Enora dismissively.

"You fucking better not lay a hand on them!" Maddie shouts.

Enora glares at Maddie, narrowing her white eyes, and her smile quickly vanishes. "And which hand would you like me not to use, Blackbird? The left one or the *charred* one?"

She draws a dark line of red on Mira's neck with her knife. It's dark, but not too dark to see the blood drip from her neck.

"Stop, please!" I cry.

"On my master's will," Mira says closing her eyes and taking a deep breath.

"Mira!" I say, shaking my head and putting my hand out. "She's not your master. You're our friend—"

"No!" shouts Enora. "You fucking liar! More lies! Mira is not your friend. She has no friends. And you don't give a shit about her. Her life is shit. Just like Beatrix. And I will have my vengeance tonight for my hand! If it wasn't for her, it wouldn't have happened!"

"All right," I say. Enora's pearl-white eyes are bulging with rage. "Please just, calm down. Let her go. I'll—"

"*For my hand! For my honor! For my circle, this is the first sacrifice before you. Sacrificium consecratum. This time, for your lies. The lies of Hawthorne shall never be forgiven! Sacrificium consecratum!*"

And Enora runs the blade across Mira's throat.

Lightning strikes overhead and clouds cover the stars and moon. The wind becomes fierce, spinning along the grass like a tornado, forcing people to tumble or crouch down. It starts to pour. But the rain is not water. It is dripping white ash. Could it be from the fire at the Billington House? This far?

Mira falls lifeless to the ground. A bolt of lightning strikes near Enora, and she's thrown on the ground.

"Oh, am I upsetting you?" Enora asks, getting up. "Huh? How 'bout my hand, Windstorm! Don't you think what you did to my hand—"

Another bolt from the sky lights up the grounds. It doesn't strike her, but Enora looks up, scared. Enora forces herself up and turns to Gus. "Here, cut the bitch's fiancé next. Do it quick before her next tantrum."

She throws the dagger to Gus, but in midair the knife stops its trajectory and veers straight down into the grass. I crawl as fast as I can to Mira with my hands still shackled.

Mira's eyes are closed, dead. It's dark, but just bright enough to see a dark red trickle of blood bubble over her neck. The white ash starts covering her like snowflakes.

It's my fault. Again. All my fault. Mira was *my* witch. From *my* coven. I failed her. I feel so heavy in my chest. The rain and ash hail on me as tears run down my face. It's my fault. Again. And I failed Alondra. She seemed so sure that I could defeat Enora. She gave me such confidence. If I'm so powerful, such a great witch, why does my friend lie dead?

Thunder and lightning crack again.

I look up at Enora. She's staring down at me with those

creepy white eyes. I rise to my feet effortlessly. It's surprising, for my hands were bound, but the ropes fall from my wrists as if they were made of paper. Those from my circle not crouching over Mira are now glaring at the red-cloaked witches in fury. When Enora gives one last nervous cackle, we lose all reason. Helen, Mandy, and Natasha charge first. Then come Hope, Frida and Tammy. They have every intention of pummeling the Abaddon coven, but when my witches are within striking distance, they freeze. Everything freezes, even Enora. It's as if time stopped. At first, I'm as surprised as they are, but then I realize that I willed it.

I walk around all the witches with my right hand raised. Everyone stands like a statue under the falling white ash. Slowly, they regain head movement. A few turn and stare at me. Gus, the beast that he is, finally breaks the spell. He lets go of Bryce, and he charges me, like an animal, on all fours. Effortlessly, I throw him. Then I turn back to Enora.

"*Vos invoco Escoba et Abigail. Relinquo. Deleo Panthera, deleo Panthera. Relinquo.*"

A bolt of lightning falls only a few feet from Enora. She's thrown, stunned by the bolt. When she regains her strength for a moment, her eyes lose their white glow. But then she shakes her head and flashes me the painted pentagram on her left palm.

"*Muta! Muta! Muta Panthera!*"

Her back elongates, her arms lengthen, and she falls on all fours. Yellow fur and a large mane appear along her neck, and she growls. She is a lion, like the lion I saw at the entrance to her cave.

The animal jumps on me with solid white eyes, snapping its teeth, trying to tear my face. The distraction is enough to stop the freezing of the witches. The moment I start rolling with the lion on the grass, I see in my periphery that the two covens are finally charging each other.

But my magic is strong. I grab Panthera and toss her across the lawn. Then I raise my hands once more. Rain falls. Torrential rain, washing the ash from the grass. Panthera, still a lion, recovers from my throw and jumps on the victim closest to her —my brother. Of course, the bitch knows this will upset me the most. Damie fights for his life, trying to push the lion's teeth away from his face and torso. I flick both wrists out.

"*Veni foras, Panthera. Veni, veni, veni foras.*"

The lion drops my brother, sliding up the muddy hill across the wet grass, pulled by an invisible force. At first, Panthera resists, but then she turns and uses the force to leap on me.

"*Hawthorne Witch,*" the lion says in a guttural male voice. "*Lux. Lux.*" Panthera's blackened right paw is aflame, and I feel burning pain as I try to hold her once more and throw her.

I will another flash of lightning. This time it's so close and bright that I have to shield my eyes. It cracks across the field. There's a yelp. Panthera falls from me. My eyes burn and I blink repeatedly, struggling to see, after the lightning strike. When my vision clears, Panthera's lying by my side, shaking. I pull myself up and grab the lion's legs. Then I toss her once more, this time nearly fifty yards, across the entire field to a group of trees. Stunned, the animal jumps back on all fours, shaking its head.

"*Hawthorne relinquo! Decipula Panthera! Decipula!*"

The tree trunks swoop down, with branches and leaves entwining and gathering up the lion, stretching Panthera until her arms dangle from the sides and her head hangs limply. While inside the tree branches, the lion changes back to Enora, but Enora remains ensnared. The trees trap her, almost like a medieval pillory.

Meanwhile, the witches still fight. I see Cordelia's ugly tattooed face under a red hood. She waves a hand and lights Mandy's jacket on fire. Even sweet Frida is rolling on the ground with one of the red-cloaked witches. Maddie's shoving and punching another. And Bryce is back to swinging his fists and kneeing Gus.

I raise my arms.

"*PROHIBE!*"

For a flash, the witches freeze again. The rain stops. The wind dies. Everything stops.

After a silence, many collapse on the grass. Some clutch their heads. Others start crying. I kneel, panting, as the rain washes down my now-drenched black hair.

That's when I notice the onlookers. Whereas before it was a handful, now there are tons of onlookers on campus and up the hill by the library.

"Windstorm! Windstorm!" I turn and one of the witches in red is kneeling over Mira. "Windstorm! Come here! Quick!" It's Courtney—you know, the witch who suggested Enora kill Bryce. Well, now she's holding Mira in her arms.

Mira's squinting and wincing in pain. I run over on the muddy grass. Mira's moving but with her eyes closed. Dark blood is collecting over her neck in the shadows.

"She's alive?" Bryce asks excitedly, sliding beside me. Mira can't speak. She just keeps wincing in pain.

"Oh, Meer!" says Courtney, shaking her head. "Meer, I'm so sorry. Can you hear me? I'm so sorry. I was afraid. I didn't dare help because I was afraid. Will you forgive me? ...Meer. Meer, can you hear us? Please wake. I love you."

"We have to stop the bleeding," Bryce says.

"She can do it," I say. Then I touch Courtney's shoulder. "You can do it. Stop the bleeding."

Courtney looks up at me, confused.

"Stop the bleeding," I repeat, touching her arm gently. "You can do it."

"Why? Why me?"

"Do you love her?" I ask.

She nods.

"If you love her, you can heal her. Use your love. Right-handed magic. Good magic. I will help you."

She looks at me funny. Then she shakes her head. "I can't. You do it. You're more powerful, Windstorm. I'm not."

"Try," I say. "Feel your love for her and touch her neck. I will try to help."

She hesitates but I don't falter. For some reason, I'm sure she can do it.

"You do love her?" I ask again.

She nods, wiping her tears with her red sleeve.

"I do too. We can do it together."

Courtney closes her eyes and presses her palms along Mira's neck. I touch Courtney's arm, and a white glow appears around her hands. Then, before our eyes, the wound closes and the bleeding stops.

"We've got to get her to the hospital," Bryce says to me.

"And call the police," I add with a nod.

"No need for that," Bryce says, shaking his head and gesturing toward campus.

I didn't see it before, but apparently the police that gathered at the Billington House have finally arrived from another disturbance in town. Red and blue lights and a bunch of police cars are blocking the main drag of campus from a large crowd of students. "We didn't do this in secret this time, Cadence."

I stand up. All my friends, even some of the red witches, are standing around us. But then I hear a scuffle. Tammy and Mandy are grabbed from behind, and I hear metal clasped. That's when someone grabs my arms and pulls my wrists behind my back. This time my wrists are trapped in metal, not rope. Fortunately, I'm myself now, so I don't do something stupid and resist. Then I see the same thing happen to Bryce and Courtney. They're arresting all of us. I don't care. As long as they help Mira, I don't care anymore.

We walk with the police, under bright lights, from two

squad cars, which are now parked along the grass. A hundred students stare. There have been suspicions on campus for two years about my witchcraft. Well, if they saw the lion flying across the lawn, their suspicions have been confirmed. I wonder if they saw the fight? They must have.

The police did. One of the cops asks Bryce if he saw where the lion went.

I pass Queen Bitch herself. Her eyes are blue. She's still imprisoned in the branches of the trees.

"How'd you do it, Cadence?" asks Enora feebly. She looks so weak.

I stop with Bryce for a second. "Hawthorne is my hallowed ground."

"But we weren't at Alondra's."

"*All* of Hawthorne is my hallowed ground."

Enora nods with a slight glimmer of a grin. Then she looks down, forlorn, and says—more to herself—"Till we meet again, Hawthorne Witch."

"Should I kill her?" I say, cocking my head to Bryce. You know, like will the branches to squeeze her chest until she can't breathe?

"You students are in a lot of trouble," says the cop beside me, grabbing my arm and pulling me away. "Come on."

As we wait, handcuffed, against the police cars, my friends mingle with our red-cloaked archenemies. We don't fight. We don't even yell at each other. We're too exhausted. And in a strange way, the people in Enora's coven look relieved. Even Gus, in handcuffs, is staring peacefully at the ground. I think they're relieved I locked their beast in the trees. I think they were afraid of her too.

Then two men run across the lawn to Mira with a stretcher.

"Thank God," I say to Bryce, gesturing to the paramedics. "I hope she's all right."

"If she is, it'll be thanks to you, Cadence."

I shake my head.

26

EXIT INTERVIEW

I'M SITTING STIFFLY IN A BLACK LEATHER CHAIR, FACING THE provost of Hawthorne University. I am holding her cell phone, watching a video of my friends and me fighting the red-cloaked witches of the Abaddon coven. Doctor Kenosha Trent is a black woman with really short black curls. She's wearing a shiny violet dress jacket and slacks and is sitting behind a mahogany desk—similar to Dr. Bainer's desk. She even has a lovely view of the outside forest behind her too.

It's a cold day and snow is falling behind her. I met the provost last year when I was sent to her office regarding my failing junior year. She's a really nice lady, unlike the history dean. But she's not looking nice now. She has her arms folded and is staring at me.

Seeing what happened is stranger than being part of it. As I watch, occasionally I see students stopping their bikes or pointing at us. I was too busy fighting to notice them. It seemed quiet outside, but a lot of people were watching us. The video was made with night vision, so everything's black-and-white and there's no sound.

Then comes the part where I'm walking in front of everybody, sticking my right hand out. Everyone's frozen. It's almost as if the video is paused, but I'm still walking with my outstretched right hand. And then the security footage reminds me of a horror movie, or some supernatural thriller, when Panthera shapeshifts into a lion and lunges at me. It's too unreal to be real, you know. The lion attacks me, throwing its claws at my face and snapping its teeth at me.

I don't really want to watch this again. I'm tired. I got no sleep last night. After a trance, sometimes releasing all that extra energy drains me. Not to mention I spent the night in a jail cell smelling of pee. Well, the police let me out after they made me review the same security footage. Apparently, although people got hurt, I didn't do anything wrong. I mean, were they going to prosecute me for sticking my hand out and fending off a lion?

I take a deep breath.

"Keep watching."

"Why? I've already gone through the footage with the police, Dr. Trent," I say, shaking my head.

"Do it," she insists, folding her arms again.

I sigh and look back at her phone.

It's at the part where my friends are staring at something outside my field of vision. This is the part where Enora's tied up in tree branches. You know, when I threw her across the grass and trapped her body between the trees. Well, you can't see Enora at this angle, but all the bystanders around us are staring in her direction.

"Rewind it," she says, leaning forward. "Go back before Enora gets trapped in the tree."

"Why? I don't understand. I...I mean, why do you—"

"Just do it, Cadence."

There's no arguing. Dr. Trent looks really pissed.

I press the screen and find a rewind button. I don't know why she wants me to see it, but I go back to where I left off—

you know, the part where everyone's freezing while I raise my right hand. Gus charges me, then the lion, Panthera—and I easily throw them off. And then I get her off Damie. The speed at which the lion is hurled seems unnatural. The lion smears along the black-and-white video as if the camera can't track the throw.

"Enora's been thrown?" Dr. Trent asks.

As a lion...yeah.

Dr. Trent nods and then sighs. She sifts through some papers on her desk. With her head in her hand, she starts writing something. This reminds me of Dr. Bainer. I just sit there and watch her. This time, I don't even have a loose nail to play with. Instead, I run my hand across my hair. God, it's so shaggy and ugly. I haven't showered for two nights. I'm just wearing a simple T-shirt and jeans, with my red coat on the chair.

I fiddle with my fingers, staring for a moment at my black nail polish.

"Am I getting expelled?" I ask, not looking at her.

"Do you know how many people witnessed this, Cadence?"

"No."

She finally drops her pen. "The security footage I showed you is only coming from the library. But on campus, over two hundred students were watching you guys as the police kept them back until it was safe. We had to confiscate everyone's phone. They videotaped you. One caught a lightning strike near your body. Another showed Enora's transformation into a lion. That part where you threw her, fortunately, looks almost like a glitch or a trick of lighting. The lion moves too fast. But..." She folds her hands and leans toward me. "Three students managed to record the trees that bent down and trapped her. Those videos were quite remarkable, and one of them was leaked on social media."

What does this have to do with me getting expelled?

"You and your friends have created quite a mess. One of the biggest messes this town has seen in over a century."

I bite my lip. What am I supposed to say to that?

"I will interview your fiancé. Then I will interview your best friend, Madison. Your brother, Damien. Then all the others. The police will deal with the non-students, the guests from Atlanta. And, of course, Enora will be behind bars. But it's not the first time she's been in prison."

"What do you want from me, Dr. Trent?" I don't like the edge in my voice, but I can't help it. I'm so tired. I just want to go home. I'm getting angry. She forces a smile and finally stops folding her arms. She leans back in her chair. Then she does something really weird. She smiles—a real smile.

"Cadence, do you still want to attend Hawthorne as a graduate student next year?"

What?

"I need to know so I can make plans."

"I... I..." *I mean, what the hell?*

"You've been through so much," Dr. Trent says, almost sadly, with a nod. "I'm sorry. I've tried to do what I can to help. And on your part, you've worked so hard to clear your name. I have to say that, unfortunately, it's affected your school record. You know, in Hawthorne, we can forgive certain things because we have an understanding, but I'm concerned for you if you apply to other schools. If you do, your record is tainted because of the things you've done. I don't feel like that's fair. I'd be willing to write you a letter of recommendation to try to clear things up, but your record stands with Cs in the fall of your sophomore and junior years. Here, as the head of the university, certain things can be, shall we say, put aside. But with the other schools, it will be hard to clear your record. If you still insist on going elsewhere, I understand. I'll do what I can."

I'm squinting at her and wondering if this is the start of my true psychotic break.

"The dean sent me his report, Cadence. But you know, Dr. Bainer can be an asshole."

Did the provost just call Dr. Bainer an asshole?

"It's up to you."

"What? What's going on here?" I snap. I'm surprised at my outburst, but I'm getting really angry. This is just too weird. I'm so tired and I just want to go home. "You made me watch a witch fight on campus. With a lion. And now you're talking about graduate school. I don't understand. What's happening, Dr. Trent?"

She nods and opens a drawer in her desk. She takes out a shiny silvery metal object the size of her palm and pushes it toward me across the desk. It's a small metal pentagram. The same pentagram, I think, that Alondra once showed me on her desk before I joined her "honors program."

"You're a witch!"

"There are many of us," she says with a nod. "Hawthorne has become the center. Escoba brought witchcraft from the Caribbean. After she hurt Abigail's family, Abigail studied witchcraft, for revenge, from the ancient Celtic sources."

Dr. Trent pauses and looks down for a moment. She reaches forward and grabs the pentagram back and places it in her desk.

"I showed you the footage to prove that I am aware of your powers, Cadence. Although there have been many witches in Hawthorne, no one has ever shown the power you hold. Maybe Enora. And Alondra once thought she could train Enora, but her heart is blackened. She is wicked." *No arguing with that.* "If the tables were turned, I don't think Enora would have trapped you in a tree. She would have killed you."

"Who are you? I mean ..."

"I'm a witch. Just like you said I am. And, yes, there are others. Many others. We are occult. But we've been shaping the world since the beginning of time. Stonehenge. Africa. The

Caribbean. Do you really think that with all the magic you've seen, there aren't others who know about our magic?"

She stops talking for me to digest all the crazy things she's saying.

"I'm not only offering you a position as a graduate student. I'm offering you a leadership position as a witch." And she's no longer scowling; she's grinning and looking friendly. This is the Dr. Trent I remember from last year.

"What do I have to do?"

"Simple channeling spells. Hold Sabbaths. Divination. Perform incantations. Conjurings. Be a witch."

"I don't worship the devil."

"Alondra delved into the workings of Satan because of her husband," Dr. Trent says with a slow nod. "That was her choice. You can choose to do or not do this. The basic nature of what we are is powerful, but I leave the direction of the pentacle up to you. I'm asking you to practice, I'm not telling you how. If you agree, you can meet with your sisters and take in new recruits, just as Alondra did for me. We will set up a new *honors program* run by you and your fiancé. Hawthorne is a hub for us, Cadence. You can be the leader Alondra wanted you to be. She believed in you. You can even continue to use her house."

"She told me it was my house."

"I see no other claim." After a pause, she adds with a smile, "So...do you want to come here as a graduate student in our history program?"

With Bryce? Are you kidding me?

27

OSTARA

"So, before I begin, do you guys all know how Bo Peep and I met?" asks Mira.

I'm cringing. Bryce is too. I feel his palm twitch as I hold it.

The two of us are facing Mira. Mira's got on this really long draping black dress that drags on the grass behind her. She looks like a total witch. She's got thick witch makeup on. The red-and-black demon tattoos along her neck don't cover up her new long, thick horizontal scar. Well, she told me she likes the scar and thinks it looks really cool. I'm wearing a lovely draping white dress. My hubby, or future hubby, is wearing white too. I have discreet red lipstick and natural makeup and have curled my hair so that it's flowing like a goddess's. (I look really good.) The only witchlike thing I'm wearing is a crown of yellow and white flowers.

Anyway, Mira's making everyone real uncomfortable, because she's got this big grin and she's pausing before her microphone, waiting for us to laugh after she called me *Bo Peep*. No one's laughing. All my friends are sitting uncomfortably in the lovely white wooden chairs we rented and set up on the wild grass. Red roses are strewn in the central aisle. And the forest, of course, is its normal loveliness, surrounding Alondra's yard. My yard, I suppose.

"Well," Mira says with her famous smile, "Katie here used to be the most innocent little girl in school. Like, she just didn't get the world. I thought it was really cute, so I teased her. I used to call her Little Bo Peep. Know why?"

The funny thing about Mira is that people who don't know her think she's shy like me, because she doesn't talk much. But she doesn't talk much, not because she's shy but because she doesn't care about anybody. Just like I don't think she cares what people think about what she's saying right now.

I turn to my left and Maddie has her eyes wide open. She shakes her head at me. She's scared about what else Mira's going to spew out of her mouth. So is my brother. He's beside Maddie in his sharp navy-blue suit, furrowing his brow. He's staring at Mira too.

"I first met Cadence at this house. She could barely say a word, she was so quiet. Then at the Billington House, Maddie invited her to summon spirits for fun. Cadence drank a lot of beer back then. Lots. Remember, Katie?"

Okay, I might have been drinking, but I didn't drink *lots*. I'll never forget that day at the Billington House. That was the night I found out my mom had passed away. Through magic.

I look around and no one is laughing or smiling. And though the spring weather is absolutely perfect, with birds chirping and not a cloud in the lovely blue sky, I'm feeling impatient and a bit claustrophobic in my heavy draping white dress.

"I really didn't like you back then," Mira says to me. *Oh, God.* "You were more focused on your looks than on the spirit world. It seemed you were always fixing your hair or looking in a goddamn mirror. Sometimes I think you still are."

Okay, now people are laughing.

"We went through tough times, you know. Katie and our

friends. And Katie was so innocent. But things have changed us." She pauses and nods. "She once asked our circle what *sodomy* means..." More laughter. It's turning into a roast, sort of. The thing is, I'm not sure Mira intended it to be. "It was weird that she didn't know, because she loves studying, but some things are just not taught in school. You know Cadence used to squirm when our friends talked about sex. I mean, she was a Little Bo Peep." She looks right in my eyes with her infamous sly grin. "You didn't think I'd say all this stuff, did you?"

No, I didn't. And I really, really hope you're finished.

"Ghosts, witches, vampires." *She's not finished.* "You know Hawthorne's really different, but since I left, I really miss it. For those of you just visiting, I don't think you know how close our friendships were." She gestures around the yard. "This place, these grounds, have been so special to me. That's what I miss. Well, Katie isn't a Bo Peep anymore. I mean, look at Bryce. Damn."

If she were drunk, maybe the guests would understand. But I see people just shaking their heads.

"And then there's Bryce."

Bryce smiles nervously.

"You know everyone in school wanted Bryce. I mean, *everyone.* I knew him before Cadence. But when he met you—damn, girl—he only had eyes for you, Katie. Why, I'll never understand."

Yes, it is a roast. And people are laughing. That was *sort of* funny.

"Okay, I'm only kidding. I'm just saying all this stuff to... I mean, what I'm trying to say is...I love you guys. I really love you. Not only as friends, but because..." She starts choking up. "Well, I can't say. All I can say is that, Cadence, you saved me. And...I'm in love too, you know. I love the girl down there on the third row. Cadence saved her too."

"I love you too, Meer!" yells Courtney.

"Sure, Courtney, anyway—"

"Can we get on with it, Mira?" Maddie says, lifting her eyebrows impatiently.

Mira nods. She brushes tears from her eyes.

I look behind me at the crowd again. There are about forty people. Most are from our coven. Frida is holding hands with her new husband, Greg. Gilda came down from Savannah with her husband and baby. And Aunt Jane is here. Everyone looks so formal, and they're all smiling. And they look "normal." Mira and Courtney are the only ones crazy enough to be dressed in black, wearing thick goth makeup.

Then I see someone in the back row. I can't believe it. It's my dad! My dad, who vowed never to come to my wedding. Well, we've been talking again. He's talking to Bryce again too. I mean, how can he not love Bryce? But he's still disturbed by the whole witch thing. He said he couldn't come to our handfasting today because he's Christian. But...he's here.

I wasn't tearing up until now.

"Ready, guys?" Mira asks with a genuine smile.

"The first symbol is the eternity symbol," Mira says. And she reaches down and grabs white ropes on a small wooden table beside her. "Can Cadence's dad please come up to the front row?"

I turn again and my dad looks as surprised as I am. I don't think anyone told him he'd be a part of the ceremony, certainly not me. He walks up the aisle, and I start crying really hard. They're not tears of sadness; they're tears of joy. And many of my witches start crying too. Bryce puts his hand on my back.

My dad faces me, looking at me with his gray eyes. He's wearing a tan suit and, although he's obviously made his decision to respect our wishes, he has a very conspicuous silver cross pinned on his coat.

"Are you okay with this, Cadence?" Dad asks.

"Of course, Daddy," I say, wiping tears on my sleeve and nodding. "Yes."

Dad looks at Bryce and smiles.

"Please face each other, Cadence and Bryce. Hold each other's right hand. One ribbon represents each family. A final ribbon represents the new joining the two of you are creating with this marriage."

Mira does this weird knot, which only she can create, on our right hands. (This is why I asked her to officiate, not for her to yap nasty things about me). Then she shows my dad the correct movements to knot the ropes around our wrists.

"Now the couple will say some words," Mira says. She puts the microphone right up to our faces.

I bite my lip. I don't want to talk. You know how I feel about that. Bryce goes first. He looks deep into my eyes and smiles sweetly.

"Katie, I'm so lucky to have met you. All I think of are the qualities of Venus when I am with you. Beauty. Not only beauty in looks, but in your heart. Your soul. I once told you your energy is of the Earth. You're an Earther. A pragmatist. I think, somehow, we've been tested. And you've grounded us. All of us. With your leadership and your heart. It's funny because—I hope you don't mind me sharing this—you said to me recently that you don't know why I fell in love with you. Cadence, truly, I don't know why you fell in love with me. I am so lucky to have found you. I love you. Will you be my wife? In sickness and in health?"

"I will." My brother walks up and helps put my diamond ring on my left hand.

Then he smiles, and for a moment, Bryce and I feel like kissing. But we can't, because it's my turn.

"Bryce ..." I'm kind of falling apart. I look over at everyone, and I try really hard to stop crying. "I don't know what to say." I look over at everyone. "I planned a bunch of stuff but I can't remember a word of it." Everyone laughs. "It's not funny."

"We should have written it down," Bryce says.

"I told you that... yeah, well... I don't know why you'd take me, either," I say, shaking my head. "I'm so lucky to have you. And I am so in love with you, Bryce."

There. I stop and he's just looking at me with a smile.

What?

Then he furrows his brow. "*Will you...*" Bryce hints.

"Oh yeah...will you be my husband?" Everyone laughs again.

"Yes, Cadence. I will." Damie helps put the ring on Bryce's left ring finger.

"The knot is tied," says Mira, tying the literal knot from our hands. Then she hands the tied rope to my dad and raises her arms. "Blessed be the two of you under Astraeus, Selene, and Gaia." She looks up. "Hecate, witness this bond. May it never break." She looks back down at us. "Now just go kiss each other already."

And we do. And everyone in the crowd jumps up and claps. I embrace my lover. Then I turn to my dad and hug him tightly.

"Congratulations, Katie," Dad says in my ear. "I love you."

Mira hugs me. She congratulates us too.

Everyone comes up. Everyone hugs. The attention is off of me and I relax while everybody's smiling, shaking hands, laughing and just being happy.

These are my friends. My family. This love, this friendship, so strong and so bound, like the knot, is something that was so special in Hawthorne and something that I will miss. For a moment, that makes my tears turn a little bitter.

Then, on the patio, I see a vision. A witch in a black cloak is standing alone. She stands there as if to bear witness to the ceremony, holding a single candle by her chest. The candle is just bright enough to show the face on the hooded shadow.

Alondra. Alondra is with me again. And her presence isn't scary; it's soothing. Pleasant. I wave and she nods with a smile. Then she fades.

Her presence eases me. Despite there being only a few months left in my final school year, things are not ending. Since Lammas, I've been dreading the end of the school year. But nothing's ending. It's beginning. And, really, beginnings and endings are just an illusion. Only the moments with people we love are important. Those moments, when quiet and reflective, never end.

Bryce jumps into my arms, startling me from my deep thoughts. I'm back with everyone, hearing their raucous shouts and laughter. Dad, Maddie, Aunt Jane, Mira, Damie, Frida, Tammy, and everyone from my coven rush over.

We chose Ostara as the day of our marriage. Ostara is the witch holiday for Easter. Bryce and our marriage are a new beginning for all of us.

THE END

EPILOGUE

Bryce is sitting on the bed in the master bedroom of Alondra's house, my house, taking off his black shoes. It's our third night here. The bedroom doesn't feel spooky anymore. And after my talk with Alondra, it feels like *my* bedroom. He's laid his white pants and dress shirt on a chair and is wearing only a T-shirt, underwear, and socks. It's late, but a full moon and the view through the floor-to-ceiling window of the master bedroom still reveal a very messy backyard. The white chairs are still in rows, and Mira's podium is still there, but no one's outside. I've already showered and am wearing a white lace nightgown, writing in my book, *Broomstick*.

"What are you doing, babe?"

"Huh, husband?"

"Whatcha doing?"

"Writing."

He removes his socks. He hasn't showered yet, but his hair is still gorgeous. He partied late with his friends at the reception.

"I like writing in this book," I say with a shrug. "It's like my diary. But I'm running out of space. It's so full and there's only one page left."

"Give me," he says and jumps on the mattress, grabbing for it. I laugh and quickly close the book and stash it under me in the covers.

"It's private!"

"I thought the book creeped you out," he says, holding me. "Why do you write in it?" Then he kisses my lips. At first, it's a peck; then it's passionate. I play with his tongue, and I feel so close to him. But while we kiss passionately, I feel him reach under my back and grab the book.

"Hey!" I say.

He snatches it and opens the book to the last page. His eyes open wide. "Weren't ... weren't you just saying this? How do you do that?"

"Magic," I say with a big grin.

We stare at each other. His lips slowly curl into a larger and larger smile. Then he jumps on me again, leaning over my body and touching my lips to his while we laugh. He pulls me very close.

"I love you so much, Katie," he whispers between kisses.

"And I, you. And..." I take off his T-shirt. "Isn't tonight the start of our honeymoon?"

His tongue dances with mine and we stay like this for a while, just enjoying our touch. I feel the fingers of his free hand inside my nightgown, running along my side and pressing along my skin, reaching over the curves of my breasts and nipples. He rubs me, kissing me hard on the lips. I enjoy his weight and reach under his shirt, rubbing his back, then lower, along his butt. Then—

Everything fades.

What do you expect? It's our wedding night. Geesh. Give me some privacy.

WITCHY ADVENTURES ARE CONTINUED IN WITCH
MIRROR, BOOK 4, IN THE HAWTHORNE UNIVERSITY
WITCH SERIES

THE SERIES

- BROOMSTICK
- WINDSTORM
- THE HAWTHORNE WITCH
- WITCH MIRROR
- RAVENS
- SHADOW CAST
- BELTANE FIRE short story prequel
- SAMHAIN WITCH short story (3.5)
- ALONDRA 20 yr prequel

THE BOXED SET

- THE HAWTHORNE UNIVERSITY WITCH
  SERIES

ACKNOWLEDGMENTS

I want to thank my beta readers Natalia Ramirez-Avila and George B. You two helped with invaluable advice in pushing action and character development. Stephanie Ward did her usual superb line editing job and Eliza Dee helped with proofreading (including those Latin incantations!) Finally, I've already heard comments about how awesome the cover is. Regina Wamba's cover art never disappoints.

I was lucky to have the same team throughout the whole *Broomstick* journey. This story, and series, would not have been the same without you. Thank you!

PARTING WORDS

What did you think of *The Hawthorne Witch*? By placing a book review, you can inform others of your thoughts and help spread the word about my book.

Want more? Periodically I like to send news regarding current or new projects. If you'd like to be privy, I encourage you to sign up to my email newsletter. Your information will remain private and you can cancel any time.

Sign up at www.alhawke.com or scan the following QR code:

AFTERWORD

With the ending of my trilogy, I thought I'd add a word about how it came to be. So, if interested, here we go …

Broomstick was inspired on a whim to write a novel on Halloween. That's it. Boring, right? But I had thought of the basis for the story many years before when listening to music by the band Dead Can Dance. The original idea involved a virgin introduced to adulthood by skeletons in a dark tower. I'll let your mind wander over that. Needless to say, the story could have turned into horror.

Then came Halloween in 2019. I was playing around with a fantasy while drinking a green tea latte in a coffee shop. The idea of stealing a cup of coffee and a virginal girl's reaction blossomed into the character Cadence. Once I liked the character, her innocence and sweetness, the rest was history. In my writing, characters are central and supersede plots. Mostly, I write my stories *around* my characters. I then endeavored to create *Broomstick*, my paranormal romance, with as much realism as possible.

After *Broomstick,* the sequels, *Windstorm* and *The Hawthorne Witch,* were challenging. I wanted to hold the same tenor of Cadence's thoughts and actions as in the first book. To achieve this, I decided to write all three books consecutively in one year without a break. Believe it or not, I don't outline. I had as much foreknowledge of the ending as you did. Well, the finished products, I believe, were three independent books that felt like one unified story.

I wrote *Windstorm* as a book of acceptance. Cadence finally accepted her job as a witch, her love for Bryce, and her place as a student in Hawthorne. The final book was designed to be the culmination of everything. Her acceptance at being, literally, *The Hawthorne Witch.* Her acceptance of her identity: a "witch" or an adult.

Completing the trilogy so soon makes me a little sad. But, who knows, there may be more adventures in Katie's life that she'll want to write about. After all, she might have finished *Broomstick,* but she can write a new Book of Shadows. She's a witch, you know.

ABOUT THE AUTHOR

A.L. Hawke is the author of the bestselling Hawthorne University Witch series. The author lives in Southern California torching the midnight candle over lovers against a backdrop of machines, nymphs, magic, spice and mayhem.

Visit A.L. Hawke at www.alhawke.com

Email: contact@alhawke.com

ALSO BY A.L. HAWKE

PARANORMAL ROMANCE

- THE HAWTHORNE UNIVERSITY WITCH SERIES I-III
- THE HAWTHORNE UNIVERSITY WITCH SERIES 4-6
- THE HAWTHORNE UNIVERSITY WITCH HOLIDAY COLLECTION
- SHADES
- HAUNTING JOY
- PHANTOM MASQUERADE

- MY EVIL EYE
- THE GUARDIAN
- NECTAR OF AMBROSIA
- CORA

FANTASY: THE AZURE SERIES

- HARMONIA
- CORA: RISE OF THE FALLEN GODDESS
- AZURE BLUE
- CORAL RED
- PRINCESS SOJOURN

SCIENCE FICTION

- CANDY SAVANT SERIES

Books available at https://alhawke.com/books